DOUBLE DIP

A DAVIS WAY CRIME CAPER

Gretchen Archer

HENERY PRESS

DOUBLE DIP
A Davis Way Crime Caper
Part of the Henery Press Mystery Collection

First Edition
Trade paperback edition | January 2014

Henery Press
www.henerypress.com

Cover art by Fayette Terlouw
Author photograph by Garrett Nudd

ISBN-13: 978-1-938383-94-6

Printed in the United States of America

For my mother.
I love her.

ACKNOWLEDGMENTS

Thank you Marilyn Armstrong, Deke Castleman, Stephany Evans, and Kendel Lynn.

ONE

The Gulf Coast has two seasons: scorching and slot tournament.

It goes from one to the other in a matter of hours.

I grew up two-hundred miles north of here in Pine Apple, Alabama, where I was a police officer for six years and where we had four seasons, the familiar ones. I moved to the Gulf to take a job with an undercover security team at the Bellissimo Resort and Casino, the tallest building in the state of Mississippi, on the beach in Biloxi, and where there are only two temperatures: 120° and 21°. With the Gulf of Mexico right out the back door, it's easy to keep casino patrons happy during Season One, but to keep them happy and thawed during Season Two, it takes slot-machine tournaments that begin the day the Bellissimo pool is covered and don't end until it's filled again. The big sign says, "Pool Closed for Slot Tournament Season! See you in April! Good Luck!"

My name is Davis Way. I'm almost thirty-three years old, almost five-foot-three, and my hair is almost red. I don't understand abrupt changes in weather, and I don't understand slot tournaments. I get tennis, golf, and ping-pong tournaments, because skill and strategy are involved. Pushing the button on a slot machine and coming out the champion takes no skill, no strategy, no pings or pongs. It takes one thing—luck.

My immediate supervisor at the Bellissimo is a man named Jeremy Coven. He doesn't have a hair on his head, not even an eyebrow or eyelash. Being terrible with names, I called him No Hair until I could remember Jeremy. By the time I remembered, it was too late. It was No Hair Jeremy who first aimed those two words at me—slot and tournament—way back in the summer. (Last week.)

We were in our Friday afternoon sit-down with our boss, Richard Sanders, President and CEO of the Bellissimo, in the back of a limo on our way to the airport. Mr. Sanders had an appointment on the other side of the globe and we were accompanying him, but only as far as his Gulfstream 650. The car had pulled to a stop on the tarmac when No Hair casually changed my weekend plans.

"Oh, one more thing." No Hair looked at me. "Davis."

I didn't need one more thing. It had been a long week already. My partner Fantasy and I had pulled quadruples, working from sunup Monday until three seconds earlier at the casino's Plethora Buffet, of all places, waiting tables, of all things. The tips were pathetic. The head chef (who did no cheffing—he supervised large lumps of frozen stuff being lowered into big silver pans, unevenly top-coated with fake cheese, then cooked to almost burnt) was going through $2,500 a week in snow crab legs, and snow crab legs weren't on the buffet. We caught him selling the nasty things—I'm shellfish intolerant—out of the back of his Kia Cadenza in the parking lot of the U-Can-Pawn. The guy was running a crab con on the Bellissimo's dime.

No Hair called it a "classic double dip."

"Everyone in that whole place double dips, No Hair. Those buffet people will stick their fork in anything."

"I'm not talking about his table manners, Davis. I'm saying he was getting a paycheck and stealing from us at the same time."

Right.

Fantasy and I, when we finally caught up with double-dip man, spoke to him about how ill-advised his program was, then passed him to Biloxi Metro, me holding my nose the entire time. The red tape had kept us from attending our regularly scheduled Friday meeting with the boss in his office, and we had one eye on the weekend when No Hair came up with the bright idea that we ride with Mr. Sanders to the airport. Which was fine—I'm always up for a road trip—except for the fact that Fantasy and I smelled like shark bait.

"You two sit over there." No Hair pointed to the little bitty bench practically in the front seat. Mr. Sanders, a football field away, asked his driver, a man named Crisp, to crank up the air and crack his windows an inch.

Richard Sanders, in addition to signing everyone's paycheck, was married to the casino owner's daughter. She's a handful. He, on the other hand, is a great boss, a nice guy, an honest man, and extra handsome. He was on the cover of *Forbes* magazine a few months earlier. "Gulf Coast's Golden Boy Gambles It All on Macau."

Mr. Sanders thanked us for solving the crab caper, then told us he'd see us on Skype next Friday, the Friday after that, and the Friday after that, because he would be on the other side of the world for that many Fridays.

"If negotiations go well, I'll be back for the big tournament." He inventoried a leather portfolio full of personal electronic devices between his shoes, then looked up. "You three keep things down to a dull roar while I'm away."

Of course, we nodded. Will do.

We pulled into the private jet airport and an electric gate slid open. The limo was a foot from the airplane when No Hair piped up with his "one more thing."

"You're going to help us kick off slot-tournament season this weekend, Davis." He passed me a skinny folder. "Fantasy," he turned to my skinny partner, who'd been my Corrections Officer in prison (long long story), "you'll be backing her up. Stay close."

"Wait!" I said. "I can't work this weekend."

The trunk of the limo popped open as Mr. Sanders gathered his iThings. He had a leg out the door. "Is there a problem, Davis?"

"No sir." I showed him my teeth.

"I'll see you all in a few weeks," he said. "Hold the fort."

I let Mr. Sanders get a foot from the limo before I pounced. "No Hair!"

"Don't start with me, Davis."

It would take two of me to make up one of No Hair's legs, so I generally don't start with him. "I have a moving truck coming tomorrow," I said. "And I haven't packed one single thing."

"Work it out." He helped himself to Mr. Sanders' recently vacated seat, rocking the whole limo in the process. "I know it's last minute, Davis, but it can't be helped. Something caught my eye, and you need to play in the tournament."

"What?"

"The slot tournament," he said. "You're playing in it."

"No," I said. "What caught your eye?"

"A little old lady. There's a seventy-four-year-old woman registered for every slot tournament from now till summer," he said, "and her home address is a church in Alabama."

"Is she a priest?" Fantasy, my wingman, stretched her legs. Which are twice the length of mine. And she's stunningly pretty. Fantasy has ink-black hair she'd recently cut into a pixie, skin the color a hazelnut caffè latte, and sky blue eyes. "Who lives at a church in Alabama?"

"Exactly." No Hair stabbed a finger at Fantasy. "I want to know who lives at a church in Alabama." He turned the finger on me. "I want to know every move she makes." Stab, stab. "I want to know who she makes eye contact with. How many cats she has. I want to know her shoe size."

"Why do you want to know her shoe size?"

"You get my drift, Davis."

I got his drift.

"Step on it, Crisp," No Hair said. "I've got to get home to the missus." He burrowed in, closed his eyes, and played possum until we were back at the Bellissimo. Crisp slid to a stop behind No Hair's car in the executive parking lot. "See you Monday, ladies."

I turned to Fantasy in a panic.

She patted my knee. "You can do this."

"I don't even know what a slot tournament is." My Bellissimo adventures, to date, hadn't included slot tournaments. I'd scrubbed shower stalls, dealt Texas Hold 'Em, and decorated wedding cupcakes, but I hadn't been anywhere near a slot tournament.

"It's self-explanatory," she said. "A bunch of people play slot machines at the same time. Winner take all. Here." She held out a hand for the folder. "Let me see."

I passed it to her.

She flipped through. "You don't even have to be there until nine o'clock tomorrow morning." She held up a DMV portrait of a Senior Citizen. "Looks like you need to find her."

She was everyone's grandmother: deep laugh lines, wire-rimmed eyeglasses, embellished cardigan sweater. (Shasta daisies.)

"And then what?" I wondered aloud. "Shoot her?"

"Get her shoe size." Fantasy passed the folder back to me. "Surely, it won't take shooting her to find out what size shoes she wears. Go home. Sleep on it. Figure it out in the morning."

Crisp let us out at our parking lot, the peasant parking lot, four miles away from anything else.

"Come with me to the office so I can find something to wear," I said. "I don't want to get here any earlier than I have to."

"Gladly." She fanned her face. "I need to change clothes anyway."

Fantasy is an excellent partner. She's up for anything, fearless, and doesn't take crap off anyone. I suppose that's how you roll after seven years as a prison guard. In addition to her job skills, she always has my back, mediates between me and No Hair, and provides valuable family and relationship counseling, two things I find myself in occasional/constant need of. We make a good team: Davis Way and Fantasy Erb, Bellissimo Super Spies. With names no one catches on the first go-around.

We swiped ourselves in, then split, taking separate and varying routes to our workspace, which is located below the casino and sea level. Fantasy and I operate as far under the radar as possible. We keep a low profile so we can infiltrate various departments within the Bellissimo, and spend just as much time posing as casino patrons, so, we travel the property independently and incognito, heads ducked and hugging the walls. Working in Stealth Mode requires us to have offices that are impossible to get to. Like Hawaii. But once there, worth it. Just like Hawaii. We made our way there. (Our offices, not Hawaii.)

We met up at an unmarked door between Shakes, an ice-cream parlor, and Gamer, a kid casino, in a no-traffic corner of the mezzanine above the main lobby of the hotel. From there, we follow a cold, dark, scary service hall, then use a keypad to enter a door that leads to an elevator hidden on a dark wall. If someone were to stumble into this space, they'd stumble right back out as quickly as possible. If someone were looking for it, they wouldn't be able to find it with a tour guide, a GPS, and a bluetick coonhound. If someone went to all the trouble of following us, then managed to hack the keypad, they wouldn't be able to activate the elevator. Admission is facial recognition only, and the elevator recognizes these faces: me, Fantasy, No Hair, Mr. Sanders, and by default, Mrs. Sanders. It's very high tech, very *Get Smart*, and well off the beaten path.

We saw the blood as soon as the elevator doors parted.

Fantasy went right. I went left.

"Clear."

"Clear."

We backed into the elevator dodging a smeared trail of drying blood that led to a puddle in the corner. Roll call. Of the five people who had access to our elevator, we knew we weren't bleeding. No Hair had just left the property, and Mr. Sanders had just left the hemisphere. That left the wife, Bianca Casimiro Sanders.

I swiped, the doors closed, and down we went.

The elevator doors opened to more blood.

We followed the trail down the hall to our office. Fantasy had her gun drawn and signaled the countdown. On one, we blasted through. At first, we thought the place was on fire. Bianca Casimiro Sanders was stretched out on one of the sofas, and from the haze of smoke that filled the room, she must have been chain smoking her long skinny cigarettes three at a time for an hour. Her face was a ten on a grayscale of eight. Her left foot was wrapped in a bloody towel, and there was blood all over our nice gold sofa.

Fantasy batted through the smoke. "Mrs. *Sanders*! What's going *on* here?"

Bianca Sanders dropped her lit cigarette in the general direction of the drinking glass she was using for an ashtray, missed, and announced, "I've been shot," before passing out, then tumbling off the sofa onto our nice, clean carpet.

I ran. Locked myself in the bathroom. The trunk full of snow crab legs, sitting the wrong way in the limo, the blood, the smoke, Bianca's feet, and I was pretty sure I was pregnant.

TWO

Our workspace is divided into three large rooms: the bullpen, the closet, and control central. The bullpen is just inside the door. It's where we have meetings, lunch, hers and hers sofas, and where No Hair catches us watching Lifetime movies. Control central is through a door to the right. It glows. We have desks, white boards, pictures of Fantasy's dogs/kids (two large dogs, three small kids,) and four different computer systems up and running at all times. Mounted flat screens march across the middle of three walls flashing live feed from the casino, count room, cage, vault, and accounting. We even keep surveillance on surveillance. On the other side of the bullpen is the closet, our very large dressing room where we step in ourselves and step out other people. For me, that used to mean hot, itchy wigs, but recently, I started airbrushing my head a different color when the occasion called for it with spray paint called Colour Couture. Two hundred dollars a whack. It takes two whacks to get my hair completely dark, a lot of work to wash out, and that stuff ruins clothes, towels, and pillows. The closet is full of clothes. We have uniforms for every department in the Bellissimo—housekeeping, restaurants, security, gift shops, pool, transportation, maintenance, spa, valet, horticulture, and casino floor. Most of the clothes, though, are street clothes. We have casual collections, so we can sit and play quarter slot machines without garnering undue attention, all the way to designer apparel that neither Fantasy nor I could afford in our lifetimes, especially me, because lucky me, I'm a stunt double for Bianca Casimiro Sanders and have to dress the lavish part. So I have ludicrously expensive clothes to match Bianca's, each with its own insurance policy. There's Chanel, Versace, Halston, Donna Karan, Valentino, and Paula Deen. (Kidding.) These designer duds are why Bianca Sanders shows up in our hidey-hole; she doesn't let me step out as her for a split second unless she approves the color of panties I'm wearing, and she shows up regularly to disapprove.

Being a dead-ringer for Mrs. Richard Sanders was how I landed this job, and exactly how I landed in jail. We look so much alike that it even fools the elevator facial-recognition software, and it was a sad, sad day when she figured that one out. The only detail that keeps us from being identical twins separated at birth (aside from our ages, personalities, politics, ethics, and net worths) is our coloring. So I have to regularly alter mine, then dress up as her and do every single thing she doesn't feel like doing, which is most things. Some of the more ludicrous things she's demanded I do in the past six months have included posing for a family portrait with her husband and son, give plasma for her at a Bellissimo-sponsored donor drive, and take an eye exam.

"But Mrs. Sanders," I'd said, "how am I supposed to pull that off?" My eyes are the same color as my hair, a coppery cinnamon color. Hers are green, requiring me to wear tinted contact lenses while I do my Bianca chores. Not to mention I have twenty-twenty and she does not.

She hung up on me, so I guess she got it. There is no doubt in my mind that any day now she's going to say, "I have a splitting headache and need you to have sex with Richard tonight." Then tell me how to fake one.

Bianca Sanders is as unreasonable and self-centered as they come, and at the moment, there was nothing between me and her unreasonably bloody foot but a hollow wooden door.

First-aid first, and Fantasy handled that, because I was still in the ladies room with a cold, dripping hand towel pressed to my forehead, my head between my knees, stars circling above me, and sirens ringing in my ears.

"I could use some help out here, Princess!" Fantasy shouted. "Get it together!"

"I'm trying, Fantasy."

"Get out here. Bring me a clean towel and some whiskey."

I picked myself up, dusted myself off, then threw open the door. "What flavor of whiskey?"

Fantasy looked up from Bianca's bullet-riddled foot. "Honestly, Davis, I don't care. I don't think she does either."

We slapped her awake. ("Easy, Davis," Fantasy snapped at me. "She's going to come to and smack you back.") We gave her sips of brandy, then stretched her out on the ruined sofa, elevating her left foot.

"We need to get you to the emergency room, Mrs. Sanders."

"Can you walk?" Fantasy asked.

She was appalled. "I'm not going out in public wearing *this*." *This* looked like a perfectly acceptable emergency room outfit to me, and *this* probably cost more than the emergency room doctor's car. The problem must be that *this* was wrinkled. And bloody.

"We'll find you something else to wear," Fantasy suggested.

"Absolutely not. I'm not sitting in a germ infested emergency room." She weakly snapped her fingers for more brandy. "Find Gregory before I bleed to death." I waited for her to say to me, "And I'm going to need your foot."

* * *

Gregory Jakeaway, MD, treats Bianca Casimiro Sanders' raging hypochondria. He's her personal physician, and as such, is expected to have a fresh batch of Botox on him at all times, never speak to her of the dangers of smoking, plus read her mind and (poof!) appear when she needs him, which is when she's awake. People magically appear to do Bianca's bidding all the time. The woman has concierge everything—doctors, dentists, diamond brokers—everyone comes to her to spare her having to go to them. She does travel by limo to New Orleans, 90 miles east of Biloxi, every three weeks to "get out of the house" (have her roots done), and makes me go there too when my hair isn't up to her standards, which is about every two weeks. Whatever she does to herself, she wants done to me, her body double, and we've only had one problem so far. Make that two.

"Miss—" she tried, "you." She shook a finger at me. "David."

"It's Davis."

"Of course. We're having our breasts augmented."

"Oh, no we're not."

For the past three months, I've had to wear bras with water balloons in them while doing my Bianca chores.

She has an in-house staff in addition to her off-site people. Bianca has two personal chefs (at a venue with twelve restaurants) and two personal trainers. She has an on-call veterinarian and a full-time dog walker for her ill-tempered Teacup Yorkshire Terriers, Gianna and Ghita. What she has the most of, though, are personal assistants. She hires and fires them regularly, and every time she hires a new one, it costs us a week of work. Fantasy and I have to vet them: background checks including credit reports, criminal, driving, marital, medical, military, and school records, worker's comp claims, bankruptcy histories, and favorite menu item at Taco Bell.

In the past few months, we'd done it three times. Twice, after all our work, Bianca changed her mind and decided she wouldn't be able to tolerate the person we'd researched all the way back to the playground. ("Her nail beds are *blue,*" and the other, "she smells like *bread.*" Tidbits we might like to have known before we spent a combined eighty hours combing through the details of their gynecological histories.) The last one, just a month ago, hadn't passed the muster—I voted no—and No Hair let Bianca hire her anyway. A largish fuss ensued.

"Don't hire her, No Hair. She lives in a P. O. Box."

"We're hiring her."

Which struck me as odd. No Hair, former MBI (Mississippi Bureau of Investigation,) isn't much of a gambler. In fact, he's rule-follower number one around here, especially when it came to protecting Mr. & Mrs. Sanders. The girl, Peyton Reynolds, was spotless. Too spotless. Squeaky spotless. Making her a bad bet. I said don't hire someone who's so off the grid she's never even been to traffic court and No Hair said I discriminated against people who don't have criminal records. (No, I don't.) "Besides," he added, "Bianca will fire her before she has a chance to do any harm."

Apparently not.

"Who shot you, Mrs. Sanders?"

"I need a cigarette." She said it with a lot of breath and even more drama.

"We don't have any cigarettes," Fantasy told her, tossing the green pack of skinny cigarettes behind her back to me. "Who shot you?"

An hour passed before she whispered, "Peyton."

"Your new assistant?" I didn't whisper.

"Maybe she didn't shoot me directly." Bianca waved toward the glass of brandy, which meant she wanted me to hold it to her lips so that she might have a sip. "But it's her fault."

"Did she or did she not shoot you, Mrs. Sanders?" Fantasy asked.

Bianca sighed and covered her eyes with platinum, diamonds, and a perfect manicure. "It was my gun, but it was her fault."

"Who was holding the gun?" I asked. Like pulling teeth.

Bianca waved the hand she wasn't hiding behind through the air, dismissing the question.

"Mrs. Sanders?" I moved in closer, something I didn't particularly want to do. "Did you shoot yourself?"

She whimpered.

"You shot *yourself* in the foot?"

* * *

No Hair had No Phone Manners. "What, Davis? *What*?"

"So sorry to bother you" (I wasn't within a mile of a so-sorry voice), "but Bianca has shot herself in the foot and refuses to go to the hospital."

"Assess."

"She's fine." I waited a beat for No Hair's life to stop flashing before his eyes. "I can't get Dr. Doolittle on the phone."

"His name is Jakeaway."

"Sure it is." I'd stepped into the closet to call him, because Bianca was well on her way to being brandy drunk, and she was lamenting her latest fear at the top of her lungs. (Shoes. She was wailing through an inventory of shoes she feared she'd never wear again.) I filled him in on what little we knew, and he said he'd get Dr. Jakeaway on the phone immediately.

"She's tried," I said. "He's not answering."

"That's because she calls him all day every day. He reaches the point that he just stops answering. He'll pick up when I call. How bad does it look?"

"To her or to me?" I asked. "Because she's acting like her leg's blown off."

"To you."

"As shootings go, not bad," I said. "It's surface. It skidded along the top of her foot. No bullet in there and no exit. Obviously, she can walk on it and the bleeding has stopped."

"Sit tight for now," he said. "I'll get Jakeaway there, then you go find the assistant."

"What?" I pulled the phone away from my head and looked at it. "For one, the assistant's probably long gone. For another, I can't go track that girl down. You've got me in a slot-machine tournament in a few hours!"

"Find that girl."

* * *

Gregory Jakeaway arrived eighteen minutes (of Bianca breaking the sound barrier with her ear-piercing agony) later. Clearly he pumped iron when he wasn't tending to Bianca Casimiro Sanders' medicinal needs. I'd bet there were more than a few steroids in his little black bag too, because the man was huge. Not larger than No Hair—no one's larger than No Hair—but he looked bigger, because he was all brawny muscle and because he wore clothes two sizes too small. I'd seen him dozens of times, and every time he'd been wearing a golf shirt that was bursting at the seams, straining against his ridiculously large neck, biceps, and chest. Tonight's skintight golf shirt was powder-puff pink. He wore absurdly small, tight, bright short shorts with the golf shirts. Year round. The only concession he made to slot-tournament season were citrus-shade sweaters he draped across his shoulders and looped loosely around his neck. He was Dr. Malibu Ken.

Fantasy rode the elevator to meet him, then escorted him to our bloody sofa full of Bianca.

"Kitten!" He rushed to her side.

(Kitten?)

He produced a syringe from one of his muscle groups, held it high to get a good look, squirted a few drops in the air, then cooed at her as he stabbed her in the hip. Lights out. Ten minutes later, he presented his findings to us. Bianca was in another realm, mouth wide open and snoring. A Kodak moment if ever there was one.

"There are twenty-six bones in the foot," he said, "and she missed every single one." He gazed at Kitten with admiration. "She grazed the metatarsal here," he pointed, "but all that really happened is the bullet grazed the exterior mid-foot—" (then there was a spiel I tried not to listen to: tissue, ligaments, planum, Chex-Mix, tendons, dorsum) "—but in the end, it's just a flesh wound."

She snored on.

"It looks worse than it is."

It looked nasty.

"And it just appears that she lost a lot of blood," he said. "She didn't lose all that much and what she did lose is probably all here."

Our bullpen looked like a blood mobile that had been in the middle of a ten-bus pileup.

"We'll probably want to do a skin graft in a few days," he said, "and of course she'll be bedridden for a few weeks," he smiled at us (2,000 watts), "but she'll be just fine."

A few weeks of bedridden Bianca was very bad news for me. No telling what was on her calendar, all of which she'd expect me to do. ("Go get my cankle lipo for me and I mean *this minute*.")

He snapped on gloves, patched up her boo boo, generously passed out pain pills, antibiotics, and instructions, then transferred her to our other gold sofa. The one she hadn't ruined. Yet.

"How long do we have?" I asked.

Dr. Jakeaway was soaping and scrubbing his muscles at the sink. "Before what?"

"She wakes up."

"Six to eight hours."

"What do you have that would keep her out for six to eight days?" Fantasy asked.

His head fell back on a laugh, and a whole new set of wiry-looking muscle things popped out of his distended throat. "Six to eight days! You're funny!"

We got rid of the good doctor, bagged everything, including the ruined sofa cushions, and tossed it all out the door. We updated No Hair and he made the decision that Richard Sanders didn't need to know about this until his plane landed.

"Do either of you know how Bianca got hold of a gun in the first place?"

We didn't.

He signed off with this: "Bianca is staying right there with you girls until you locate the assistant and find out what happened up there."

There was no telling what happened up there. Bianca said it was the assistant's fault, but Bianca passed out fault like it was bubble gum. The girl could have run Bianca's bath one degree too warm, or served her a martini with three stuffed olives instead of two. For all we knew, Bianca could have blown the assistant's head off simply because it was Friday, left her in a puddle, then dragged her own bloody foot down here without saying a word about the dead body upstairs. I could hear it now, "Yes, I failed to mention it, because she wasn't going to get any deader and at the time I was in danger of losing an *appendage*!"

And she was snoring like a bear.

To put off the possibility of a dead body in the Sanders' residence for a few minutes, Fantasy banged around at the bar and produced a bottle of Jack Daniels and a glass. She poured herself two inches and tipped it my way. "Fortitude."

"Where's my fortitude?"

She tossed it back, then poured another. "Davis," she said, "you can't drink."

Like hell. I was a champ.

"If you think you're pregnant," she said, "don't drink."

I hadn't said a word. Not a peep. Not even to Bradley Cole.

THREE

Before we met, Bradley Cole was my landlord. After we met, he was my criminal defense attorney. Through it all, he's been the absolute love of my life. Lately, though, I've worried that I'm not his, and the second I started down that road, I began wondering if I'd *ever* been.

Three's a crowd, and we have a third: Mary Harper Hathaway. I believe, in addition to having a stupid name, Mary Harper Hathaway wants Bradley Cole to be the love of *her* life, and she definitely has the upper hand, because for every ten minutes he spends with me, he spends ten hours with her.

Bradley Cole—sun-kissed, six feet tall, golden blonde, center of my universe, perfect teeth, brilliant green eyes—is lead counsel at the Grand Palace Casino, a much smaller and very different resort than the Bellissimo. We welcome the masses; Bradley's casino caters to the ridiculously rich gambling golfer. Bradley and I live together in a one-bedroom condo between the two resorts. He takes a left and drives seven miles to work. I take a right and do the same.

We'd been living together for six months (think six-month honeymoon) when Bradley came home from work one day, covered me with kisses, then said, "You are not going to believe what's happened. We got slapped with a lawsuit today."

"Don't you get slapped with lawsuits every day?"

"A lot of days," he said, "but this one's different."

Understatement of the year.

The Grand Palace has no slot machines, just tables: blackjack, craps, roulette, and seven hundred different kinds of poker. A woman named Bonita Jakes, who'd dealt Mississippi Stud at the

Grand Palace for fifteen years, had gone to her doctor, who told her that her work environment was killing her. She got a lawyer.

"What's she claiming?" I asked.

"That second-hand smoke has made her pre-cancerous."

"You are kidding."

"I am not."

A casino employee playing a No Smoking card? Casinos are Yes Smoking. There isn't a venue on Earth where smoking is more welcome than casinos. Casinos are a smoker's paradise, there are more ashtrays than money. It only stands to reason that if you're going to *work* in one, you're going to be around smoke.

"She'll never win it, Bradley." We settled on the sofa with two big glasses of wine.

"I don't think so either," he said, "but it's already a nightmare. We've had four senior dealers up and quit in the past two weeks," he looked at me, "no notice whatsoever, and it's obvious they plan on joining her suit or filing their own."

"So it could get really big?" I asked.

"This thing might get *huge*, Davis. I'm not sure we can handle it alone."

Hello, Mary Harper Hathaway. Come save the day, Ole Miss Law, Tri-Delt Southern Belle, Toxic Tort Litigation Specialist, Home Wrecker.

At first, I didn't say a word about the long hours, constant phone calls, and cute little quips about Mary Ha Ha's brilliance. How could I? I was happier than I'd ever been in my life and I loved every single thing about Bradley Cole. We'd been together less than a year when that crazy lady filed the smoke suit, so I chose to wait it out rather than whine, because for all practical purposes, we should have still been in the getting-to-*really*-know you stage, not the you-think-she's-prettier-than-me-don't-you stage.

Two weeks in, he began watching me out of the corner of his eye.

"Is everything okay, Davis?"

I swallowed it. "Fine."

"Fine?"

"Fine!"

"You know, Davis? If you met her, you'd see that you have nothing to worry about."

"I'm not worried, Bradley." I was full-blown freaked.

Bradley Cole and I covered so much ground so quickly that we'd skipped a few steps. Maybe we should have started at the beginning instead of in the middle.

Bradley came into our relationship as clean as a whistle. I came in with blonde hair (quickly corrected), a prison record (big mix-up between me and Bianca Sanders), two divorces (but only one ex-husband), a Southern Baptist mother who badgered me incessantly (left lengthy phone messages questioning my "unusual" roommate situation), a sister (Meredith) who popped in regularly with my seven-year-old niece (Riley) in tow to drop off my eighty-two-year-old grandmother (Granny Dee) who thought sitting around Pine Apple watching the grass grow wasn't nearly as much fun as staying with her granddaughter (me) in Biloxi and playing slot machines at her (I wish) casino.

Granny Dee is the very reason we began looking for a bigger place.

It wasn't hard to keep the fact that we were living together from Granny Dee. She couldn't hear a bomb going off, couldn't see her own hand in front of her face, and swallowed a small mountain of pills every night, the little blue one assuring her a good night's rest. Of course, we gave her the bed. The *only* bed. The minute her head hit the pillow, she was gone for eleven hours. La La Land. It was only a couple of nights a month and Bradley assured me he didn't mind the sofa bed as long as I was in it. (See? He's so perfect.) He waited to come home from work until I had Granny Dee tucked in, which was about 6:15. He'd call. "Is the coast clear?"

Granny Dee would, on occasion, sneak out of her chemical stupor and yell, "DAVIS? IS SOMEONE HERE?"

I'd scoot to the bedroom door. "NO, GRANNY, THAT'S JUST THE TELEVISION!"

"OKAY, DEAR." And off she'd go.

I'll tell you one thing she could see and hear—slot machines.

Granny Dee was an almost perfect human, and she had, in turn, produced one in my father. I worship the ground the man walks on. My father is the Chief of Police and Mayor of Pine Apple, and for years, on his day off, he's driven Granny Dee to Sprague, Alabama, home of the Fortune Casino. Daddy would get Granny Dee settled at her favorite slot machine, Diamonds and Devils, get a big cup of coffee, then read one of his cold-war spy novels until Granny began showing signs of wear and tear from the Diamonds and Devils, which is to say when she fell asleep on the slot machine. Before that, it was church bingo. Before that, throughout my childhood, it was Canasta Tuesday with her girlfriends.

But things change, and Granny's game had to change with them. Her canasta friends, one by one, had gone on to the Big Canasta Tournament in the Sky. Bingo night came to a screeching halt when it was discovered that Brother Bob was the only one winning. Just in time, the Fortune Casino was built—a 20,000 square-foot prefab metal building stuffed to the brim with penny and nickel slot machines—close enough to Pine Apple for a day trip. But then more change last year, when Daddy had a heart attack and subsequent triple-bypass. His recovery has been amazing, but none of us, including Granny Dee, wanted him off on a field trip one day a week, so my sister Meredith began chauffeuring Granny back and forth to the Fortune, which was right about when a major Alabama gambling storm that had been brewing for years finally broke wide open and everyone involved was either mad, indicted, or dead. In an attempt to contain the chaos, temporary injunctions and cease-and-desist orders were slapped on slot machines around the state. One day it was the Fortune Casino, the next an indoor flea market. For the first time in her life, Granny Dee had no game.

Leave it to my mother to come up with the solution: Granny could stay with me a few days a month and get her gamble on. I was just across the state line, and Mississippi had no qualms about gambling. Mississippi said bring it on.

"What is it, Davis?" my mother demanded. "Do you have *secrets* you don't want Granny to know?"

"Of course I don't!" *Of course I do!* "It's our home, Mother. And we only have one bedroom."

Ooops. Until that exact moment, my mother believed in her heart that she'd raised me right and that Bradley and I were very mismatched roommates. That's how delusional she is: I'm thirty-something, I've been married twice, I *love* Bradley, and this isn't 1953.

Once the Mary Ha Ha program began, though, I was thrilled to have Granny Dee stay with me, because at least I had someone to shout to.

"DO YOU WANT MORE LASAGNA, GRANNY?"

"Thank you, honey." Granny reached up and patted a few hundred of the five hundred curlicues on her head. "Monique mixes this shade herself." Monique is Granny's eighty-seven-year-old hairdresser. Granny's hair is cornflower blue.

Bradley called a hundred times the first month to tell me how sorry he was that he wasn't going to make it in until midnight. Again.

"IT'S OKAY, GRANNY'S HERE."

"*Davis!*"

"Oh, sorry!"

Month two of Mary Ha Ha Daze, Bradley began throwing me bones.

"We're going to take a quick break, Davis. Come have a drink with us."

"Pass."

That invitation came when Fantasy and I were in the middle of a swimming pool project, serving giant frozen vodka drinks—Summer Slushes, Electric Lemonades, Blue Bahamas—to people who were, for the most part, still drunk from the night before. Our uniforms were red bikinis with floral sarongs the size and bulk of a single Kleenex. We were on the pool job because, as everyone knows, prostitution is illegal. And those cabanas are for changing clothes. Fantasy, whose skin is not all that dark, had slathered herself in sunscreen the first day.

"You'd better lotion up, Davis."

"Why? It's not that hot out."

I was sunburned beyond recognition. I jumped on the sunscreen train the second day, but it was too late. I was already the exact color of the bikini. I wasn't about to sit across from Miss Porcelain Skin Law Review.

There was precious little time to talk to Bradley about anything, because he was always with Mary Ha Ha. When we did catch up, it was about the lawsuit. The day after the news broke about pre-cancerous Bonita Jakes suing the Grand, an attorney based out of Birmingham, Alabama, Jerry McAllen, took to the airwaves. Every other commercial on every local channel showed him in a $4,000 suit, sitting at a bar with a gorgeous young woman wearing a cowboy hat and boots, not much in between, in a fog of cigarette smoke. The commercial began with him fake coughing and fanning away the smoke. His big, fat, diamond pinkie ring zigzagged across the screen.

"*Have you ever worked for the Grand Palace? Even for a day? Do you work there now? Do you plan on working there in the future? Then call me. Jerry McAllen. Let's talk about the Clean Air Act. Let's talk about your God-given rights and Mississippi's promise to provide you safety in the workplace.*"

The camera panned the girl, then zoomed in on her cleavage.

"*I was a cocktail waitress at the Grand Palace for three months on my way to being a country music superstar.*" Cough, cough, cough. "*Now my dreams are gone.*" Cough, cough, cough. "*I can't sing a note because the Grand Palace didn't protect me, so I called Jerry McAllen.*"

Jerry McAllen reached out and patted her bare knee, poor little thing, then solemnly faced the camera head-on with ominous parting words: "*Has the Grand Palace stolen your dreams and your ability to support yourself in the future too? Then call me. Jerry McAllen.*" Next, the television screen filled with the phone number: 1-800-NO-SMOKE.

Bradley and Mary Ha Ha, plus several other attorneys working the case, fought a tough opponent, and not the ambulance-chasing Jerry McAllen. They were up against the Big Picture. The charge wasn't that the Grand Palace broke the law, because Mississippi doesn't have a comprehensive indoor smoking ban. The charge was negligence—the Grand Palace should have taken better care of its employees by having adequate ventilation, air-purification systems, and mandatory clean-air breaks.

One thing has kept me going. A few times a week, since the start of this mess, Bradley has snuck in and woke me up with kisses, sometimes five or six hours after I've climbed into bed alone. He doesn't turn on a light and we don't say boo to each other. We skip all formalities and preamble. In the wee hours of the morning, we recharge our relationship batteries. These are the only times it doesn't feel like Mary Ha Ha is in the room with us.

One night Bradley snuck in and almost recharged Granny Dee's batteries. I honestly didn't know my grandmother could move that fast, hit that hard, or scream that loud. The next morning, he left a note: *Davis, let's look for a bigger place.*

We found one. A really nice one. Moving Day was hours from now. I wished my boss's wife hadn't shot herself in the foot. I wished her personal assistant wasn't missing. I wished I didn't have to play in a slot tournament instead of moving. More than anything, though, I wished Bradley and I had been paying a little more attention to formalities and preambles.

FOUR

Fantasy and I went through passed-out Bianca's pockets.

"I found her key."

"Good," I said. "I found three hundred dollars and an earring."

"Let's see the earring."

I held it up.

"Pass."

We left Bianca sleeping on our sofa and rode the elevator to the Sanders' place a mile above us.

"We should have changed clothes." I fanned the front of my fishy Plethora Buffet uniform.

"Stop, Davis. You're stirring it up."

The Sanders' home was palatial, beautiful, and empty, as far as we could see. The staff that should have been there had probably scattered during the shootout. We snapped on gloves and tiptoed through, keeping our eyes peeled for dead bodies and the like.

"The mystery of Bianca Gets a Gun is solved." Fantasy pointed. "She borrowed yours."

It *was* my gun. A girl knows her gun. "Damn."

Downstairs in our closet we have a hidden vault drawer in the middle of the shoe racks where we keep our guns and ammo. Just in case. Apparently the hidden vault drawer isn't hidden enough. We were two feet into Bianca's dressing room when Fantasy spotted my Smith & Wesson Bodyguard 380 on the floor beside the chaise lounge. So Bianca had gone downstairs and helped herself to my gun. No big surprise. She'd helped herself to my ex-ex-husband last year. She could have him, but it's not nice to take someone's gun. Not that I ever said Bianca Sanders was nice.

I took the right and Fantasy dropped to her knees on the left side of the long chair. We used our gloved fingers to comb through the thick carpet for the brass casings that eject from the gun as it's fired. With six in the clip and one in the chamber, Bianca could have pulled the trigger up to seven times.

Fantasy rose from her side of the chaise with four casings.

I had three.

"Let's go." Fantasy shook the empties in her closed palm like they were brass dice. "We have to find all seven rounds."

The dressing room had three doors. We'd entered from the hallway. Another door led to the Sanders' bedroom, and the third door led to Bianca's office, a deceptive designation because Bianca didn't do anything that remotely resembled work. The wall spaces between the three doors each held Jackson Pollock abstracts. In a *dressing room.* The ones to the right and left of the office door each had .380 blowouts. We admired the two mutilated paintings.

"Who shoots art?" Fantasy asked.

"She double tapped this one," I said. My painting had twin blasts.

"I've got one," Fantasy said.

We found the fourth and fifth rounds embedded in the baseboards on both sides of the office door. I stretched out on Bianca's chaise lounge, aimed a finger gun just above my feet, and determined the one to the right seemed, trajectory wise, to be the most likely candidate to have skidded along the top of Bianca's foot before finding a home. We turned up a sixth round that had whizzed through the doorway and into the office, hitting one of Bianca's dogs between the eyes. Actually, it hit an oil portrait of the dogs, not a real dog.

We didn't find the seventh round, or Peyton, the assistant.

Here's hoping they're not together.

We'd gone over the surveillance footage a dozen times before we came up here. Peyton Reynolds had not left the thirtieth floor unless she'd jumped off the roof and after two hours of searching high and low, we decided she was not in the Sanders' residence either. We looked absolutely everywhere.

Where was Peyton Reynolds?

I pulled my phone out of my double-knit pant pocket. "No Hair. We found seven spent casings, but only six rounds, and the assistant isn't here."

"Holy, holy hell," he said. "I'm on my way."

He called in extra security and a nurse, then gave us permission to have Bianca transferred to her own living quarters.

Fantasy and I staggered to our cars.

"Good luck in the slot tournament tomorrow, Davis."

"Good luck finding Peyton."

* * *

When I finally stepped inside my own front door it was after two a.m. I draped a hanging bag full of slot-contest clothes across the sofa, then used the walls to hold me up as I stumbled to the kitchen. There was a note in the middle of the table.

Davis, We're on our way to Corporate. Last minute, couldn't be helped. I tried to call you ten times. X, B.

Not *Love, B*, not *XOXO, B*, just *X, B.* I don't know if *X* was for a hug or a kiss. Either way, I could have used a little more. I crumpled the note and bounced it off the refrigerator. Corporate was the Grand Palace, Las Vegas. We was Bradley and Mary Ha Ha. I checked my phone. I had seven missed calls from *X, B*, and that made me feel a little better. I felt my way to the bedroom, turned in the general direction of the bed, fell on it, still in my fish clothes, and slept until the doorbell rang.

A large man waved a pink sheet of paper in my face. My eyes focused just enough to see the logo: *777 MOVERS.*

"Twenty-two hundred Beach Boulevard? Cole? Unit three-oh-seven?"

"We can't move today," I said. "I'm running in a slot-machine race."

"My grandmother plays slot tournaments," one of the three men said.

"Tell her I said good luck." I closed the door, started a pot of coffee, and stepped in the shower. Thank goodness the movers had woken me up. The slot thing started in an hour.

* * *

I showered, got gussied up, sprayed my hair medium-spice brown, poked contact lenses into my eyes until they were medium blue, poured a cup of coffee, then checked my phone. Nothing from Bradley. There was a message from No Hair letting me know that Peyton Reynolds was still nowhere to be found. He said that he and Fantasy would be hot on her trail today and when I wasn't in the slot tournament tracking down the little old lady who lived in a church, I'd better be on the thirtieth floor getting information out of Bianca. Stay in touch. Acknowledge receipt of these pointed instructions.

No Way was I calling No Hair. It was entirely too early.

I sat down at the kitchen table with my coffee and the folder of marching orders, then fired up my laptop to cram for the slot-machine test. The Bellissimo website told me there were three types of tournaments. The first, in a category all by itself, was the official kickoff to Slot Tournament Season, the mother of all Bellissimo slot events, and it was right around the corner. Only high, high rollers played in this one, limited to fifty invited guests—an intimate slot gathering with fantastic odds and fantastic-er prizes. I didn't need or want to know about that production, so I concentrated on the others. They fell into two categories: free and not free, regular and irregular, no big deal and big deal.

The free tournaments are weekly for the duration of Slot Tournament Season, at the crack of dawn every Thursday morning, and the password to get in is probably Geritol, Depends, or Polident. Thursday mornings at the Bellissimo are set aside for seniors. It's a traffic jam of walkers, wheelchairs, and motorized scooters until noon, when the slot tournament and two-for-one buffet are over, then the old folks scoot home for their naps. No pre-registration, entry fee, or red tape is required, just show up with your Medicare card and bang on the one-armed bandits. The weekly winner receives a thousand dollars in cash. Thank goodness No Hair didn't have me in the Thursday senior tournament. I sprayed my hair gray once and it had been a nightmare. I looked like I'd dipped my head in a bucket of sidewalk. Never again.

I was in the medium-sized tournament, the middle child tournament—not the huge one that made headlines, but not the weekly senior event that wasn't the least bit newsworthy either. Today's tournament was the first of six. These shindigs are held once a month for the season, invitation only, and themed—Cashanova, Pirate's Treasure, Christmas Cash, Break the Bank. And little old lady who lives in a church was signed up for all six. They required a three-day commitment, an entry fee, and you have to be a registered guest at the hotel to participate.

It all looked perfectly sane to me, as sane as casino events go, so I turned to the next order of business, the folder from No Hair. I pulled out the photo of the little old lady. Her name was Jewell Maffini. Jewell didn't look like she could hurt a flea, but she was my mark. No Hair's sticky read: *All known associates and details of her connection to the church.*

If history repeats itself, and it certainly does around here, No Hair already knew who this little old lady was associated with and he already knew her connection to the church. If I were a betting man, and there's certainly a lot of betting around here, I'd bet No Hair sprang this on me with the singular goal of confirming what he already suspected.

Wonder what he already suspected.

Under her photograph, the details. I was on my way to the Mystery Shopper tournament, with an entry fee of $2,500. The best news? I was booked in a Lantana Suite for two nights.

The invitation was an elaborate print production that started out like an oversized greeting card. Inside was a folded, glossy shopping bag with *Bellissimo* stamped in gold with braided gold ribbon handles. It pulled open to reveal silky cards, individually wrapped in creamy, thin tissue paper, secured by a sticky gold seal with a raised script *B*.

Fancy shmancy. Tiffany's should see this.

The first card was a wedding invitation. Upon closer inspection, it turned out to be the who, what, when, and where of the slot tournament. The second card listed the fabulous prizes, including the grand prize. One of the hundred participants was to be crowned the Mystery Shopper and a ridiculous cash payday was in store. The third card was a coupon for a forty-percent-off shopping spree in the Bellissimo shops, and the Bellissimo shops were nothing to sneeze at, so that meant for the duration of the tournament, the participants could get $5,000 socks for $3,000 or a $7,000 ink pen for $4,200.

The one thing about casino work that I really couldn't get used to was just how much money was involved-- $5,000 dresses, $7 donuts, $10,000 bets, $400 lobsters, $12,000 watches. All under one roof.

I grabbed my things, hopped in my VW Bug, and got myself under the one roof.

I made my way to the convention level, a venue above the casino that I'd not had the pleasure of and where all slot tournaments took place, which is another reason I didn't know a thing about them. Not only had I not played in one, I'd never been anywhere near this part of the extensive Bellissimo properties to even walk by one.

The Bellissimo Convention Center was, like the rest of this place, plus-sized, impeccably dressed, and mostly red and gold. Unlike the rest of this place, the lobby was as quiet as a library. And speaking of impeccably dressed, I looked great, thanks, for the most part, to the styling talents of Mr. James Perse. I was wearing his beach-blue, short linen shirt dress with drawstring waist. It was glorious, and I was glad to squeeze it in one more time before it got too cold to wear it or it took any more squeezing to get in it.

Note to self: start taking the steps and stop eating the whole box of Pop Tarts for lunch.

Over the dress, I wore a BCBG pale gray, jersey knit, cropped jacket that was as soft as a baby blanket. Below the great dress, I had on Michael Kors four-inch cork and leather sandals. Above it all, I was a blue-eyed medium-spice brunette.

I followed discreet Mystery Shopper signs to the ballroom. I didn't even know there was a ballroom. I stepped up to the desk to find out that No Hair had registered me, set me up in the hotel, but hadn't paid the entry fee. Dammit.

"Are you sure?"

The lady sighed. "Yes. I'm sure."

"Can I pay it later?"

"No. There's an ATM right outside the door."

There were more ATMs than anything else at the Bellissimo. There were ATMs in the bathroom stalls. (Kidding. There weren't.) I dug through my bag, a Gucci medium tote, and came up with nothing but my own bank card. I drained the money out of my account, paid the entry fee, drew a number out of a hat, seventy-six, and found a corner seat to watch for the little old lady who lived in a church while waiting for my turn to play.

The ballroom had to be twenty-thousand square feet. The walls weren't fabric covered so much as they were fabric upholstered, all the way up, in a gold fleur-de-lis patterned silk. The ceiling was a mile high, arched, and gold. Everything else was black: carpets, linens, staff. Bright lights from somewhere above were aimed at four long rows of slot machines in the middle of the room; everything else was backlit or candlelit. Clearly, the slot machines wanted to be the star of the show, but just then the brightest Bellissimo star appeared. The slot machines saw him, gave up, and powered down.

(No, they didn't.)

Celebrity sightings weren't all that unusual at the Bellissimo. They headlined the theater acts every weekend, other times they were simply VIP guests. Last year, the entire ensemble of a television real wives show piled in. They brought a camera crew, a production team, and a trailer load of ill will and Spanx. The next weekend, it was an MVP NBA forward, his latest wife, and his fourteen very tall children. Several months ago, there'd been a convention of *governors*. Forty-eight of them. In addition to the A-list musicians, politicians, comedians, authors, actors and athletes, we had our own internal celebrities, Richard and Bianca Casimiro Sanders at the top of that list. Bianca, especially (and I knew this first hand), didn't go anywhere on the property where the crowd didn't part and gasp, and when Mr. Sanders entered one of the restaurants, all forks dropped. ("It's the *president*!") They were pretty, the Sanders, both of them. They were often more of a presence than the real celebrities; the crowd loved nothing better than a good, up-close Sanders sighting.

But no one, absolutely no one, at the Bellissimo had the star power of the man who'd just entered the ballroom. I was busy scanning the crowd for my little-old-lady mark when the air changed. I looked around to find the source, and it didn't take long.

Matthew Thatcher.

The domed ceiling could have parted with Elvis descending on a fluffy cloud with wings, cherubs, and harps, and he wouldn't have been given more than a glance, because everyone in the room was so completely smitten with Thatch. He was a real guy, one of us, and I'd heard that he, like me, was from next-door Alabama. And here he was. In the flesh. I'd certainly heard of Thatch, and had seen him dozens of times from across the casino (you couldn't miss him), but none of my Bellissimo assignments had taken me anywhere close to working around him. He'd been in the ballroom one minute, and already his name was being shouted from every corner.

Matthew Thatcher was the Bellissimo's resident Master of Ceremonies. If a microphone was ever turned on Thatch was at the other end of it. He emceed all contests, drawings and promotional events, including, it would seem, slot tournaments. Twice a week, a brass cage the size of a car was rolled to the middle of the casino floor. Based on points earned, gamblers were given entry slips to drop into the cage. Every hour on the hour, Thatch, with a lot of hoopla, pulled a name out of the big brass hat. The prizes varied: cars, cruises, free casino money, spin the wheel, scoop up cash. Everyone knew him, loved him, and begged him to call their name. His resident rise to fame had happened well before I arrived on the scene and while I was aware of the Thatch Phenomenon, I'd never seen it up close. Until now.

A well-dressed woman at least twenty years older than me had taken a seat at the table next to mine. She was alone with a cup of coffee waiting, I assumed, like me, for her turn in the tournament. I caught her eye. "What *is* the big deal about this guy?" I asked.

She glazed over. "Isn't he something?"

Something was busy working the crowd. Had there been babies, he'd have been kissing them.

"They say," the woman didn't take her eyes off Thatch, "that if he walks by you, you'll win."

"Really?" I half-laughed.

"He's like," she sighed, "a lucky charm."

Apparently, I wasn't immune. All of a sudden I was overwhelmingly dizzy; the room spun around me at warp speed. It was like someone had turned off all five of my senses, and I wondered if it might be possible to faint while sitting down.

"Are you okay?" It was a voice from a thousand miles away. "Should I get someone?"

The cloud began to lift and I heard a loud siren ringing in my ears. My vision slowly cleared and it seemed I'd lived through whatever had just happened without having to be picked up off the floor. Ten very long seconds had elapsed, but it felt like ten hours. When was the last time I'd eaten anything? What in the world was *wrong* with me?

Oh.

FIVE

My paycheck is ridiculously large. I have two jobs, so I receive two salaries, but just one check every other Friday. Direct deposit money dump every other Friday. Once or twice a month, I pull up my banking information just to stare at the big numbers.

The negotiations had gone down shortly after my release from prison earlier this year.

"At this point, Davis, you know what I expect of you in the corporate realm." Richard Sanders was on his side of the desk. I was in the hot seat across from him.

"Yes, sir." Under No Hair's supervision, our team solves pesky internal problems that are part of the fabric of day-to-day casino operations. Simply put, cheating at games probably dates back to dinosaurs in cahoots with pterodactyls who spotted for them during boulder bowling for a cut in on the bucket-of-turtles jackpot. Today, with the eleven thousand cameras and a security staff of one-eighty at the Bellissimo, things hadn't changed much. All players want an edge, and there will always be those who are willing to go over it.

Surveillance systems are in place for the small-time casino cheat. Purse snatchers, chip scoopers, past-posters, and dice sliders are expected. They show up regularly and are promptly shown the door, where they're introduced to the Biloxi Metro Police. Tough sentences discourage apprentices; time served for emptying out a bank vault runs neck-and-neck with time served for marking cards at a blackjack table in Mississippi.

There is, however, another layer of cheating, the one No Hair,

Fantasy, and I wallow in. The Bellissimo employs almost four thousand people, and let me assure you, they're not all true blue. It takes more than a security suit and videography to catch a dealer partnered with a gang of counterfeiters, or a front desk manager skimming and selling random guest credit card information. Our team covertly immerses ourselves in the problem area, sniffing out the bad guys.

That's my first job.

Bianca Casimiro Sanders is my second.

"I don't know how this will work, Davis," Mr. Sanders had said that day. "But I can't imagine it will take that much of your time."

(Wrong.)

Richard Sanders, Nevada native, UNLV graduate, mid-40s, blonde-athletic-handsome, is a stand-up guy and scary smart. The one area of his life that doesn't fit the rest is his marriage.

"It's not a bad idea for you to impersonate Bianca on occasion," he said, "but I'm at a loss to set parameters or assign a value to something so unprecedented." He shrugged, tapped a silver pen against his desk. "I think the Bellissimo will benefit from the goodwill Bianca's stronger presence will bring." (Behind every good man and such.) "But more than that," he dropped the pen, "she's dead set on it."

Why wouldn't she be? I honestly think that it had more to do with the fact that I was ten years younger than her (and let's face it—five pounds lighter, seven on a skinny day) than anything else. At the time Richard Sanders and I sat down, I'd attended two events pretending to be Bianca—the Biloxi Mayor's Breakfast and a ribbon cutting at the new children's wing of Biloxi Memorial—and while she'd cut out her own tongue before admitting it, I think she liked the good press. A few days after the ribbon cutting, she'd tossed me an Oscar de la Renta Picasso Newsprint swimsuit. She added a sheer jacket, red stiletto heels, a hoola-hoop sized hat with matching straw bag, and four hundred dollar sunglasses. Then she sent me to the Bellissimo pool.

"Don't take the shoes off."

I guess that meant no swimming.

I had zigzag sun marks on my feet for two weeks.

People gawked all day, and it could have been that the swimsuit, folded, could have fit in my ear. If my father had walked up, he'd have thrown a quilt over me. The pretty pool boys, four of them, never spoke directly to me, and never left my side. They spritzed me with chilled Evian water. Brought me iced, spiked lemonade. Fed me grapes. (Kidding about the grapes.) My photograph appeared, a half-page, in an oversized, glossy New Orleans lifestyle magazine a few weeks later with the caption *The Bellissimo's First Lady of Leisure*. The man who does our hair, Seattle, had it enlarged, matted, and framed, and I see it every time Bianca makes me have my eyebrows threaded.

Here's what I think: Bianca is aging, and she's not being very graceful about it. She wasn't going down without a war either. The specialist's surgery suite was her battleground, and the strongest weapon in her arsenal was me.

And here's something else I think: If the Sanders' marriage playbook hadn't changed, everything would have been fine. But it did, and the reality of the new rules staring her right in her Juvidermed face had resulted, I was soon to learn, in her shooting herself in the foot.

After the first round of the slot tournament, I had to go see Bianca.

Knock-knock. "Mrs. Sanders?" It was a scene from The Princess and the Pea. The bed was a linen parking lot. A family of five could sleep in it comfortably. It was a study in pillows, too many to count, several propping up her injured foot, which was swathed in a silk Gucci scarf featuring green horses. I noticed she had a brand-new perfect pedicure. (Ouch.) Her little dogs were adrift somewhere in there, I could hear them snarling at me.

"You look terrible, David. What is *wrong* with you?"

"It's Davis."

She waved me off.

"I think I have a virus."

(No, I didn't.)

She dove behind pillow number seventy-three. Her muffled outrage escaped. "You need to leave immediately!" One of her arms shot out from the many fluffy duvets and I caught a glimpse of fur flying as she scooped her rat-dogs under the covers and away from my germs.

Ha ha.

"Just one thing, then I'll go," I said.

"Make it quick," the pillow said.

"Why did you shoot Peyton?"

The pillow came down. "Because Richard is sleeping with her."

* * *

One of the two elevators inside the Sanders' residence went directly to a hallway behind Mr. Sanders' office. And by directly, I mean in a hurry. Like a bomb. When it came to a stop (three seconds later), I found myself contemplating my lifelong adultery theory. Be it lack of opportunity, libido, or pulse, I've held fast to the belief that there was a slice of the male population pie immune to cheating. With each passing birthday, Democrat, and marriage (of mine), the slice has thinned. With this news, it may be gone.

In spite of my opinion that he has every reason to, there was no evidence of Mr. Sanders being unfaithful to his wife. There's never been a whiff, hint, or trace. I found it hard to swallow that he'd start now, and in his own home.

But I've been wrong before, and in *my* own home.

My father could make anything work, even being married to my mother. The parts of their lives that aren't perfect are her fault. Because he is. (Perfect.) Like any other family, though, we'd had our share of dysfunction. Sadly, most of that can be chalked up to me; I've had a few bumpy years/divorces.

I remember very little of middle school—the childbirth movie, pre-algebra, the 8th grade trip to Six Flags—but one thing our family never talks about-slash-will never forget is the two-year chill that settled in our home after Daddy returned from a week of hostage-negotiating training in Montgomery, as if anyone in Pine Apple would ever take anyone else hostage. At the time, I paid very little attention. I was busy twirling my baton. And I'd all but forgotten it until a few years ago, when Mother and Daddy were at odds as to how to repair the toll the tanking economy had taken on their 401K, and Mother went behind Daddy's back, moving the money without his blessing. It got ugly. Meredith said, "This will be worse than the time Mother caught Daddy with that hostage-training woman in Montgomery if they don't get this worked out soon."

I walked around without blinking for a week.

From behind Mr. Sanders' office, I regained a little of my equilibrium as I made my way to a second elevator ride that would take me to the Bellissimo lobby. From the lobby, I wove my way through the casino and from there, I took a steep escalator ride to the convention level. And by steep, I mean straight up. Like a missile.

The real question, though, was this: Would Bradley Cole ever cheat on me?

I made it inside the door just in time for Round Two of the Mystery Shopper slot throwdown. A lady with sliver hoop earrings as big as bicycle tires checked me in and passed me a slip of paper. I barely perched on the edge of a chair before I heard Matthew Thatcher call out from behind his microphone. "Where's number sixteen? Number sixteen! You have less than a minute to get to your slot machine!" I looked at the slip of paper in my hand. Sixteen.

I shot up and the lights went out.

* * *

"You *what*?" Fantasy asked. "You *fainted*?"

"Yes," I said. "I passed out cold."

"You stood up, then went down."

"That's what happened."

"And this was last night?"

"Round two of the tournament. On my way to round two."

It was too early Sunday morning. Weekends meant nothing around here.

"So the old lady who lives in a church is still on the loose?"

"I never saw her."

"She won." No Hair came barreling into Mr. Sanders' sunny office, our appointed meeting place. Around his neck, a noose. His tie was a noose. The hang someone kind. In all my time at the Bellissimo, I've never seen No Hair wear the same tie twice.

"She what?" I asked. "Out of all those people, she won?"

"Jewell Maffini won the Mystery Shopper grand prize. Twenty-five thousand in cash." No Hair didn't seem happy for her. "And you missed it." Or with me.

I opened my mouth to defend myself but he stopped me by holding up a huge paw. "I'm pushing the pause button on her," he said, "until we find *her*."

He slapped a picture of Peyton Reynolds in the middle of the round, glass-topped conference table. We all took a seat, and Fantasy added a file containing our painfully thin background report. No Hair looked at me. "Don't say it."

I zipped my lips.

"What'd you get out of Bianca?" No Hair asked.

"Brace yourselves."

Fantasy grabbed the edges of the table with both hands.

"Bianca thinks Mr. Sanders is having an affair with Peyton. And that's what all the shooting was about."

After five minutes of total stunned silence as they contemplated the improbable possibility, No Hair cleared his throat. "What else?"

"Nothing else," I said. "She wasn't in the mood to talk." Not that I had been in the mood to listen.

"Make your calls," No Hair said. "Cancel whatever you have going. Inform your loved ones. We're staying on this until we find this girl." He slid the assistant's photograph closer to us. "My best guess is that she ran," No Hair tapped the picture, "because there's nothing up there other than her fingerprints. Not a shred of evidence that she took a bullet." He leaned back in his chair. "So she ran. You two figure out where, why, and how the cameras missed it. Get back up there with Bianca." (He lobbed that one at me.) "Get her to tell you exactly what happened, and find that seventh round."

"Is he?" I asked.

"Is who what, Davis?"

"Is Mr. Sanders having an affair with the assistant?"

No Hair took a deep noisy breath. "That's none of our business."

And that was our cue to scoot. Fantasy and I began gathering our things, minding our own bee's wax, making a run for it, when No Hair stopped us. "One more thing."

I *hate* it when No Hair says those words.

"Davis."

I hate it when he says that word, too.

"Is it true Thatch caught you?"

Fantasy dropped her purse and her jaw. "*No*!"

I dropped back into my chair. "It really wasn't that big a deal."

"*Matthew* Thatcher?" Fantasy asked. "Mr. Microphone?"

"I don't know that he caught me so much as he was holding me when I came to."

"Whatever," Fantasy said. "What'd he smell like?"

I turned to No Hair. "How do you even know about that?"

"First," he shook a finger, "I know everything, and don't forget it. Second, he called."

"You?"

"He called Richard," No Hair said. "It got routed to me."

"Why would he call Mr. Sanders?" I asked. "To tell him someone fainted at the slot tournament?"

"No," No Hair said, "he called because he couldn't find the someone who'd fainted at the slot tournament."

"Why was he looking for me?"

"I don't know, Davis." No Hair laced his big fingers across his barrel chest and tipped his chair back. "Why would he be looking for you?"

"Mr. Microphone is a notorious boy-slut," Fantasy said. "He *likes* you, Davis! He wants to play *doctor* with you!"

"Oh, poo." I could feel my face turning red.

"That is why he called."

What?

"He looked you up."

"How and why," I asked, "did he look me up?"

"He called your room to check on you," No Hair kept going, "then called here because there wasn't a marketing portfolio set up on you, which he found odd." He took a beady-eyed swat at Fantasy, who was in charge of base-covering when it came to aliases.

"How and why," I asked, "does he have computer clearance for marketing portfolios?"

"I found it odd, too," he spoke directly to Fantasy, "that there was no marketing portfolio."

"Oh, brother," Fantasy said. "Don't turn this into a federal offense on my part, No Hair. You're the one who sprang all this on us. There were probably ten new players in the tournament whose portfolios weren't complete. We'll just call her a new player and leave it at that."

"The microphone guy shouldn't have access to player information." Could anyone even hear me?

"That'll work this time," No Hair said to Fantasy, "but these little details—" after that, it was blah, blah, blah, and yada, yada, yada. I didn't hear another word until "—so I gave him your number."

"You what?" I shot straight up.

"Davis. The guy asked for your number. I told him I'd look into it and get back with him, and I had two choices: Tell him who you are or give him a contact number. I gave him a contact number."

"What number?"

No Hair reached into his jacket, pulled out a burn phone and tossed it to me. "This one. And he's called you twice. And it sounds like he does want to play doctor, or something, with you." No Hair snickered.

"You *listened* to the messages?" I was offended. "My *private* messages?"

Fantasy was clapping with glee. She was, like the rest of Harrison County, including Mr. Sanders, a huge Matthew Thatcher fan.

"What am I supposed to tell Bradley Cole?" I demanded.

"He knows you have a job to do, Davis," No Hair said. "No one's asking you to sleep with the guy."

Just then, the burn phone rang. I tossed it through the air hot-potato style. It landed on the floor in the middle of the room. We all stared at it as it sang its ring song.

"Answer the phone, Davis," No Hair barked. "And find that girl."

SIX

There were two ways into the Sanders' residence: the private elevator, which spilled you out at a security desk and you had to have your blood typed to take another step, or the super-duper-rocket private elevator from behind Mr. Sanders' office that spilled you out in the middle of their home, but your surname had to be Sanders to ride it up. There was a third way, via the helicopter pad on the roof, but climbing up the side of the building, then rappelling over the edge to crash through a thick pane of hurricane-friendly glass was time consuming.

I avoided the 30th floor with all my might, but some days there was no getting around it. My choices were the security desk, which meant a disguise and a fairy tale, scale the side of the building (too hot for that today), or get Bianca to grant me a ride on the family elevator, which meant getting her on the phone. Most of the time she ignored my calls, but miraculously, twice in a row, yesterday and today, she answered, and agreed to beam me up. She communicated this by hanging up before I finished speaking.

Making my way there, I listened to the message from a sleepy-sounding Matthew Thatcher. I will say this, a large part of his star power stems from his intoxicating voice. If he ever lost his emcee job, he could get a job leaving people seductive messages. "*I tried reaching you twice last night and struck out both times, so I thought I'd try you early. This is Thatch, your friendly knight in shining armor, and I want to see how you're doing. I've had beautiful women swoon at the sight of me before* (oh, brother), *but not as beautiful as you."* He left instructions to meet him for dinner tonight in the Bellissimo's private dining room, then gave me directions. I knew exactly where it was, because I'd *served* dinner there before. (Shrimp and grits, orange-avocado salad, strawberries in Chantilly cream. Wearing a little boy's tuxedo. No kidding.) Thatch didn't ask if I wanted to have dinner or if I were available for dinner. It was more edict than invitation.

I didn't swoon at the sight of him. I just swooned. For no reason whatsoever. Random swooning.

Bianca was stretched out on a velvet sofa, her wounded foot airborne, and in her usual good mood. (Not). And she greeted me with her usual hospitality. Make that hostility. Most days, she didn't speak, but cut her eyes in my general direction as if to ask, *What?* Most days I gave it right back to her, today with a sharp inhale. *You're the one who shot yourself in the foot, Bianca, not me.*

I was, today, and all other days, eternally weary of her attitude.

"You know, Bianca? You're a bitch."

(I did *not* say that.)

"Hello, Mrs. Sanders."

(That's what I said.)

She looked up, batting a manicured hand through the air, dismissing me.

"How's your foot?" I asked politely.

Just then, smelling fresh blood, her little dogs came in for the kill. Sidestepping them, which is to say hopping like a bunny until they settled down, I started my business so I could finish my business. "Mrs. Sanders," hop-hop, "we need to find Peyton."

"*We* don't need to do anything," Bianca said. "*You* need to find her, and *I* need a new assistant," Bianca said. "I am in my very hour of need, and without help."

No telling what she needed. A Q-Tip, maybe. Or a page turned in a magazine.

"Has she, by any chance, tried to contact you?" I asked.

She gave me another non-verbal response. This one I easily translated, *No, you imbecile.*

I didn't think so. "I'll need to see her desk," I said. "Her work area."

"Help yourself." Bianca reached for her long, skinny cigarettes.

I waited. And waited. "Where is Peyton's office, Mrs. Sanders?"

She lit, then took a long drag of cigarette. "I'm not sure."

After a treasure hunt through the service area of the penthouse, I found Peyton's office, which was more like Peyton's closet. It was behind a produce humidifier room that was behind a pantry, and there was some unrecognizable produce in the glassed-in humidifier. Seriously. Foot-long tentacle-looking things, bulbous purple things the size of soccer balls, and bunches of green things that looked more like weeds than anything else. Who eats this stuff? The whole kitchen reminded me of the Disney movie, *Ratatouille*, which my niece Riley and I have watched ninety-nine times. Speaking of rats, this would make an excellent storage space for Bianca's little furry canine rodents, Gianna and Ghita. I made my way past kumquats and giant onions with thick green stalks as big around and long as my arm, to double-louvered doors. I pulled them open, and found Peyton's workspace.

I sat in her chair, pulled gloves out of my pocket, snapped them on, and started digging. After an hour of sifting through Bianca's shoe receipts (found one for Christian Louboutin coyote fur boots—price tag $4,900), I had nothing but a headache. In a last-ditch effort to find anything—ticket stub, gum-wrapper, ten-dollar bill—I pulled the desk drawers all the way out to see if anything might be wedged between or taped under. I was force-feeding them back into their slots when something stuck against the back frame of the desk caught my eye. I looked like a pretzel, I'm sure, stretching for it. I finally connected with a corner and pulled it out. I recognized it immediately. It was a wedding invitation to the Mystery Shopper slot tournament I'd been kicked out of. It was addressed to Jewell Maffini, One God's Boulevard, Beehive, Alabama.

Well, I'll be dipped.

* * *

I would have made up something or another to get out of going to dinner with Thatch the Great, had it not been for the fact that my boyfriend was in Las Vegas with Mary Ha-Ha the Lawyer. That, and I was hungry. The distance I covered from Peyton's office up near heaven to mine and Fantasy's down near hell, if horizontal, would probably cross a state line. I keyed myself, then poked my head in the door of control central.

"Whatcha got?" I asked Fantasy.

She looked up. "Not much." Peyton Reynolds' face was on the left sides of four computer screens, with flashing images zipping by on the rights. "I'm running her picture through every database in cyberspace, and so far haven't turned up a thing. This girl doesn't even drive a car."

"Check Beehive, Alabama."

"Beehive? As in the little old lady who lives in a church, Beehive, who won the tournament?"

"The very same."

"Seriously?"

I dropped the Mystery Shopper invitation on the desk in front of her. "Found this in Peyton's desk."

"Jewell Maffini," Fantasy read. "This is way more than a coincidence."

"I agree," I said. "See if you can find anything on Peyton in Beehive while I get dressed for dinner."

"Dinner who? Where? Why?"

"Matthew Thatcher," I said.

"Can I go?"

"No." I turned for the closet.

"Why is Beehive one word when Pine Apple is two?" Fantasy shouted at my back.

"I have no idea!"

I grabbed a dress, shoes, earrings, blue contacts, a push-up bra, a bag, and was almost out the door when I remembered that I had to be a medium-spice brunette. I pulled my red hair up, twisted it, twisted it more, stuck four hundred bobby pins in it, covered my face and clothes with a towel, and yelled across the bullpen to Fantasy. "Can you come spray my hair for me?"

"No!" Fantasy shouted back. "I've got something in here!"

I did a quickie on my hair, holding my breath. I checked the back with a mirror, sprayed a spot I'd missed, then scurried across the bullpen to control central.

Fantasy rotated the computer screen my way. "Check this out." It was Peyton Reynolds, the missing assistant, both on the right and left of the screen.

"Well, how about that." I stepped into my shoes. "Where'd you find her?"

"Beehive High School alumni database," Fantasy said. "And that's not all. Take a look at her name."

I leaned in and read *Peyton Beecher Maffini, Class of 1998.* "The little old lady and the missing assistant are related."

"By marriage."

We said it together. "Road trip."

* * *

The best thing about dinner with Mr. Microphone was the food. Delicious.

Another great thing was my outfit. I was a fashionista below my medium-spice updo. I was Armani business-casual in a herringbone jersey dress, a little on the short side. It had a very scooped neck, a banded waist, and cap sleeves. I looked like I'd been poured into it. Lots of shoe: black, block-heeled pumps that took me from five-two to five-six. Also Armani. Pewter satchel bag. Target.

A not-so-great thing about dinner, and I found this out quickly, I was dining with the President of the Crazy for Thatch Club; the guy was beyond egomaniacal. I didn't have to worry about my cover story, explain why I'd fainted, or divulge any details I might need to remember later, because he didn't ask. All I had to do was make sure I didn't have spinach in my teeth, and even at that, I'm not so sure he'd have noticed. Come to think of it, there was no spinach, so the whole thing was no challenge whatsoever, unless you count staying awake.

From the moment I sat down, he began answering questions I didn't ask. How he got his job and how shocked the professionals ("flown in from major media markets coast to coast") he beat out for it were. How difficult it was in the beginning, because he didn't start out with a staff feeding his earpiece with the proper pronunciation of the crazy gamblers' names that he had to call out. ("I don't know what people are thinking when they're naming their kids. How do they even come up with some of this stuff? I mean, look at my name"—huge pause—"Matthew Thatcher. Say it. No, really. Try it on. See how it rolls off? A strong, masculine, solid name. Easy without being common.") How difficult a time he had keeping a low profile and private life with his celebrity status. ("The last time I went to the mall, I was *mobbed*." Chuckle, chuckle at the memory. "My assistant takes care of all that now.") No, he can't rig anything so that it's my name pulled out of the hat for this or that. ("Now, there are other ways I can guaran*tee* you'll win." Wink, wink, wink.) (Gag, gag, gag.)

I got a very few words in edgewise. "I hear you're from Alabama."

He weighed his response, trying to decide whether or not he was going to admit it.

"My family has strong French roots."

Not.

And he had strong auburn roots. His fluffy chestnut hair was straight out of a bottle. Or a spray can, like me. I wouldn't bet on it, but I strongly suspected Mr. Smokey-Eyed Thatcher knew his way around an eyeliner pencil too. Or maybe his assistant takes care of all that now. I couldn't help but compare him, and all other men, to Bradley Cole, as he was the bar. Bradley Cole would stand at the mirror smudging on eyeliner in about one gazillion gazillion years.

The last of the china was whisked away, and, out of nowhere, a man showed up.

Thatch half stood. "Laura Kasden, Rodney Whitehead."

What? Who? I was used to the alias thing, and I sure hoped I was the Laura Kasden at this gig and not the Rodney Whitehead.

"Rodney is my publicist," Thatch said to me, which made me Laura. Whew. "And I hope you won't mind a photo op."

I minded it very much. No Hair would have a cow and blame me.

"I'll make sure you get a signed copy," Thatch assured me.

"Scoot in a hair, Miss Kasden, if you don't mind." That was Rodney.

"Smile!" Thatch said, pasting on his own. "Look up at me through your eyelashes, chin down," he spoke through his mask, "and don't say cheese, say *home*."

The whole thing was over in three seconds.

"You wouldn't believe," Thatch dismissed Rodney, checked his seat for crumbs before taking it, then smoothed his tie, "how much mileage I've gotten out of you fainting." He shifted positions, crossing his legs the other way, picking at the pleat in his pants. "Word spread like wildfire. Five hundred people have asked me who you are, how you're doing, and have made me promise to catch them if they fall."

I'd known for a while that this wasn't about me, so I didn't pout.

"Hope you won't mind a little Page Six." He winked. "Follow up for my peeps, you know."

Page Six in *The Biloxi Sun Herald* was a bigger deal here than Page Six in *The New York Post* was there. Page Six was the casino news. Several local casinos reported not only the amounts of huge slot machine wins, but the machine serial numbers and locations too. There were lots of winner photos, restaurant specials, and a Q & A section where gambling experts weighed in. Page Six was the addicted gambler's bible, complete with daily gaming horoscopes, which had every sign under the sun winning. Thatch, believing me to be from out of town, was explaining the relevance and privilege of Page Six to me. "I kept a scrapbook the first year," he said, "but I'm in it every other day"—he threw his hands in the air; what's a boy to do?—"and I couldn't keep up. I have a *huge* Page Six following."

No Hair wasn't going to have a cow. He was going to have a tractor.

"Marketing wants me take a first aid and CPR course," he said, "just in case an opportunity like this comes up again."

I could see the publicity possibilities, so I smiled an *Oh, really?*

"But rest assured," he leaned in. "Mouth-to-mouth is Thatch choice only."

Gross.

He reached under the table and pulled out a gift bag. "I have a treat for you."

"You shouldn't have."

"Oh, but I did." He placed it on the linen between us. "Go ahead."

I pulled out tissue paper, then a thick sealed envelope that I placed on the table for later. No doubt it was an autographed studio portrait of him for my nightstand. I shook out the treat. It was a T-shirt, size S, bright red. On the front, the Bellissimo logo. On the back, the whole back, in letters large enough for an interstate billboard, it read *THATCH! PICK ME!*

"Is the color okay?" he asked. "They come in every shade in the rainbow."

I knew this. Thatch had a whole line of T-shirts, and casino patrons wore them all the time. *Thatch, call my name! I* (heart) *Thatch.* One had a quip he'd made famous around here, his stock greeting when he stepped up to the mike: *Who wants Thatch to call their name?* The crowd went nuts when that particular question boomed out of the sound system. You could buy them in the gift shops, and I'd been in the casino before when he'd come through accompanied by half-naked girls shooting them out of guns. They were part of the Thatch phenomenon, and now I had one of my very own.

"It's lovely," I lied.

"Wait," he said. I was rolling up the shirt. "Look closer."

He'd signed it. *Saved by the Thatch! –Matthew Thatcher.* Big fat Sharpie letters. EBay, here I come.

"Open the envelope." He nudged it.

It was an invitation to a slot tournament, die-cut, shaped like an ice-cream cone, two scoops above a gold cone, the individual scoops loose slips of pastel silk. Everything was sprinkled with dots of cubic zirconia. I lifted the strawberry silk scoop to see that the buy-in was $25,000 per player. I lifted the chocolate scoop to see the theme—Double Dip.

"This," he leaned in, he needed a Tic-Tac, "is the hottest ticket in town."

"I'm honored." I wasn't.

"It's a spectator pass, mind you," he said, "but you won't want to miss a minute of it."

* * *

Bright-eyed and bushy-tailed the next morning after a great night's sleep in my slot-tournament hotel room, I speed dialed Fantasy at eight on the nose. "What are you doing?"

"Waiting on you," Fantasy said. "How was dinner? Is he bigger than life?"

"His head is." I was zipping through the Bellissimo lobby, overdressed in last-night's clothes for today's early hour. I passed the T-shirt to the first person I made eye contact with. "Listen, I'm going by my place real quick for some people clothes. Pick me up there in thirty minutes and we'll head that way."

"I was hoping you were calling to tell me we didn't have to do Alabama today."

"We'll hurry." A porter held the door for me. "We'll find Peyton, check her for bullet wounds, snap a few pictures for No Hair, then be back by dinner."

"The chances of it going down that way are slim to none, Davis."

On the drive home I listened to the messages that had parked themselves on my phone for two days. Bradley had left a quick one: The movers called, they were going to charge us $2,500 for the $1,200 move because we hadn't let them know in time. (In time for what?) Surely something could be done. (One would think.) He was up to his eyeballs; could I handle it? (Handle *what*?) Bradley again. Where was I? Could I possibly call the movers and work something out? (Work *what* out? Reschedule the move?) Then my sister, Meredith. Same question. Where was I? She hoped I remembered. (Where I was? She hoped I remembered where I was, or she hoped I remembered something else? Was it our mother's birthday again already?)

I stepped into the front door of our condo, my Armani shoes starting an echo that bounced off the walls. There were three things, and only three things, in the whole condo: dust hippopotamuses, my grandmother, and my ex-ex-husband, Eddie Crawford.

SEVEN

"You're kidding, right?"

Fantasy drove a mom car, a white Volvo XC90. I stood beside it, in front of the building Bradley Cole and I—news to me—had already moved out of. I looked in the backseat. I waggled my fingers, then said to her, "No, *you're* kidding, right?"

Fantasy twisted in her seat. "Don't move." Her long legs came out of the car, the rest of her followed, and she crooked a finger at me. I turned, held up a wait-a-sec finger to my crew, and followed her.

"Are your grandmother and your ex-husband going with us?" she asked.

"Is your *kid* going with us?"

Fantasy's smallest child—I never could remember her sons' names because they all started with the letter K, so it was either Krane or Keef or Kite—was in the car, poking on a noisy electronic handheld game.

"You're the one who said we were zipping down there, snapping a few pictures, then zipping right back," she said.

"It's up." I pointed. "Alabama is zipping up there."

Fantasy smiled at her small child. "He asked if he could ride. I said yes. Besides," she said, "you brought Granny and your ex. You win."

"I didn't bring them," I said. "They were here when I got here."

"Why?"

"I got here three seconds ago, Fantasy. I haven't figured it out yet."

"Can you leave them here?"

"No." I looked up at the building Bradley and I used to share. "Apparently, we've already moved out."

"When did you do that?"

"Four seconds ago."

It took an additional ten thousand seconds to get on the road. Both Granny and K, the small child, had to visit the facilities in the empty condo, and Eddie Crawford, that sorry bastard, refused to get in his car and leave until I bought him a tank of gas. My sister, Meredith, who usually shuttles Granny to and fro, was busy, and with zero consideration for me, had roped Eddie into driving Granny down for her gamble, which I'd completely forgotten about. Eddie, who all but refused to work, would use any excuse to get to Biloxi, his old hangout, and would give a ride to the devil himself to get here. He was, for a long list of reasons, eighty-sixed from the Bellissimo, but there were a dozen other casinos he was more than welcome in.

"How much, Eddie?"

"I like your hair that color."

"Shut up. How much?"

"Two." He batted his long black lashes at me. (As if.) "Hundred."

"Two hundred dollars for a tank of gas? That's not gas money, you jerk, that's gambling money, and I'm not giving it to you." I didn't have a dime on me had I wanted to. Which I didn't. "Granny?" She was shuffling our way, K bringing up the rear, still poking on his game. "Do you have any cash?"

"Honey, we already ate," my grandmother said. "I'm full as a tick."

We piled in, Granny in the third row of seats, a mile away. "IT'S NICE AND ROOMY BACK HERE." Fantasy's kid clapped his hands over his ears. "YOU NEED ONE OF THESE CARS, DAVIS."

Eddie was following us to a convenience store two blocks away so I could buy him a tank of gas (what an ass), but his rattletrap car, a relic Lincoln Continental the size of a tugboat, died across two and a half lanes of busy Beach Boulevard.

I dug in the bottomless pit of my purse for my phone. "I'll call a tow truck."

"No," Eddie the Ass said, "let the city get it. Scoot over, kid."

I almost jumped out the window at every mile marker until the stowaways fell asleep. Two were drooling. All three were snoring. Fantasy and I were breathing sighs of relief. I caught her studying Eddie the Flea in the rearview mirror.

"He's a total waste of pretty," she said.

My ex-ex-husband was famous for his dark, swarthy, Danny Zuko-vibe good looks. "Let's call him a total waste," I said, "and leave it at that."

Welcome to Pine Apple, Alabama. One four-way stop. One water tower. Fifty goats.

My sister owned a curiosity shop, The Front Porch, that was the ground floor of a restored antebellum on Main Street. She and Riley lived upstairs. We dropped everyone off there. Meredith was none too happy about it. "We'll be right back," I said. "Sometime this afternoon. Maybe tonight."

"*Dammit*, Davis!" You'd think that was my name, Dammit Davis, because it's almost always how my sister addressed me. (She loves me.) (I love her, too.)

"Dammit, Davis?" I was practically in Fantasy's lap trying to get through the driver window to get to my sister. (The one I love.) "What were you thinking sending Granny with *Thing*," my right arm shot out in Thing's direction, "to my *home*! How about dammit, Meredith?"

"Dammit!" My niece Riley announced.

"Dammit!" Fantasy's small child stamped a Jordan. Super.Fly.

"Jesus," Fantasy mumbled.

"Hey." Eddie the Thing was stretching off his nap. "Whenever you all wind this up, I'm going to need a ride to my place."

"First of all, Eddie," I turned to face him, "you don't have a place. Say, 'I need a ride to my parents' mobile home.' And second of all, walk." Then to Fantasy, "Go, go, go!"

There were two hours of road between Pine Apple and Beehive, a lot of it standstill traffic in Montgomery, and Meredith let us get through all the 85/65 exchange construction before she called and said, "I hope you know Granny's sleeping in the back seat."

I looked in the rearview mirror. Granny was awake, upright, and smiling. Her hair was awake, upright, and screaming. "I COULD USE A LITTLE SOMETHING TO WET MY WHISTLE, DAVIE."

I hung up on Meredith.

We found a diner in Shorter, Alabama. We chose a booth. Granny sat beside me. Fantasy pulled a thick file folder out of her bag, and I turned to Granny. "We're going to work a few minutes while we wait on our pie."

"The secret to a perfect pie crust is ice water and a wooden rolling pin." Granny was wide-eyed, her little head bobbing. "And you can use your rolling pin to bop someone over the head if need be." Then my eighty-two-year-old grandmother reenacted a rolling-pin head-bopping, complete with soundtrack. "THWACK."

"What happened to your grandfather?" Fantasy asked from behind her hand.

"We're not sure," I said from behind mine.

Fantasy's eyes were wide. Granny patted her blue hair. I patted Granny's little bird arm.

"Why do you have a picture of Jewell?" my grandmother asked.

Double take. I flipped the eight-by-ten black and white and moved it as close to Granny's nose as I could. "Do you know this woman, Granny?"

A crooked finger shot out. "That's Jewell Maffini."

"How do you know her?"

"From the Fortune Casino," Granny said. "She played there before it was shut down. You know who her grandson is, don't you?" Granny dragged Jewell's picture an inch closer.

"No," I shook my head. "I don't know her grandson."

"Mr. Microphone," Granny said, "at your casino. If things

don't work out with you and your new young man, I could have Jewell introduce you."

And this would be what caught No Hair's eye. If Jewell Maffini is related to Matthew Thatcher, and Jewell Maffini is related to Bianca's missing assistant, Peyton Reynolds, then Matthew Thatcher and Peyton Reynolds are connected.

"Of course, I'll always have a soft spot for Eddie," Granny said. "He's a hunk."

* * *

Beehive, Alabama. Who knew?

I knew the necessities, because I'd grown up not too far from here. It was one of many small Alabama towns named, surely, over pints of ale.

"Let's call ye ole town Flabbergast Foot."

"Thee's crazed. We shall call it Horse's Large Member."

"What hast happened to thou?"

"A bee's hive hath dones't dropped on mine head."

Well, there you go. Beehive. Every time I'd heard mention of Beehive, Alabama, it was either about the church we were here to take a look at, rumored to be outrageously large, or cheeseburgers, rumored to be heavenly. And also outrageously large.

Population: roughly five thousand. Beehive was more an exurbia of Auburn, Alabama, twenty miles away, than anything else. It was mostly residential, make that mansionential, the four corners of the city made up of subdivisions named after horse race tracks. Fountains, statues, magnolias, and elaborate guard houses announced entrances to Churchill Downs, Belmont, Saratoga, and Pimlico.

"These people have some *money*," Fantasy commented.

"I'll say."

"DO YOU SEE A LADIES ROOM ANYWHERE, DAVIS?"

We found an elegant strip mall, complete with valet parking, that had a coffee shop, *Bistro de Jesus*. ("I'LL BE BACK IN A JIF-

FY.") On one side of the coffee shop was a burger joint, *Our Daily Burger*, home of the heavenly burgers, and on the other side, a fancy steak house, *Holy Cow*.

The next few blocks of Beehive were not as blatantly religious, but just as noticeably stylish. There were fancy banks, fancy topiary gardens everywhere, and a string of fancy mountain-stone buildings with arched stone breezeways connecting Beehive's elementary to middle to high schools. Everything in Beehive was professionally manicured. We saw one gas station, and even it was pretty. We thought we'd reached the end of main street, which was God's Boulevard here, having missed the church, when the road took a sudden sharp left and the church loomed before us in the distance like a divine palace.

"Good God." Fantasy hit the brakes.

"Amen."

"PRAISE BE."

A vast parking lot circled the castle of a church like a concrete moat, and was sectioned off like Disney's, segregated by reminders: Wisdom, Understanding, Counsel, Fortitude, Knowledge, Piety, Fear of the Lord (who'd park there?), and Daisy Duck (kidding).

"I wonder if they tailgate," Fantasy said.

I turned to her. "We're on the Polar Express and this is Holy Santa's Village."

"IS THIS A NEW CASINO?"

At least fifty SUVs filled several long rows of Fortitude. God's staffers, it would seem, favored Lexus. We worked our way to the front, then drove through a massive stone archway leading to the main entrance, and, stupefied, read the sign.

WELCOME TO THE
SO HELP ME GOD
PENTACOSTAL CHURCH
MARION BEECHER, SENIOR PASTOR
COME ONE, COME ALL

"Beecher?" Fantasy turned to me.

"*Beecher*?" I was dumfounded. "Isn't that one of Peyton's names?"

"Holy crap." Fantasy shook her head. "What is going on?"

"WE GOT COMPANY."

A black, four-door sedan came out of nowhere and angled itself ten feet from Fantasy's front right bumper. Another one pulled up behind us, counter, on the back left bumper of the Volvo. NFL linebackers (they had to be) exited the cars, two each, everyone wearing black, and surrounded us. One guy behind us, I could see in the side mirror, was poking on his phone, running our plates. Fantasy and I exchanged a quick look, mapping a plan. She put an elbow on the console between us, ready to snap it open should she need its loaded contents, and with her other long arm, reached over and pressed the button that lowered the driver window.

"Gentlemen?" She smiled.

"Ma'am," one said. "Can we help you?"

"We're here to see God." Fantasy nodded in the direction of the massive stone sanctuary.

"He's not in." The man reached inside his jacket and I had to clamp down on Fantasy's arm to keep her from shooting him. He pulled out a printed card, not a firearm, and held it in the open window. I let go of Fantasy's arm. "Here's a list of worship services, Ma'am. You'll need to either call and make an appointment with one of our counselors, or come back during one of these times."

"YOUNG MAN!"

Oh, God.

"DO YOU HAVE A LADIES ROOM?"

"Didn't she just go?" Fantasy whispered. I shrugged.

"Yes, Ma'am," linebacker said. "If you'll follow the gold signs to our gift shop, you'll find facilities there."

Gift shop?

"WHAT'D HE SAY, DAVIS? I DON'T HAVE ALL DAY."

Another one of the football players spoke up. "I'll tell you what," he said, "just follow us."

The gift shop was Holy Smokes Saks: shiny marble floors, sacred symphony music, and soft chandelier lighting. We followed a woman wearing a dove-gray suit through a large section of leather coats (chained to the hangers and emblazoned with the church logo) to the Ladies Lounge. Fantasy and I waited outside the double doors, smiling gratuitously, scratching things that didn't itch, and shuffling our feet. Our four escorts kept their distance, but escorted nonetheless. We checked out their surveillance and exchanged a look agreeing that they had as much, if not more, spying going on than at the Bellissimo. Granny finally emerged, smelling like a hooker.

"THEY'VE GOT EVERYTHING IN THERE, DAVIS. LINEN TEA TOWELS, DIPPITY-DO, AND WIND SONG."

"What's dippity-do?" Fantasy took a giant step back.

"She means hair spray," I said.

"What's wind song?" Fantasy fanned her face.

"PERFUME."

Fantasy sneezed.

"I feel like shopping," I said.

"Let's do it." Fantasy shot off.

We bypassed the book section that featured the church's two bestselling authors: Marion Beecher and God. We zipped through Casual Apparel, men's on our right, ladies' left, with Granny between us, and stopped near the front of the store to look around. I spotted security linebackers out of the corners of both eyes. So Help Me God's Emporium had case after case of fine jewelry, gold, silver, and platinum pen sets, engraved this and that, and crystal everything: praying hands, miniatures of the main sanctuary, and busts of the Reverend Beecher. I turned to a different gray-suited salesgirl. "Are there photographs of the pastor?"

"Oh, absolutely!"

"Is there anything that tells the history of the church?" Fantasy asked.

"Oh, absolutely!"

We followed her, turned a corner, and found ourselves in a

shrine to the Reverend. His likeness was on T-shirts, coffee mugs, and oven mitts.

The salesgirl checked us out. "Cash or charge?"

"Cash." Fantasy and I said it together.

The girl wrapped and bagged our purchase, explained the no-refund-no-return policy, and sprinkled some blessings on us. We could not get Granny in the back seat fast enough. We couldn't get out of the parking lot fast enough, and we couldn't get out of town fast enough. We didn't lose our black-sedan tail until we were safely on I-85 on our way back to Pine Apple to drop off Granny and pick up Fantasy's small child before heading home to Biloxi.

We pulled over at an IHOP to unwrap our gift.

We found what we were looking for on page 277. A small photograph. In it, Marion Beecher sat on a throne. Bold script cut through his middle: *Pastor Beecher*. Below it: *God Bless*. Crossed hands rested on his left shoulder. Attached to the hands, standing, was a perfectly preserved, stylishly dressed middle-aged woman. The wife. On the hem of her skirt in dainty cursive: *Praise Him, Helen*. On the other side of the reverend were two adults. The feminine handwriting across both their middles read *In His Name, The Maffinis, Peyton & LeeRoy*. Except it wasn't the Maffinis, Peyton & LeeRoy. It was Peyton Reynolds, Bianca's AWOL personal assistant, and Matthew Thatcher, our own Mr. Microphone.

We stared at it for the longest.

* * *

The traffic through Montgomery had doubled.

"It's not too hard to connect these people to each other." I used my fingers to tick off a list. "Matthew Thatcher was a preacher before he worked at the Bellissimo, he was married to Peyton, who is a preacher's daughter, and he's related to the little old lady who loves slot tournaments. I guess our job," I scratched my head, "is to figure out what they're up to at the Bellissimo."

Fantasy sneezed three times in a row.

"GASUNDHEIT."

Fantasy pulled up the hem of her shirt and was dabbing her eyes with it.

"Are you crying about this?" I asked.

"No, Davis." Her eyes were red, swollen, and pouring. "That perfume of Granny's is killing me." We drove the rest of the way with most of the fourteen car windows down. The polluted air felt good.

"Are you okay back there, Granny?" Her blue hair was airborne.

"IT'S PONDS COLD CREAM," she said. "I SWEAR BY IT."

EIGHT

I spent my first night in our new condo alone. It was a wreck. The whole place was an obstacle course of furniture clusters and box towers packed by the 777 Movers. The first box I opened contained these things: a dish towel, three screwdrivers, an empty shampoo bottle, a television remote, a lone lawyer shoe of Bradley's, hardback books, a potato smasher I'd never seen before, and his-and-hers clothes. All of it beneath an emerald green water-balloon bra that had been splayed across the top. Very funny.

My living quarters have always included an assortment of hand-me-downs and mix-and-match Ralph Lauren florals, overstuffed everything, and homey touches, like quilts and antiques scattered here and there. I've always been surrounded by, and not so much by choice as by birthright, more than a few ruffley things, almost all monogrammed. Bradley's spaces, before us, were traditionally more mahogany, glass, and stainless-steel, with a general color theme of chocolate. There was no middle ground between dark contemporary and cabbage-rose yard sale that we could come up with. So, with both of us snowed under at work all the time, we hired a decorator. She'd used the words "soft palette" often, which, I could see now, translated to "stark-raving white like the pure-driven snow." Had we signed off on all of this?

The condo itself was the stuff of decorator magazines—travertine floors, granite, inlaid mosaics, built-in this and thats, a screened and shuttered terrace (no view of the ocean) on one side, an open liana (view of the ocean) on the other, and even a butler's pantry. A butler, we did not have. We did, however, have *two* guest rooms, a total of four powder-your-nose rooms, and the master bedroom was a master piece. It was large enough to hold four beds, had his-and-hers closets and dressing-rooms separated by a show-place of a marbely bath, and it all spilled into a step-down den-entertainment-office corner with a full Gulf view.

We chose it for two reasons: the private elevator, and Bradley picked it up for a song on the courthouse steps at a short-sell auction after the owner (surprise, surprise) gambled away his oil-rig business. I don't pretend to know what all that involved. We loved it empty, paid no more for it than a starter home, and signed on each of the four hundred lines the nice lady told us to. There weren't many condos in Biloxi, certainly not many new and spiffy choices (think post-Katrina), and everything else we'd looked at had neighbors I couldn't be neighbors with and stay anonymous at the same time. There were Bellissimo department heads up and down the beach, and I cared very little about sneaking in and out of my own home so no one would make me.

I fell onto the circular sofa, a hundred-thousand marshmallows, and felt like I was getting it dirty. It would take my sister, who was a wizard in the taste-style-transformation department, to make this space livable.

Digging into a second box total strangers had packed willy-nilly, I found a fleece blanket that smelled comfortingly like our old place. I found a pillow in the fifth box I opened, along with a tea kettle (I've never had a cup of tea in my life, and I'd bet the same was true of Bradley Cole) and a lampshade. Making my way to the masterpiece, I heard an unfamiliar trilling sound. It was my purse. Digging, I located the source: the burn phone. Mr. Microphone was calling me. Or should I say Mr. Maffini. To get to the noise, I'd passed an unfamiliar bulky drug-store bag. Handwritten on the front were the words *Housewarming Gift!* in Fantasy's handwriting. Inside, a home-pregnancy test.

I didn't take Mr. Microphone's call for a number of reasons, the main one being I opened the door to the dark masterpiece bedroom and was assaulted by an odor so horrific the only thing it could be was a big dead body and I was too tired to deal with a big dead body. I backed out, pulled the door to, and slept on the marshmallow sofa with the fleece blanket that smelled like Bradley Cole, dreaming about dead bodies and weddings.

* * *

Richard and Bianca Casimiro Sanders hadn't married so much as they'd merged. It had been a business deal fifteen years ago. I'm not judging; I married twice for the wrong reasons, the same idiot both times. To understand why I'd do something so self-destructive, you'd have to grow up in a town of four hundred and have no idea a man like Bradley Cole even existed. All that was behind me now, thankfully. It would be farther behind me if Eddie the Sloth would move to the Mohave Desert, or grow up and get a job, or just stay the hell away. From me. From my family. And without a doubt, from my boss's wife.

Somehow, the Sanders have stayed together. He's kept the marriage intact, I believe, for the sake of their son, Thomas, who is far, far away at school. Mr. Sanders moved him a year ago, when Bianca's lifestyle became so atrocious he decided it was best his son not witness it. At the time, he was working twenty-five hours a day, and Thomas was being raised by a male nanny who his mother, as it turned out, was also sleeping with. It was all very Jackie Collins. No Hair, Fantasy, and I were paid royally to keep our mouths shut and look the other way.

Mr. Sanders, fed up with it, cut her a deal. Instead of divorcing her—and this was right around the time (two minutes after) I agreed to be her body double—he told her she could sleep with whomever she wanted, whenever she wanted, but from that moment forward, he would too. That's all it took to settle her down.

Settling down meant Bianca stayed in town, which turned out to be somewhat of a problem for me. She parked herself in Biloxi, found plastic surgeons she liked, and trained a hawk eye on her husband. She became more active in the community. (She did not. I became more active in the community.) She found her inner humanitarian. (She did not. I found it for her.) She played the dutiful hostess when her husband couldn't attend five-hour dinners with high rollers, famous golfers, and secretaries of agricultures. (She did not. I secretly yawned through those.) Bianca insisted she had "no time for that kind of nonsense."

I woke up Tuesday morning on my marshmallow sofa staring at the vaulted ceiling of our new home thinking about something she's had plenty of time to do but hasn't bothered: take some target practice. The woman couldn't shoot a gun straight to save her own life. If the idea ever did pass through her brain, she'd want me to take the target practice for her, and I was already a sharp shot.

Bang.

The ceiling of our new condo was more cathedral than vaulted, because all the slopes were equal, meeting in the middle.

I knew where the seventh bullet was.

Bang, bang.

All of a sudden, I knew *exactly* where it was.

No way was I going into my bedroom. Something nasty was going on in there I'd have to deal with later. Much later. I drove to work in my pajamas.

* * *

"Dammit, Davis."

"Good morning, Meredith!"

"Where are you?"

"On my way to work. Where are you?"

"I'm at home with Granny, who is supposed to be in Biloxi."

"Can you bring her?"

"I don't have much of a choice, now, do I?"

"What do you want me to say, Meredith? I'm sorry I have a job?"

"You know what I ought to do, Davis? I ought to let Mother bring her."

"Meredith! Do you *hate* me all of a sudden? First you send Eddie here, and now Mother?"

"Get dressed!"

I pulled the phone away from my head and looked at it. "Can you actually see my pajamas?"

"I was talking to Riley, and no, I don't hate you. Why are you driving to work in your pajamas?"

"Long story."

"Tell me the long story about why Granny is here instead of there."

"I had to go to Beehive."

"Why?"

"Long story."

"Tell the long story about Granny first."

"I couldn't leave her alone in Biloxi, Meredith, so I took her with me. And she could have ridden back with me last night, but she was so tired I just couldn't do it to her. She needed to be home in her own bed."

"You dropped her off here, Davis. Her own bed isn't at my house. You snuck her in, grabbed Kyle, then hit the road."

"Who's Kyle?"

"Fantasy's son!"

"Right. Granny was pooped, Meredith. She needed you."

"I guess so. You dragged her all over Alabama."

"She had fun."

"She smelled vicious."

"Yeah, she got a hold of some Wind Song perfume. I think it was as old as she is."

"Speaking of old, are you in your new place yet?"

The words I'd been waiting for. "Almost. I need your help, sweet sissy, my best friend ever; I'd step out in front of a train for you; I'll give you a kidney if you ever need it."

I waited.

"I'll give you all my kidneys. Right now."

And waited.

“Dammit, Davis.”

* * *

He was waiting for me in control central.

“Did you know Bianca’s assistant was Matthew Thatcher’s ex-wife?”

“Do you know you’re wearing pajamas?”

Fists on hips.

“Yes,” No Hair said. “I knew.

“Why didn’t you just tell us?” I found a chair and fell in it.

“There wasn’t much to tell until his grandmother registered for all the slot tournaments.”

“What’s he up to, No Hair?”

“That’s just it, Davis.” No Hair’s tie had Dalmatian spots on it. “I have no idea.”

“How much of this does Mr. Sanders know?”

“He doesn’t.”

We sat in silence until I said, “We’ll get to the bottom of this, No Hair.”

Flashing images from the monitors mounted the walls cast light and shadow on No Hair’s bald head.

“Davis?”

“Yes?”

“Do you know my name?”

I nodded.

We listened to the mainframe whir.

“Davis?”

“Yes?”

“We have to find the girl and figure out what Matthew Thatcher is up to before Richard gets back.”

“We will.” Go Team.

Fantasy burst in and went straight for No Hair. “Did you know Bianca’s assistant was Matthew Thatcher’s ex-wife?” Then to me. “Why are you wearing pajamas?”

Which reminded me. "I know where the seventh bullet is."

"Is it in Peyton?"

"No."

"Good," he said. "Now tell me you know where *she* is."

"Not just yet."

"Find. That. Girl." He stood, then crossed to the door in one giant step, scaring the floor to death. He turned. "You two listen up—" Then there was a whole lot of do this, and even more do that. Do the other. Just do it.

* * *

I did it. I could hack Santa's List.

One of my degrees is in Computer and Information Science (the other in Criminal Justice), and like everything else at the Bellissimo, my mainframe was Five Star. What would have taken me three days on any other system took a little more than an hour at my desk in control central.

Lee County, Alabama, issued a marriage license to Peyton Elaina Beecher and *Pastor* LeeRoy Gerard Maffini ten years ago, then granted them a divorce five years later. Peyton was the only child of the Reverend Marion and Helen Beecher, of So Help Me God Pentecostal Church fame. Those details out of the way, I set my sights on the church. My first quick search turned up nothing. Donate here. Join us for worship at these times. Isn't our preacher Godly looking?

Hackity, hack, hack, hack.

So Help Me God Pentecostal Church had an operating budget of $45,000,000 and change, with fifty-three percent of that going to salaries and benefits (that's a lot of salary), but with $61,000,000, give or take, in contributions last year, So Help Me God was way, way, way in the black, black, black.

Honestly, does the Bellissimo have these kinds of numbers?

Which begs the question: If you had a few extra million sitting around, taking up valuable counter space, what would be your best bet? A casino or a mega-church? The only difference I could see was that one was very upfront about taking your money, while the other, I'm not so sure.

Who are these people pumping up the church numbers? Where was the church getting all its dough?

So Help Me God was a non-profit organization. (Now, there's a funny.) As such, it was tax-exempt, somehow satisfying the requirements of section 501(c)(3) of the IRS Code. It paid payroll taxes, along with Social Security and Medicare, on almost three hundred employees, but that was it. Which meant it could prove to the IRS that each of the sixty-one million dollars they'd collected last year was used for religious, charitable, or educational purposes, none of the net earnings benefited any private individual, and it wouldn't dare attempt to influence legislation.

Please.

The video tour of So Help Me God's property (straight from their own security feed) made it look like a small oil country. There was a health center, a rehab center, a huge assisted-living and retirement housing complex, an organic-food market, two gift shops (including Holy Smokes Saks), a concert hall, a golf course, a down-home-cooking restaurant, three cafés, podiatrists and hearing specialists on site, and a full-service auto-repair center (for widows and single parents). And no profit in there? Anywhere?

The number I found that looked the most skewed was the warm-body one; there weren't enough people there to support all the auto repair. Staff, yes. Congregation, no. In a church that could hold 24,000 (what a fire hazard), average attendance on Sunday morning was 4,200. That's the whole town of Beehive. Were there 4,200 people in southern Alabama who could give a church $15,000 a year each? Were there 4,200 people in southern Anywhere who had that much extra loot lying around? Let's check and see.

While So Help Me God might not belly up and tell all to the federal bean counters, its customer base would surely brag about it.

Deduction City. I pulled ten random names off the church directory, plugged them in one-by-one, looking in every cyber nook and cranny the IRS owned, and came up with absolutely nothing. These people didn't pay taxes. Nor did the next ten, or the next.

Lord, help.

The corner of my computer screen said it was nine-thirty in the morning on Tuesday. I was still in my pajamas. All of a sudden my cell phone blew up. *Why do you have a pregnancy test?* I stared at the phone until the next text came. *I'm going to need a credit card.* I stared at that until the next text message arrived. *Dammit, Davis! Do you know that your movers packed the contents of your REFRIGERATOR into a MOVING BOX? And that it's been sitting in the sun in your BEDROOM?*

What a relief! She would have killed me if it'd been a dead body.

Why wouldn't the movers have just thrown the things in the refrigerator away?

I texted her back. *There's a big garbage chute behind a door in the butler's pantry. Don't fall in.*

I amaze myself.

I picked up the phone and conferenced myself with Fantasy and No Hair. "I know where Peyton is."

NINE

"You might as well be asking for the blueprints to the vault, Davis," No Hair said. "Richard is the only person who has access to security schematics."

"What's so secure about garbage?" Fantasy asked.

"We'll have to call him," I said.

"And tell him what?" No Hair asked. "That you think Peyton Reynolds is in the garbage?"

"Tell him Bianca lost something," Fantasy said. "Accidentally threw something out."

"One of her dogs," I suggested.

He ignored me. "I'll get him on the phone, and you two get dressed."

"I am dressed, thank you!" Fantasy pointed. "She's the one in yoga pants and a Saints T-shirt."

"Get dressed in something appropriate for a visit to Waste Management." And to me, "You just get dressed."

Before I logged off, I saved all the dirt I'd found on So Help Me God, then logged into the Bellissimo system. I dug through my fake credit cards and driver's licenses, found a quick match, then booked myself into an unoccupied two-bedroom suite a mile over my head. Status: VIP Level Five. Levels below five don't get fruit baskets, Godiva on the pillows, or spa robes. Next, I produced four room keys: one for me, one for Granny, two to lose. After that, I electronically gave myself unlimited credit to watch pay-per-view movies, eat everything in the mini-fridge, and charge small appliances to the room. I wasn't going back to my new place until Meredith finished having her way with it. I reached for my phone and tapped out a message. *Bring Granny for her gamble. I booked us a suite, and the keycards are in an envelope with your name on it at Shakes.*

She texted back right away. *What's Shakes?*

Me: *The ice cream shop*

Her: *Can't you just leave them at the front desk?*

Me: *No*

Her: *Dammit, Davis*

"Hey!" Fantasy called from the closet. "Are you coming, or what?"

"On my way!" But my phone went off again, ringing instead of buzzing. It was Bradley Cole. Finally. "Hello, you!" After that, I didn't say another word. I just listened. Fantasy appeared in the doorway and tapped on her wristwatch. I lowered the phone, pressed it into my leg, and loud-whispered. "Get a paper! Go upstairs and get today's newspaper!"

I put the phone back to my ear. "...like a promo for a porn movie!" Bradley Cole was having a hissy fit.

"Bradley, he was barking instructions at me. Say this, do that, put your nose here, put your chin there."

"The picture looks like you're about to put your *head* in his *lap*, Davis!"

Bradley was still in Las Vegas. I assumed Mary Ha-Ha was still with him. And he was not happy about the Page Six photograph of me and Matthew Thatcher. Kirk Olsen, Grand Palace Casino co-counsel, office next to Bradley's, had woken up Bradley with the news that he'd better get online and look at page seven of the *Biloxi Sun Herald*, which was a full-page ad taken out by the ashtray-chasing lawyer Jerry McAllen, announcing that the case was going to trial soon and urging those who hadn't yet jumped on his gravy train to do so while they still had a chance.

"I had to see Page Six to get to page seven, Davis."

It went on for a while longer, with Bradley conceding that he was stressed (get in line), tired (again, behind me), aggravated about the move going down the way it had (an additional $1,300 for them to physically pack us), and he missed me. (Me too!) (Missed him.)

I gave him the SparkNotes on most of what I'd been juggling, and eventually we ended up on the same page. Six-and-a-half.

"Why'd he want them to tow his car? Why didn't he put gas in it and drive back to Pine Apple?"

Bradley knew way more than he wanted to about my ex-ex Eddie.

"So he'd have an excuse to come back."

"Does he not understand that Bianca doesn't even remember him? What makes him think she'd give him the time of day if he *did* manage to get in the same room with her?"

"Eddie doesn't even understand the concept of Tuesday, Bradley, so it's safe to assume he doesn't get it about Bianca."

"Sit him down and talk to him, Davis. Explain that he's wasting his time and it's disruptive for us when he pops in."

I could hear Las Vegas in Bradley's voice. He was never in Vegas for routine matters. Vegas meant Grand Catastrophes, and if my phone were smart enough, I'd use it to dial down the tension that was spilling over from Bradley's no-smoke lawsuit and into our relationship.

"And say something to Meredith while you're at it," he added. "If she'd stop using him to run her errands, it would help."

"I had that chat with her yesterday, Bradley."

"Have it with her again, Davis."

We had a much larger issue than Eddie to discuss, but something told me this wasn't the right time. "I will."

"I swear, sometimes I think he's after you, Davis."

"Bradley. That's ridiculous."

"Not when you're talking about a guy who doesn't understand Tuesday."

So much for being on the same page.

I asked him when he'd be home. He said he had no idea, as soon as possible, he'd call again when he could.

Fantasy dropped Page Six in front of me.

Don't ever ever ever ever say "home" instead of "cheese." Ever.

"Did you tell him?" Fantasy asked.

"Tell him what?"

"Davis."

"No, I didn't tell him."

"Did you take the test?"

I sniffed.

"Why didn't you take the test?"

"I haven't had time to study for it."

* * *

We dressed in shades of beige and grabbed insurance-fraud investigator identification. To perk up the beige, we added mint-green latex gloves and surgical facemasks. No Hair burst through the door with the garbage bible. We spread it out, then quickly traced the path from the chute on the thirtieth floor to the waste-treatment unit into which the Sanders', and everyone else's, refuse found final rest.

No Hair made the call and shut down the garbage machine. "Hurry," he said, "before this place turns into the city dump. Find that girl and find her fast."

* * *

"If you're right, Davis," Fantasy hesitated before she pushed the elevator button for the thirtieth floor, "she's probably not alive. How could someone survive from Friday night until Tuesday morning in a garbage chute?"

"Haven't you heard those stories about people being rescued two weeks after an earthquake?"

"Sure," she said, "but I think they're staged. They make up that stuff when donations start slowing down."

I turned to her. "Surely you don't believe that."

"And that people on the moon business is all Hollywood, too, Davis."

We were taking the scenic route to the Sanders'. I poked the unmarked button to make the elevator go faster. "What about the Loch Ness Monster?"

"Real," Fantasy said as the doors parted. "And we're about to see the Wicked Witch of the Bellissimo. Also real."

We found her sunning herself and chain smoking.

"Good morning, Mrs. Sanders," I said.

"Are you here because you've found me an assistant?" she greeted us. "A very large, masculine assistant?"

It occurred to me that No Hair fit that bill. We'd been there long enough (two seconds) to panic Gianna and Ghita, who rushed to the foot of Bianca's lounger and locked their furry sights on our jugulars. Bianca cooed at them—she uses that tone of voice with the dogs and only with the dogs—after which, they toned it down a little.

"We've been very busy, Mrs. Sanders," I said. "We still haven't located Peyton."

"Who?"

Fantasy, not one for wasting time, said, "We need to see your dressing room again, Mrs. Sanders, and we need to know why you think there was something going on between Peyton and Mr. Sanders."

We did? We needed to know that? I swear, Fantasy wasn't afraid of anything. Not even Bianca.

"I'm weary with the subject of Peyton," she said on a long sigh. "I'm ready to move on. Put my life back together." All of Bianca shifted except her injured foot, which was wrapped in an Emilio Pucci scarf today.

Fantasy folded her arms across her chest and began tapping a foot.

"She had condoms in her purse," Bianca said.

What? Did they have Mr. Sanders' name on them? Who goes from woman-of-childbearing-age-has-birth-control straight to she's-doing-my-husband? (Bianca.) Who goes through someone's purse? (Bianca.)

"Where's the purse?" Fantasy asked.

"I threw it out," Bianca said. "It was a ten-year old Kate Spade clutch."

We were headed to the garbage anyway. Might as well retrieve the condom-filled purse.

"Show me the bullet," Fantasy said.

"Follow me."

The seventh bullet was right where I thought it would be, the only place we hadn't looked, fourteen feet up, imbedded in the base of a strip of crown molding in Bianca's dressing room.

"How'd you know?" Fantasy asked.

"I figured it out when I was staring at the ceiling."

We looked at the sooty scar in the white wood from several vantage points, trying to determine what Bianca could have possibly been aiming for, and decided she hadn't been aiming at all.

"She can't shoot worth a shit," Fantasy said.

* * *

We started at the top, the litter that hadn't yet left the Sanders' residence.

"I doubt you'll need the masks." A tall, thin man with no sense of humor whatsoever, Henry Armor, Head Steward of the S.S. Sanders, met us at the security desk.

"We're good," Fantasy said from behind hers.

"We like them," I said from behind mine.

Henry gave us the garbage speech using his library voice, and only after we followed him far away from civilization. Our journey began in a carpeted hallway between Mr. Sanders' study and the media room. We entered what should have been a coat closet, but was a narrow hallway instead, our destination a service room behind a service room that was behind a service room. Along the way we passed stainless steel shelves full of small power tools, Christmas decorations, luggage (all Louis Vuitton), golf clubs, a really big oil painting of Bianca Sanders all but in the buff (cover that thing up), and snow skis. Bicycles hung from hooks on the walls. It was your basic thirtieth-floor garage, but no lawn mower. And no car.

"Waste is collected throughout the residence several times a day," Captain Henry whispered, "or as needed. It's brought here and sent down the lift." He opened one last door. There were five or six swollen garbage bags piled around a metal door. And he said we didn't need our surgical masks.

Captain Henry jerked. "There must be a problem!"

"So there usually isn't this much garbage in here?" Fantasy asked.

"Never," he whispered. "I'll speak to maintenance right away." He pointed to the metal door. "All of this should have been sent down the lift."

The door looked to be just under three-by-three. Let's put it this way: I could get in it if I wanted to. (I did not.) I did, however, walk to it and pull it open. It was your basic dumbwaiter with no dumb waiter. Just dark, open space, cables, and pulleys along the back.

I knew it. Another way to and from the thirtieth floor.

"Will there be anything else?" He held a starched, white handkerchief over his nose and mouth. "I must speak to maintenance."

"We're good," Fantasy said. "Give us fifteen minutes."

"I will wait for you in the hall."

He backed out. Creepy guy.

"Go ahead," Fantasy said, eyeing the plastic bags.

"Oh, no. Ladies first."

With a heave and a ho and some sailor language, we tore into the bags.

There are many, many ways Bianca Casimiro Sanders might become a better citizen (many), and recycling was promoted to the top ten. The woman threw everything, I mean everything, out. We shouldn't have been doing this anyway—no one should dig through anyone else's garbage—but in less than five minutes, Fantasy found a very personal crumpled note that our boss, Richard Sanders, had written to his wife before he left for Mow-Mow (would she be interested in tacking on a few Mr. & Mrs. days to their upcoming Parent's Weekend at Thomas' school), and we agreed that more than the cold coffee grounds were stuck on everything (gross), it was the voyeurism that bothered us the most. I didn't want to know what flavor of mood enhancer Bianca ate like M&Ms (Xanax), or why Mr. Sanders always smelled so good (Jack Black—how appropriate—shampoo and Beard Lube Conditioning Shave Cream). What we didn't find was a Kate Spade clutch full of condoms, or its owner.

Fantasy stuck her head in the dark shaft. "Peyton? Are you in there? Can you hear me?"

Nothing but echoes.

"Let's throw something down there," I suggested, "to see where it stops."

"Like what?"

I looked around. "A brick?"

"If she is in there," Fantasy said, "and if she's still alive, you want to kill her with a brick thrown from thirty stories?"

Maybe not. We didn't have a brick anyway.

We left a great big mess for Henry's people to clean up, then traveled silently, changing elevators three times, from 30 to B3. My ears popped.

Fisher Iboch, Director of Waste Management, was in his early forties, and he didn't have much on me in the height department. He had two tufts of hair, one front, one back, and a bundle of energy. The man was in an amazingly good mood, considering he was in charge of the trash at the Bellissimo and that his massive work space didn't have one single ray of natural light. What it did have were twelve employees, a compressor, a coin catcher/counter, and an incinerator, two of those items the size of mini vans.

Mr. Iboch seemed pleased to have visitors. "After it's separated, it drops into a bin. From there, it's disposed of. If you'll follow me," he bounced, "I'll show you."

"How is it separated?" Fantasy asked from behind her surgery mask.

"The easy answer? Recyclable and non."

"Who separates it?" I asked from behind mine.

"There's no who. It's more what. Hydraulic arms use sensors, grates, cameras, and lasers to separate it."

"Where are they?" I asked.

Fisher Iboch used both arms to point up. "Right above our heads."

Nifty.

"Paper, glass, plastics, metals, and compost materials never reach this level," he said. "They're extracted. I call it the Recovery Program."

"Where does it go to recover?" I asked.

He pointed up with both his arms again. He looked like he was parking a plane. "They're mined and sorted during the screening process, then redirected, which is to say, recycled. By the time it gets here, the volume is significantly reduced, there's very little toxicity, and you might notice," he beamed, "very little odor, because we neutralize it, too."

"What's with the coin machine?" I asked. It was the size of No Hair.

He stopped. "The Bellissimo vacuumed more than forty-thousand dollars in loose change last year."

"Whaaaaa?" That was Fantasy.

"Who designed all this?" I asked.

"Waste-management engineers," Fisher Iboch said, "including myself."

"You're an engineer?"

"Georgia Tech," he said. "Buzz!" He used his arms for bee wings and buzzed a zigzag path in front of us. This guy needed companionship. Maybe a dog. Or a bee farm.

We continued on a concrete path through the dumpster parking lot. Some of the bins were filled to the brim. Unidentifiable stuff dropped from overhead chutes, in no particular pattern—here, there, here, here, there—like popcorn popping. Or random gunfire.

"Big place," I noted.

"We generate one-hundred and fifteen thousand tons of waste a year," Fisher Iboch said. (Seriously?) "And through our integrated waste-management procedures, we reduce our waste by eighty-five percent, so we end up with fifteen percent of what we started with."

"How?" Fantasy asked.

We'd finally reached the end of the line. Fisher Iboch used both arms to direct our attention to the massive burning contraption. "I call it," he paused to let the tension build, "the *Dragon*."

It was an iron box full of hell, inside a chain-link fence. We were looking at the front and top of it. I had no idea, nor did I want to know, how far back or down it went. "What do you do with the fifteen percent?" I asked.

He held an open palm in front of his face and blew, fairy-dust style. "It's ash, at that point."

Fisher Iboch didn't need a dog. He needed community theater.

"Are you saying the Bellissimo blows fifteen tons of ash into the air?" I asked.

"No. That's not what I said. Don't put that in your report."

He assumed the posture of someone about to give a long lecture I cared nothing about hearing, so I ceremoniously looked at my watch. "We need to get moving, Mr. Iboch."

"Certainly." He bowed. (See? Thespian.) "So Mrs. Sanders misplaced an article of jewelry?" he asked.

"She thinks so," Fantasy said. "A big ole diamond. She thinks she may have thrown it away, and we're here to look for it."

"Very well. Follow me."

Four miles later.

"It's empty." Fantasy's whole head was in the bin.

"It can't be." Fisher Iboch stuck his head in too.

Two heads in the garbage bucket were better than three. I held back.

Fisher Iboch produced a flashlight and a ray gun from somewhere around his middle. Maybe it was a barcode gun. Whichever, he aimed it at a panel on the side of the bin, then pulled it to his nose. "This bin hasn't dumped in five days!" (Barcode gun.) He stuck his head in again. "There's no way it should be empty!" His voice echoed around. "The elevator must be stuck."

"Let me see your flashlight." I held out my hand. His flashlight was a ten-inch Maglite. I knew it well from my years with the Pine Apple Police Force. It could go from spot-to-flood with a twist. I chose flood. We took a look. The chute above the bin was your basic scary, dark, steel opening, and at first glance, nothing looked out of order.

"There's something." Fantasy pointed.

"Where?" I aimed the beam.

"There." Fantasy pointed to a corner. "It looks like a shoe."

We'd just been through several Hefty bags of Bianca's rejects. A shoe wouldn't be out of the question. Fifty shoes wouldn't be out of the question.

"Oh, my word," Fisher Iboch said. "No telling how much waste is behind that shoe." He disappeared, then reappeared, crow bar in hand.

"What are you doing?" Fantasy asked.

He was climbing in the garbage bin was what he was doing.

"If the shoe is stuck, I'll shove it out of the way. That might release the lift."

"If it works, Mr. Iboch, won't you be smothered in garbage?" I took a giant step back. "Won't it all fall out?"

Clank, clank. "It doesn't matter," he said. "I'm not tall enough. I'll have to call maintenance."

I smiled at my ten-foot-tall partner. (She really is almost six-feet tall.)

"No way," she said. Then after a full minute, "Dammit, Davis." She hiked her skirt, then lobbed a long leg over the side of the bin, trading places with Fisher Iboch.

She aimed and pushed with the crowbar one time before we heard a mechanical growl. She'd hit paydirt. She scrambled to get out of the bin before the lift released its load, but didn't quite make it. Peyton Reynolds fell out on top of a mountain of garbage. She was either very dead or very close to it. Fantasy was somewhere underneath.

TEN

"Stop calling her Mr. Microphone's wife, Peyton Reynolds, Bianca's bitch, the preacher's daughter, and everything else under the sun, Davis." No Hair had No Patience. "I don't have enough time to figure out who you're talking about. The prints came back Peyton Beecher, so we're calling her Peyton Beecher, and that includes you."

After taking care of almost-naked, almost-dead PEYTON BEECHER, we were back in our offices, which we now knew weren't all that far from Waste Management.

"You're on the other side of the property, Davis." No Hair was far from concerned. "You might as well be in a different time zone."

"Says you, No Hair," said me. "We want new offices and a bunch of stock options."

"And new cars," Fantasy added.

"Tough."

Tough didn't begin to describe what we'd been through. There wasn't a car out there that would make up for it. My plan was to never set foot in Waste Management again, or even use the words "waste" or "management" again for the rest of my life.

Fisher Iboch and I passed out cold (my new and annoying trick) upon the discovery of the pile of Peyton, which left Fantasy alone to swim up from the waste and then see if the girl had an ounce of life left in her. From the far end of a very dark tunnel, I heard Fantasy call for a bus and our bus-shaped boss, No Hair.

When I came to, Fantasy greeted me with, "Lie back down before you faint again, Davis."

I was in no position to argue. "Is she alive?" I asked from the floor of the garbage department.

"Barely," Fantasy said. "Looks like a head wound, but it could be cocktail sauce."

Fisher Iboch resurfaced as well, mumbling, "Shit, shit, shit, oh, help us, Jesus."

Fantasy's head snapped up. "Give me your shirt."

I began fumbling with buttons.

"Not *you*, Davis." She pointed at Fisher Iboch. "You." He stripped off his shirt and tossed it through the air. Get this: he was covered, *covered*, in tattoos. A dragon's head filled his chest, it's disproportionately smaller body slid down his abdomen, with a dragon tail snaking up one arm, trailing across his shoulders, and wrapping around the length of his other arm.

I edged as far away from Fisher Iboch as I could manage. One hand clapped over my mouth, I said through my fingers, "Give him his shirt back, Fantasy."

Just then we heard pounding footsteps from a distance. "Over here!" Fantasy waved her arms. "Over here!"

The EMTs took in the scene, especially tattoo boy, but mostly, they hopped to. A man and a woman climbed into the dumpster, trading places with Fantasy. The other two responders lifted a stretcher above their heads, and within a minute, they'd boarded the girl. They lowered her to the floor, then swarmed. Tool boxes snapped open, a mobile IV appeared, and radios began squawking. I heard the usual medical words through the din—pulse, BP, heart-rate—and the words "penetrating head wound" and "ketchup" were tossed around. They discussed her age (early thirties), general appearance (filthy), and apparent state of severe dehydration (I guess so).

"Is she going to make it?" Fantasy asked.

One guy said over his shoulder, "Ma'am, we have no way of knowing that."

And they were off.

"Wait!" I scrambled up. They slowed, and I got my first good look at her. She was out cold, wearing a torn and stained jersey-knit camisole and matching bikini panties holding on by a single thread. Her right thigh had an ugly two-inch gash that looked days old, and she was covered in purple-black bruises and black specks of something. Probably coffee grounds. (Gross.) Her hair was mid-length, mid-brown, and in bad need of shampoo. I snapped a photograph of her face, then slid my phone under her right hand, letting her index finger rest on the screen, and took another picture. Without a word, the EMTs sped off. I poked my phone, and within a minute, got a hit on her prints. (How cool is that?) "It's Peyton," I told Fantasy. "Her prints come up Peyton Beecher."

"What about the jewelry? The diamond?"

We turned to Fisher Iboch, still sprawled on the floor, still tattooed, who we'd forgotten was there.

We ran.

* * *

It was early in the evening of the longest day of my life. Fantasy, on her end of the sofa, had just tossed back a double shot of tequila. I was on the other end, working my way through a party-sized bag of Cool Ranch Doritos. No Hair was at the hospital with PEYTON BEECHER.

"It can wait," Fantasy said.

"Let's just get it over with."

We went into the closet and changed into Bellissimo Property Management jackets and uniform black pants. She made the call.

"Inventory? This is Cheryl in Property Management, and I just got my butt chewed out because twenty-three doesn't have a new sofa."

I yawned and stretched.

"What? I sent the requisition this morning, and I copied your boss. Maybe he got it."

I should change shoes.

"She, then. Maybe she got it, and maybe you're not hearing

me. I have a suite with no sofa. A guest set the sofa on fire and somehow maintenance has managed to get the carpet replaced and the wall painted, but you guys haven't delivered the new sofa. We're sold out you know."

I checked the pockets of the jacket. Nothing.

"Well, twenty-three's sold out. Completely. Every room."

My hair was two different colors. I'd been too busy to fix it.

"I can't help it if you can't keep up with your paperwork."

I pushed my cuticles back.

"Your schedule is your problem."

I thought about snips of my phone conversation with Bradley Cole...

"No," she said, "a gold one. And not a used sofa, either. A brand-spankin' new one."

I remembered I hadn't checked on my grandmother all day.

"I'll tell you what," Fantasy said. "You get it strapped on a dolly and I'll be there in ten minutes." She hung up. "Let's go, Sunshine."

Thirty minutes later, we had our new sofa. Fantasy was stretched out on it and I was sprawled all over the one Bianca hadn't ruined when No Hair blasted through the door. "Did you two put your old raggedy sofa upstairs beside Shakes?"

From the brand-new sofa Fantasy said, "No. Why?"

He shook his head. "It looks like a damn yard sale up there."

We shrugged, smiled.

"You," he said to Fantasy, "go home, get some sleep. Your shift at the hospital starts at seven in the morning. Be there when Peyton Beecher wakes up."

He pivoted. "You." (Me.) "You're up in the hotel tonight?" I nodded. "Go get some sleep, but get back down early," he said, "and figure out why Peyton Beecher followed her ex-husband here."

* * *

Granny was sitting straight up in her Bellissimo bed, mostly in the dark, her blue hair twisted around bright yellow Velcro curlers, wearing a flannel nightgown buttoned up to her nose. She was propped on pillows snoring through a movie. Full blast. The walls were shaking. I located the remote and poked as fast as I could, then tucked her in. It was 7:30 in the evening.

Next, I heard a shrill bell, and looked at the clock to see it was 7:31, but the lights were on. I didn't remember getting into my own hotel bed or turning on all the lights, but here I was. I pulled a pillow over my head to block out the light, but a load of flowers on skinny legs shuffled in. Who could sleep through that?

"Davis, honey? Are you awake? DAVIS?"

Now it was 7:32. The next morning.

I jumped up. "Granny, give those to me." There were twice as many flowers as there was Granny.

"Don't you want to know who they're from?"

"Not just yet." I looked for a space large enough to hold the arrangement, and settled on the bathtub. Granny was right behind me. We stared at the ridiculous display.

"That's a good idea," Granny said. "You're full of good ideas."

"I need to get full of coffee, Granny." I rubbed away the last traces of sleep, then yawned the rest of the way awake.

"I'll fix you right up." Granny shuffled out, but not before snatching the card from the arrangement.

We sat at an oblong glass-top table in a large sitting room between the bedrooms in our Bellissimo suite, which had two of everything one could ever want. I was looking for the edge of the ocean, sipping coffee, while Granny opened the envelope.

"It says," Granny cleared her throat, "'*Had to come back and see me this soon? Dinner tomorrow night. Eight sharp. Violettes. Thatch.*'" She looked up. "What's a violette?"

"The French restaurant downstairs."

"Ah." Granny tipped a sixteenth of a teaspoon of Amaretto into her coffee. She held the teeny bottle up in offering.

"Gotta pass, Granny."

"Don't you tell your mother about this." She stirred. "And what's a thatch?"

"It's Matthew Thatcher," I told her. "Your friend's grandson? The announcer here?"

"I never said she was my friend," Granny said. "I said I knew who she was."

I grabbed the television remote, which I'd read was the absolute germiest thing in a hotel room, ever. I clicked until I reached the guest portfolio screen and saw the name I'd booked the suite in: Laura Kasden. That was how he knew I was here.

I showered at my end of our swanky hotel room (in a streaky medium-spice brunette, out a redhead), then dressed for work in Ray-Ban Wayfarers under a Zephyrs baseball cap above a Property Management blazer and black pants. Granny showered at her swanky end (in a pink plastic shower cap covering her blue curls and singing Nikki Minaj at the top of her lungs), then dressed for the casino like a polar bear with a cardigan sweater over a cardigan sweater set above double-knit pants, all the color of lime Kool-Aid.

We stepped into an empty elevator and I pushed M for Mezzanine and C for Casino, which anywhere else would have been L for Lobby. I went to work; Granny went to gamble. My purse rang as I stepped into control central. The caller ID displayed the number of the home I'd grown up in.

Oh, dear.

I generally communicate with my mother through my sister. "Tell Mother to stop hanging up when she calls and Bradley answers the phone. It's rude." And, "Meredith, tell Davis that she needs to stop letting strange men answer her phone." And, "Meredith, tell Davis Dr. Bubba has sent three postcards reminding her that it's time for her to get her teeth cleaned and be sure to point out she only gets the one set of teeth." And, "Tell Mother to tell Dr. Bubba that I don't live in Pine Apple any longer and have a new dentist in Biloxi. One that doesn't work out of the back of his moonshine liquor store and climb on top of people to yank out their perfectly good teeth with needle-nose pliers."

When Meredith wasn't handy to pass notes between us and Mother was forced to call, three out of four times I let the machine get it. I'd logged on to all four computers before she finished.

"Davis!" Her discontent bounced off all four walls; her disapproval filled the room. "What's this I hear about you taking your grandmother to Beehive? If I *ever* hear of you taking her to Beehive again, I will skin you alive. I have a good mind to tell your father, and the only reason I'm not going to is because I don't want to upset him. Your grandmother doesn't even have enough money to get into that place, and even if she did, do you honestly *want* that for your grandmother? Who put you in charge of your grandmother, Davis? Sometimes you think you're the only person in the family with a lick of sense, and it would do well for you to remember that I am also a college graduate. And besides, you're the one always going on and on about how busy you are. Do you have time to go to your grandmother's funeral?"

Finally, she took a breath.

"One. Last. Thing."

I would bet my bottom dollar that there would be more than one last thing.

"I told Eddie and he said he'd tell Meredith, but I'm telling you to tell your sister, because you know about as well as anyone how unreliable Eddie is. I had to call six or seven times in a row before he would even wake up and answer the telephone. Half the day already gone and him still in the bed. Anyway, I told him to tell Meredith, and you make sure he did, that Riley has a homework assignment to do a...hold on...diorama? Whatever that is? There's something here called a...hold on...rubric? Whatever that is? I don't do this new math, you know. Meredith needs to get back home and help her daughter with this because it's the biggest bunch of nonsense I've ever looked at. You tell her, because I don't think Eddie was half listening. He's just like his father. Pickled all the time."

She took another big breath.

"I meant what I said, Davis."

My fingers flew across the keyboards. I pulled up the list of So Help Me God benefactors who didn't exist yesterday—no federal taxes, no DMV records, no Social Security activity. I ran them again, this time through Lee County, Alabama's Department of Health Statistics and the SSDI, the Social Security Death Index.

Why would my mother leave a message for my sister (who is here) with my ex-ex-husband Eddie the dumb-dumb (who is there)? It made no sense—my mother rarely did—although she pointed me in the right So Help Me God direction. The people putting money in the church plate were dead.

ELEVEN

The Bellissimo has a monster public-relations department, full of first-rate spin doctors. Things happen around here all the time that the general public never hears about. Gamblers pull into the parking garage, key the lock on a back seat full of children, then merrily stroll into the casino to power drink and gamble away their child support checks. At least two or three times a year, someone dies of natural causes in one of the 1,700 guest rooms. Other things needed "managing" every day of the week. Medical emergencies in the casino are more common than anyone would guess. Number one? Choking. Once this year, to death. But he choked on three $1,000 chips he swiped from another player's stack, denied it, then unsuccessfully tried to swallow the evidence. Other repeat offenders: heart attacks, strokes, diabetic comas, Charley horses and hangnails. (Kidding.) Fist fights, dog fights, and fights with ATMs and slot machines occur almost hourly. In June, we had a live birth between two crap tables. It was a boy. The mother named him Shooter. A few weeks ago, a guest stumbled off the elevator and halfway through the casino wearing nothing but a black G-string before Security tackled him. The same day, a woman came in carrying an extra-large purse, then went from slot machine to slot machine trying to find homes for the calico kittens she had stuffed in her bag.

None of it made the news. If it did make the news, Marketing made sure the Bellissimo was left out of it.

So when No Hair called, interrupting my So Help Me God research to tell me that PEYTON BEECHER had disappeared from the hospital, my first thought was that this would be the lead story at five, and it would start with Bianca Sanders unloading a gun on the girl. There would be no way to keep it out of the news cycle, and there wasn't a doubt in my mind that the three of us were headed for mall security jobs.

"What?" I could hardly process his words. "She got up and walked out?"

"She didn't get up and walk out," he said, "she had help."

"Where was Fantasy?"

"Barricaded in the bathroom."

"Is she okay?"

"She's pissed."

I realized I was up and pacing a circle. "Who helped Peyton out?"

"An unidentified man. The hospital's never seen him," he said. "Their cameras got one good shot, but he was all decked out in surgery garb so he didn't set off any alarms and all you can see are his eyeballs. I'm sending it your way."

The email containing the grainy photograph popped into my in-box. I tapped, tapped, tapped on the keyboard and began running it through our facial-recognition software. On another screen, I blew up the photo, and in spite of the low resolution I could see from the deep crow's feet and thick white eyebrows we weren't looking for a young surgeon. Not that he was necessarily a surgeon. I've never heard of a surgeon absconding with a patient.

"What name was she registered under?"

"Peyton Beecher," No Hair said.

"You should have registered her under a different name."

"When I want some Monday morning quarterbacking from you, Davis, I'll ask for it." Then he said, "Find that man and find the girl. Sit there until you do."

* * *

At six that evening, I gave up on following every vehicle leaving the hospital property that could have possibly held PEYTON BEECHER. If I looked at one more minute of Biloxi traffic cam feed, my eyeballs would pop out of my head and roll across the floor. I stepped into the closet to dress in camouflage casino clothes, then tracked down my grandmother nodding off and on at a Frog Princess Deluxe slot machine.

"Granny." I shook her little shoulder. "Granny wake up."

We had meatloaf, mashed potatoes, turnip greens, pickled beets, butter beans, cornbread, banana pudding, and a pitcher of syrupy sweet iced tea at Dixie, the family-friendly restaurant past the cashier's cage in the casino. The tablecloths are red-checkered and every menu item is hidden under glossy butter, creamy sauce, or peppered gravy.

"THAT'S A HEALTHY APPETITE YOU'VE GOT THERE, DAVIE."

"This food is delicious."

I tucked Granny in at seven-thirty, then went right back downstairs for more eye strain. I didn't even try to look for PEYTON BEECHER again. I went back to matching death certificates with So Help Me God patrons. I have no idea what time it was when I finally found a benefactor with a beating heart. He was Jewell Maffini's neighbor. The man's address, like hers, was One God's Boulevard.

* * *

Something was so wrong with the coffee the next morning, both in my Bellissimo suite and in Beans, the lobby café, so while Fantasy was busy cleaning out Matthew Thatcher's closet full of skeletons in control central, No Hair was at the hospital watching parking garage surveillance feed and threatening to snap necks over Petyton Beecher's disappearance, and my little worn-out grandmother was sleeping above me, I decided it might be a good time to sneak out and check on Meredith at mine and Bradley's new condo. I knew I could get a cup of coffee there that didn't taste like aluminum foil, and we needed to work out something to get our grandmother back to Pine Apple. A little casino goes a long way with an eighty-two-year old.

"Fantasy?" I breezed in. "What do you think about me ducking out for an hour or so?"

She peeked over my neatly stacked printouts of So Help Me God on a table between us. "Considering you worked all night, I say go for it." She stretched her long legs. "How late were you here?"

"Late enough to figure out the church is making a fortune off the old folks who live there and reporting it as donations from dead people."

"You don't say."

"I do say. The profit center is the senior citizen housing."

"What's so profitable about senior citizen housing?"

"That," I said, "is a good question."

"And where do we fit in?"

"That," I said, "is an even better question."

"So what's our next move?"

I tapped a thick stack. "Run all the people who live behind the church through our system and see if anything pops.

"Let's do it," Fantasy said.

"We can't," I said, "not yet. The resident's identifications are encrypted. I couldn't stay awake long enough to crack the code. My brain hurts from trying and I need coffee."

"You're holding coffee."

"I need better coffee."

"I'll take it if you don't want it."

I passed it to her.

"This coffee is good, Davis." She blew across the top and took another sip. "Come look at this."

I skirted around the table and propped myself up on elbows at her desk. All shapes and sizes of LeeRoy Gerard Maffini a.k.a. Matthew Thatcher dirt was on the screen. She had everything but him in short yellow pants wearing a bowtie sitting on the Easter Bunny's lap. "It's so nice to know someone's real name and date of birth."

"This coffee is *so* good," Fantasy said. "Where'd you get it?"

"So this guy was a preacher back in the day," I clicked around, "but has a master's degree in finance?"

"And now he's the Bellissimo frontman," Fantasy said. "Go figure."

"Maybe he can't decide what he wants to be when he grows up."

"His original application doesn't say a word about any background in finance."

"It doesn't say his name is LeeRoy Maffini either."

"Mr. Microphone has secrets."

"So does that big church." I gave a nod to the stacks of dead-people financials.

"I'll tell you one thing that's not much of a secret," Fantasy clicked. "Did you see this?" She pulled up two photos of Mr. Microphone, one from his preacher days and a recent Bellissimo press shot. "This nose job." She tapped the eraser end of a mechanical pencil between the wide bumpy nose on the left and the sleek movie star nose on the right.

"Good work, Ms. Erb. And look at his ears." They flapped out of his shaggy auburn hair in the old shot and were pressed tight against his neatly-coiffed chestnut head in the new.

"He makes a better looking emcee than preacher," Fantasy said.

"Amen."

The phone rang with an announcement from No Hair: Peyton Beecher had left the hospital in a silver Porsche Boxter. No discernible plates, but run down that car anyway, and do it now.

I slumped against a wall.

"Go on, girl," Fantasy said. "I got this."

"Are you sure?" I shouldered my bag.

"Granny, right?"

"In the end, yes."

Fantasy shooed me out the door.

I listened to local news on my drive to the new condo (we weren't on it) (yet), then I listened to piped mood music in the condo elevator (Diana King's "I Say a Little Prayer"), and the next thing I heard was the harmony, tranquility, and serenity of home.

My sister is a miracle worker.

She'd added two colors to the whitewash: raspberry for me, and a pale celery green for Bradley Cole. Upon closer inspection, the color she'd added the most of was a fieldstone gray, fifty shades of it, but it blended so well I didn't see it at first. There were rugs, lamps, art, and pillows I'd never met, in textures and patterns I wouldn't have chosen in a million years, and they all played so beautifully against the backdrop of the Gulf that I sank into the marshmallow sofa, drank it all in, and decided to never ever ever leave. I couldn't wait for Bradley Cole to see it.

But just then my ex-ex-husband Eddie exited one of the guest rooms, as naked as on the day he was born, saw me, laughed, then stood there, dangling, idly scratching his stupid chest.

Something about the scene made me very, very ill. I ran, shoving past him, locked myself in the masterpiece bathroom, kicked a thick silver rug out of my way, then stretched out on the icy-cold tile floor to wait it out. Several minutes later, when long shadows of that naked rat bastard Eddie Crawford's toes fell into my line of vision, I rolled over and let the other side of my body cool off. He jiggled the doorknob. "Go away, Eddie." I barely got the words out. "Get out of here."

"What's the matter with you, Davis?"

"You, Eddie! You're the matter with me! Get out!"

"Let me in and we'll talk about it."

"NO. And put some clothes on." I rolled onto my back when I heard him pad away, growling and grumbling, but three seconds later I heard the doors to the His dressing room slide open. I dragged myself up from the floor and threw open the bathroom door to shout, "Not Bradley's clothes, you idiot!"

I turned to the vanity, splashed cold water on my face, and grabbed for a towel the size of a king-sized bed sheet. I tossed it to Eddie the Ass as I passed him. "Come on." By the time we reached the living room, he'd wrapped the towel around his hips, but I made him stand anyway. He wasn't sitting on any of our new furniture, ever. I fully intended to burn the towel he was wearing and the bedroom he'd slept in. "Where's Meredith?"

"Said she was going back to Pine Apple." He tucked the towel. "Something about homework."

"Why are you here, Eddie?"

"What's it to you, Davis?"

"This is my *home*!" I yelled. "And I don't want you in it!"

He yawned. Not a care in the world.

"You need to go, Eddie. Get your stuff and get out."

"Hey." He stabbed a finger my way. "Lose the attitude. Your sister has worked my ass off. 'Move this, nail that.' She's as bossy and bitchy as you are. She gave me a ride so I could get my car, and she told me to stay here until Granny was ready to go."

"Here? She told you to stay *here*?"

"She might've meant Biloxi," he said, "not so much here." He said it on a yawn. "Nice place, though. I like it."

If I had a loaded gun on me, this room would get a whole new color scheme.

"Do you have your car, Eddie?"

He rubbed his jaw. "Not just yet."

"Not just yet," I repeated. "When are you thinking you'll get it?"

"As soon as I drum up enough money to get it out of hock," he said, "if it'll run."

"And where do you plan on getting the money to get it out of hock?"

"I'm going to hit up the Tiger here in a little while."

He was talking about the cheesiest, greasiest, slimiest casino in Biloxi, The Lucky Tiger. It was a hole-in-the-wall last-resort joint, smelled like a gutter, and catered to a sad, sad local clientele. Business was brisk on the days government checks hit mailboxes, but otherwise, it was a ghost town. No one ever won a penny at the Tiger, and once or twice a year, either the Gaming Board or the Health Department chained the doors for any of a laundry list of offenses, like now. I'd seen it on Page Six, not far from the porn photo of me and Mr. Microphone, a pardon-our-progress-for-the-next-few-weeks ad, which was really a we've-gone-and-screwed-up-again ad. "No you're not, Eddie." I said it on a long, weary sigh. "The Tiger's closed."

"Dammit." He scratched his stupid ear. "Now what am I supposed to do?"

I spotted my purse at the door, and pointed to it. "Go get it."

Smelling money, Eddie and his towel hustled.

I dug for my checkbook. "How much?"

He had an instant smirk on his face. Eddie Crawford had been taking my money for a decade, and here we go again. "I'd say five hundred ought to do it."

A bargain. I scribbled out a check. He broke out in a sweat.

"What about Granny?" he asked. "I'm supposed to wait on her."

"I'll take care of Granny." I tore off the check. "You leave."

Eddie, eye on the prize, closed the space between us with one giant step. He was so close I could smell the fabric softener on the towel. He held his hands out—gimme, gimme—and as he did, the towel he was wearing dropped to the floor. Before I could scream, shove him away, or throw up, the front door burst open and Bradley Cole stood in the threshold of our new home holding a spray of white roses tied with a long, white, silk ribbon.

I froze.

Eddie laughed.

Bradley gently placed the roses on the demilune table to his right, took a giant step back into the elevator, and left without a word.

The space around me took on a carnival funhouse quality. Everything was distorted. Eddie's mouth was moving, noise was escaping, but I couldn't make a bit of sense of it. When my head finally stopped spinning, he, however, had no trouble understanding my words. He got my message loud and clear.

* * *

We call it Pine Apple Highway; others call it Interstate 10. It connects Greenville to the east with Camden to the west. Pine Apple is the halfway point, but everyone calls the middle mark Dead Curve. Many nights of my childhood sleep came to abrupt ends with the screeching wail of brakes, then the crushing pandemonium of steel, metal, glass, and twice, explosions, as Dead Curve, less than a mile from our quiet country home, claimed another midnight victim. It was the finality of the silence after my father's rapid footfall past my bedroom door that horrified me so. It was knowing there was no turning back the clock ten minutes. It was the silence that terrified me.

My vision shifted between the two things that could break the silence I found myself in after Bradley walked out. My phone could ring with his call or the door could open and usher him back in, though neither would invade the ominous still, no matter how hard I stared at them.

At the one-hour mark, the foyer buzzer sounded. I rose from the sofa and crossed the room.

"Ma'am, my name is Herbert Baldwin. I'm a bellman with the Grand. I'm here to get a few of Mr. Cole's personal belongings." Thirty minutes later Mr. Baldwin left with, among other things, Bradley's Sonicare toothbrush base. Which meant Bradley Cole had no plans to return anytime soon.

* * *

He would not take my calls. I drove to the Grand, but security wouldn't let me through to the offices. When the phone beside me finally rang, it was Mary Ha Ha, who stopped whatever she'd been doing (probably my boyfriend) to tell me he was in a meeting, would be in a meeting, had fourteen meetings after that, so there was no point in me waiting. She suggested I have a nice day, then hung up.

"Davis." Fantasy was talking me off the cliff. We were in the bullpen, on the new sofa, with enough So Help Me God on the table in front of us to start a bonfire. "Your ex-husband was standing an inch from your nose buck naked. You need to give Bradley some time to get that image out of his head."

I wish I could get that image out of my own head.

"If you could have seen the look on his face," I said. "He was a total blank. He stared at us, dropped the roses, then he was gone. I don't understand why he wouldn't have stayed long enough to at least let me explain. How can he decide I'm guilty without letting me defend myself? And Eddie? In a million years it wouldn't happen. If Eddie Crawford were the very last human on the face of the Earth it wouldn't happen. And Bradley knows that!"

Fantasy patted my shoulder. There, there. "What'd you do with Eddie?"

"I put his ass on the street."

"Okay, Davis," Fantasy said. "Let's turn the tables. Let's say you walked into Bradley's office and the lawyer Mary was sitting in his chair, like you were sitting on the sofa. And standing one inch from her is Bradley. And he's naked."

"Oh, come on, Fantasy."

"Seriously," she said. "What would you think? What would it look like to you? What would you do?"

I had to admit, if only to myself, I'd probably have a fit. There might be some biting, scratching, and hair pulling. I know one thing I wouldn't do: walk out without a word.

"Which puts a whole new wrinkle in it for you, Davis."

"I have enough already, thank you." I unconsciously reached to smooth the space between my eyebrows where Bianca kept telling me I was getting "elevens."

"You two need to sit down and talk," Fantasy said, "but you'd better save the big news until you cleared up the Eddie business."

"What big news?"

"Davis. Bradley needs to know you're pregnant."

I clapped my hands over my ears and began singing, "La la la la la!"

She raised her voice. "For that matter, you need to know."

I sang louder. "LA, LA, LA, LA, LA!"

Fantasy pulled my hands away from my ears. "If he thinks there's something going on between you and Eddie, it paints an entirely new baby picture."

I would happily share whatever frantic, desperate thought Fantasy's observation prompted had I had one, but her words paralyzed me.

"And you need to get to a doctor, Davis. You've fainted twice this week. You need to have blood work done. A mosquito has a higher iron level than you. You need to be on prenatal vitamins."

"No way. Those things are horse pills."

"How late are you?" she asked.

"Dinner's at eight," I said.

"You know what I mean."

I held up two tentative fingers. I reluctantly added a third.

"Days?"

I shook my head no.

"*Months*?"

"No!" No. Not months.

Just then, No Hair keyed himself in. He aimed at me. "Did you send your grandmother all the way to Pine Apple, Alabama, in a Bellissimo limo, Davis?"

Ooops.

"We've got way bigger fish to fry, No Hair." Fantasy to the rescue. "These church people," she waved a So Help Me God brochure, "are running a senior-citizen scam. They're getting old folks to sign over every dime they have to the church, locking them up in their Senior Living Center, then making a killing off them."

No Hair was still staring at me. "Where have you been all morning?" He turned to Fantasy. "That's a very sad story, Fantasy."

"It gets sadder," she said. "We think they're recruiting their old people *here*, No Hair, at our slot tournaments."

TWELVE

Peyton Beecher Maffini had been a troubled youth. You know what they say about preachers' kids. Her juvenile records were sealed, and had she misbehaved in any state other than my home state of Alabama, I doubt I'd have been able to get to them. Lucky for me, I had an Alabama Ace. My dad.

At age fourteen, Peyton had chained herself to the step railing in front of Beehive High School in protest of fetal pigs being mutilated at the hands of the ninth grade science teacher. According to the police report, she claimed the massive slaughter was "wreaking environmental genocide" and "represented animal brutality at its worst." She used bright orange organic spray paint on the teacher's white Chevrolet Impala. *KILLING BABY PIGS DOESN'T TEACH ANYONE ANYTHING* started at the driver's door and wrapped all the way around.

At sixteen, she went on a hunger strike to protest school pizza. She decorated school hallways with a disgusting collage of photographs featuring rotted and decaying cafeteria offerings, and claimed Beehive High School was perpetuating "the gross obesity of an entire generation." She broke into the school after hours and destroyed a snack machine and its companion soft drink machine with a sledge hammer. Two weeks later, when she was supposed to be in study hall, she slashed three tires on a food-service delivery truck. The girl had a knack for vandalism.

Her records show she was suspended a total of thirteen times between eighth grade and graduation. Five of those for refusing to go on mandatory school trips, because they wouldn't let her ride her bike and she wouldn't contribute to the hole in the ozone by traveling via bus or car.

Naturally, she started smoking pot, so by the time she reached the eleventh grade, the effects of her breakfast, lunch, and dinner marijuana kept her subdued. Still, her student-conduct incident file didn't know the difference, because the drug offenses kept it fed.

Her twenties were a blur of protest—Kuwait, Iraq, Israel—five of those years married, with two short stints in jail for occupying foreign embassies. (How'd she get that far on a bicycle?) Then? Nothing. She wound up here. Lots of blanks to fill in. One thing seemed obvious to me: Had her parents not been so busy managing their fortunes in senior-citizen estate wealth, they might have sent up a prayer or two on this girl's behalf. Peyton had not lived an easy life.

Photographs, starting with the one I'd taken of her after she was pulled from the dumpster and dating back to her high-school mug shots, would indicate that she'd had lifelong issues with cosmetic and hygiene products. She didn't look as if she'd ever met a pair of tweezers, a bottle of No Frizz conditioner, or tube of lipstick. She was five-seven, one hundred twenty pounds, with hair and eyes of no discernible color, but both on the wild side. As such, she was easily lost in a crowd, and her looks, at first glance, were bland underneath her hair and Boho wardrobe.

However, the years of biking everywhere with an organic mango for lunch had caught up with Peyton Beecher Maffini. The wild teenager had grown into a tough and beautiful woman. I knew she was tough: She'd tumbled down a thirty-story garbage chute and survived for almost five days. And I could see that she was beautiful. At some point, she gave up her Cousin Itt coif and began lassoing her hair behind her head, resulting in corkscrew tendrils that framed her very pretty face. Her skin was flawless, her body even more so. Let's put it this way: if she'd been pulled out of a dumpster in New York City or Los Angeles, someone would have slapped angel wings on her and sent her down the runway.

Bianca Casimiro Sanders popped out of her bubble long

enough to notice. It's possible that her husband noticed too.

Was Peyton Beecher Maffini here as part of, or in protest of, the scam under the steeple?

I queued all four office computers with our face-rec software and asked it to zero in on choke points—all entries and exits from the Bellissimo properties at which hiding your face from the cameras was not an option. I went back three years, which was when Mr. Microphone's reign at the Bellissimo began, and, worth noting, when casinos in Alabama began closing their doors. I got more than 1,700 hits. Peyton Beecher had worked here off and on the entire time her ex-husband had, in every entry level position Human Resources could think up. She'd pushed vacuum cleaners in the casino, she'd chopped vegetables, she'd served steak sandwiches, she'd pulled weeds in the gardens and had been on the midnight pool-cleaning crew. All under assumed identities, and all under our noses.

With twenty minutes to spare, I remembered I had a dinner date with her ex-husband. I raced from the office to the dressing room, where I caught my own reflection in the wall of mirror. I slowed down and stared at myself. What I need to do is slow down and work things out with Bradley Cole. I love Bradley. I really, really love Bradley. I till-death-do-us-part love Bradley.

* * *

I went all Ralph Lauren Black Label for dinner. I wouldn't have gone at all had it not been for the fact that my dinner date's former better half had spent five days stuffed in a dumpster elevator, and No Hair would stuff me in a dumpster elevator if I bailed.

The evening's hot couture was a sleeveless silk dress with matching sheer wrap, that were, for the lack of a better word, purple. Perky purple. I couldn't pull it off with my natural red hair, but sprayed medium-spice brown with medium-blue eyes, I was good to go. I went a little heavier on the eye makeup than usual, because

I looked like I hadn't had any sleep in a week. (I hadn't.) I scooped out two handfuls of things from my real purse and dumped them into a Prada pleated clutch, including cell phones, Hershey's Kisses, a lip gloss, and for all I knew, a toaster. On my feet, which hurt because I'd been on them so long, I wore Ralph's Italian camel suede five-inch sandals with ankle straps. Here's hoping I didn't have to do any running.

I arrived at Violettes two minutes late to find that Mr. Microphone wasn't there at all. He was in the casino, a city block away, calling out names for the eight o'clock drawing.

"This is for you." The maître d' passed me a folded note.

Laura, I double booked myself! Duty calls!
My car is out front. Go ahead. Enjoy it.
I'll be there in 20. Or 25.

Gripping the note, I made my way through the lobby and out the front doors. The night was clear, nippy, and smelled like the sea. Three valets appeared, then looked straight down the front of my dress. "Mr. Thatcher's car?" Three arms swept west, but their heads didn't move. I probably should have worn a bra.

I'm not much of a car person, but there was no ignoring his. It was a silver Porsche Boxter.

Oh, dear.

The personalized Mississippi tag read EMCEE. No surprise he drove an obnoxious vehicle. No surprise at all. (Bradley Cole—sob—drives a very Republican black BMW 528). And no surprise that his was the car that had pulled away from Biloxi Memorial with Peyton Beecher in it. If we hadn't had eight million irons in the fire, we'd have looked in this direction first. What did stop my $600 RL shoes in their tracks was the sticker in the corner of the Porsche windshield, driver side.

It was a small, red coat-of-arms for The Regent.

Mr. Microphone lived in the building I'd just moved into, Bradley Cole (whimper) had just taken his toothbrush out of, and

Peyton Beecher Maffini was probably holed up in.

A twelve-year-old valet was guarding the car with his life.

"I need the keys." I held my hand out.

The boy choked. I showed him the note written on Matthew Thatcher's personal stationary that clearly invited me to go ahead and enjoy it.

"He's waiting on me." I tapped one of my RLs, and the boy passed me two electronic fobs on a ring. One for the Porsche, one for the Regent.

Where did all the keys go?

* * *

"You *what*? You stole his *car*?"

"I didn't steal it," I said to No Hair as I ground the Porsche gears (so crunchy) and ran a red light (barely). "His note said 'Go ahead.' What does 'go ahead' mean to you?"

"It doesn't mean 'take my sixty-thousand-dollar car for a joy ride,' Davis."

"I can get Peyton out of his place in ten minutes," I said. "But you've got to keep him distracted in the casino."

"Turn around right this second and take the man's car back, then we'll go together and get the girl. For one, you don't know that she's there. If she is, you don't know that she *wants* out, Davis, and you can't go in there without backup."

I hung up on Plan A and called Plan B.

"Davis," Fantasy whined. "Seriously? I have one foot out the door."

"Give me fifteen minutes, Fantasy."

Plan B hung up on me.

Good communication among coworkers is vital and I facilitated most of it among the three of us all by my lonesome.

A few miles north on Beach Boulevard, I was on two wheels taking a right into the Regent. I didn't know this place all that well, having spent so little time here, but I did know how to get into the parking garage. I pushed Thatch's fob into the slot and the pearly gates parted, just like with my own fob.

Regent residents parked on an interior level in the middle of the building, which I thought was clever. No running to and from the car in the weather. To get there, we scaled an interior concrete corkscrew that you'd think a Porsche would be good at. It wasn't. At all. There must be something wrong with the steering in this car too, because I had a small right fender scrape on the first bend and a medium right fender scrape near the top. Finally, I got the damn thing to the parking level.

The fob was unmarked, so if you dropped it on the street, someone picking it up wouldn't know where to go to wipe you out. By the same token, if you dropped it on the street and someone picked it up who knew to go to the Regent to wipe you out, that person still wouldn't know which private elevator led to your unit. That someone would have to traipse around the parking level, trying the fob in every private elevator until they found the one it fit, which is what I did. In five-inch heels. There were twenty-six units in the Regent, so twenty-six elevators, and I only knew one that it wasn't. That left twenty-five that it might be. I knew to start at number twenty-six and work my way back to save time.

Matthew Thatcher's unit was number three.

I had to hike back to his car (in seven-inch heels) (they'd grown), grind it into reverse, park it where it was supposed to be, in front of the Unit Three elevator, so it wouldn't look out of place. You'd think it would be easy to park such a small car straight, but it's not. I accidentally bumped the garage wall—ooops—and had to find reverse *again*. I did *not* like this car. Too sensitive.

The private elevator that led to my unit was oak-paneled. Thatch's was five solid sheets of mirror. Ceiling too. Disgusting.

My knees were knocking when the doors parted and Matthew Thatcher's living quarters were laid out in front of me. It was deathly quiet, dark, and it smelled like footballs.

I stuck my head out of the elevator. "Peyton?"

As soon as I said it, an electric shock ran through my body, and I jumped straight out of my skin. When it happened a second time, I decided it was a phone in my Prada bag. The text was from Fantasy.

I PICKED A FIGHT WITH A DRAWING WINNER, CLAIMING SHE WAS IMPERSONATING ME, AND SHE HAS ALL BUT KICKED MY ASS IN THE MIDDLE OF THE CASINO, THANK YOU, DAVIS. SECURITY HAULED US BOTH OFF. THEY'RE GOING TO OPEN THE DRAWING AGAIN AND LET BOTH OF US HAVE A TURN. I'LL DRAG IT OUT AS LONG AS I CAN, BUT HE'LL BE OUT THE DOOR IN JUST A FEW MINUTES. HURRY.

I texted back. I'VE GOT TO HAVE MORE TIME!!!!!

YOU'D BETTER GET YOUR BUTT BACK HERE, DAVIS.

And my last text. FAINT. FAINT DEAD IN THE FLOOR IN FRONT OF HIM.

"Peyton?" I finally let the elevator go and took a step inside that sounded like a one-ton TNT bomb detonating. I slipped out of my nine-inch heels and tiptoed barefoot from there.

The floor plan on this side of the building was flipped from mine; everything was to the right of the foyer—kitchen, study, bedrooms—where in our place (sniff), everything was to the left. All the lights were on sensors, because with each step I took, another spotlight came to life. The general decorating theme of Matthew Thatcher's home was Concrete, Leather & Mirrors. The walls were covered with reflective surfaces of all shapes and sizes. The floors and countertops were cold, stained concrete, and everything else was leather. The *rug* under my bare feet was leather. Every stick of furniture was dark, distressed leather. He probably had leather towels.

The first room down the hall appeared to be an office, complete with a wall of fame displaying framed photographs of Thatch cozied up with visiting Bellissimo celebrities. I'm sure that beyond the photos there was excellent stuff in there, but I didn't have time. Next was the master bedroom where I found more of the same: mirrors, photos of the owner, concrete, and leather. I made a U-turn to the third closed door, which I guessed would be a guest room.

It was. There was a guest. Peyton Beecher Maffini was gagged, bound, and tied to the bed.

I rushed in. "Peyton!" Digging through her Rapunzel hair trying to locate the source of the gag, I wished I'd taken a second to notice that she was none too happy to see me, thrashing around beneath the restraints, screaming into the gag, and that the look in her eyes was one of sheer terror. Had I taken the time to make even one of those observations, maybe I wouldn't have been so shocked when I loosened the gag and she bit the holy shit out of me.

I let out a scream to wake the dead. From now on, she was Jaws to me. I shook my hand up and down. "Why in *hell* did you do that? I'm here to *help* you, Peyton."

"Get away from me, you crazy bitch!" She bucked all over that bed, her wild hair flying, while I stared at my hand, watching the teeth marks darken. "I don't even know your stupid husband!"

What? Who?

I had No Hair on the phone. Jaws of Steel Peyton had earned her gag back, thank you very much, and my whole arm was throbbing.

"She thinks I'm Bianca."

"I don't care if she thinks you're Mother Goose. Get her out of there and get that car back here." The phone went dead.

"Listen up, Peyton." I began popping the hooks on the bungee cords snaking around her feet, legs, and the bed posts. There were about four hundred of them. Somebody was missing a few Boy Scout badges. All the while, Peyton was desperately working the gag, trying to bite through. "I am *not* Bianca Sanders. See this hair?" I shook my head. "Red! See my eyes?" I widened them to saucer size. "Brown! Ish!"

She'd worked the gag to her chin. "How crazy *are* you, lady?"

I looked up to catch a glimpse of myself in one of the many mirrors. I'd forgotten I was Laura Kasden. My hair wasn't red at all. My eyes weren't brown. Ish. And I suppose, in dim lights and

$7,000 worth of Ralph Lauren, Laura Kasden favored Bianca Sanders. "You're going to have to trust me on this one, Peyton. I'm not Bianca."

I finally popped the magic bungee cord and the rest fell away, just in time for Peyton Beecher Maffini to twist, grunt, then land her foot squarely in my chest, drop-kicking me to the concrete floor. I was too stunned to get up and now my butt *and* my hand hurt. I batted around for my Prada bag without taking my eyes off Crazy, found it, fished around, then tazed the crap out of her before she killed me.

THIRTEEN

It was the middle of the night, either Thursday or Tuesday, I wasn't sure.

I wasn't about to take Peyton back to the hospital, if for no other reason, I didn't want to drive the irritable Porsche again. Especially with her in it. So I dragged her to my place, which was the least amount of fun I've had this decade. She was absolute dead weight and I stepped on her hair twice.

No Hair sent a limo after Dr. Jakeaway—who he tracked down at The Penthouse Club on Highway 49, where, as it turns out, Jakeaway is a frequent flyer—to give Peyton Beecher Maffini the once-over. Dr. Doolittle entered the room, stopped short, then delivered his professional opinion. "She looks marvelous." His eyebrows danced. "I like the restraints. Classy."

I explained her hands and feet were cuffed to the iron railings of the guest bed because she was out of control. Not for his viewing pleasure.

"She's been a little hard to handle," I told him.

"*She's* a crazy bitch!"

"Peyton." I turned to her. "Do you want your gag back?" She didn't bark or growl. "I didn't think so."

Then to the happy doctor. "I had to taze her three times just to get her in the bed. She bit the fire out of me," I showed him, "and she's staying in those cuffs until she settles down."

I winked. He winked back.

"Settles down."

I winked. He winked.

We did this until ridiculous.

"Settles down? Like you settle Bianca down?" I hissed the last part on low volume through clenched teeth.

"You can't drug me, mister!" Peyton screamed. "I'll have your license yanked so fast you won't know what hit you!"

She might be able to pull that one off. She certainly had the résumé for it.

"Peyton, do you drink?" I asked. "Would you like some" (What's the strongest stuff out there?) "moonshine?"

"I would," Jakeaway said. "I'd like some moonshine."

I turned to him. "You've had enough. You need coffee." A strange distant alarm sounded. "Watch her."

"Just a nip." The gap between his index finger and thumb measured about five inches.

The noise was coming from a small speaker on a panel beside the elevator. I pushed a black button. "Bradley?"

"It's us." Fantasy. "Buzz us up."

No Hair, just the square footage of him, settled Peyton down. His tie might have helped—it was riddled with bullet holes. (Not real. He hadn't been shot.)

We were all stuffed in the guest room. Dr. Zhivago declared Peyton's blood pressure, pulse, respiration, and heart rate all in the normal range. (He said "normal ranch" then corrected it to "formal range".) After which, he made himself at home, sniffing candles, poking on an antique Royal typewriter my sister had placed in the middle of the guest-room desk. "This is so cool," he said. Poke poke. He found the carriage return lever and annoyed us with that ten times. "Groovy!"

"Jakeaway!" No Hair shot him a vicious, threatening look. "Get your act together."

The tipsy smile slid all the way off the doctor.

No Hair turned to the patient. "Now, Peyton." His voice switched to the soothing channel. "I know you've had a rough week. I understand you had an incident with Bianca, were trapped in a garbage chute for days, taken from the hospital, held against your will, and I want to hear all about it from you. You talk, I'll listen." No Hair sat back and folded his big arms across his bullets.

"I want everyone to leave," she said. Her eyes brightened with the promise of tears. "And I want out of these restraints." She rattled the cuffs against the iron. "I want something to drink," she said, "and then I'll talk to you."

No Hair's thumb shot up, showing us the door.

I sat Dr. Seuss down in front of the television with the remote, and he went straight to the golf channel. Groovy.

Fantasy was banging around in the kitchen. "Davis, you have a teapot, but you don't seem to have any tea."

"I don't even know that teapot," I said. "Make her coffee." I curled up in a raspberry print loveseat that guaranteed me a great nap if only I could get all these people out of here.

"Surely we don't want her drinking coffee at two in the morning." Fantasy was opening and closing every cabinet and drawer in the kitchen. And not gently.

Dr Pepper's head swiveled around. "No caffeine for the patient."

"It's coffee or Heineken," Fantasy said from the kitchen.

"I'll take a Heineken."

"I'm not your waitress, Jakeaway."

"You tell him, Fantasy."

I only meant to rest my eyes for two minutes, but I don't remember a single thing after that.

* * *

Growing up in the Bible Belt has its advantages. Southerners don't gossip; Southerners pray for one other. Of course, you have to know the details of the sinner's sins to get any good praying done, then you have to recruit others to pray, and they need the details too. It's called Prayer Circle.

Another Southern convenience is blessing people's hearts. Say anything you want about anyone, but follow it up with a blessing.

"Why would she keep having kids when the three she has are so ugly? Bless their hearts." It works when you lead with the blessing, too. "Bless his heart, he smells like a pack of dead wombats."

But the best is hiding behind the Bible. Look long enough and hard enough, and you can find Bible Backup. "I sure did beat him within an inch of his life with a tire iron. God says don't be coveting another man's wife." (God did say that.) "And that means don't be buying her beer when I'm gone deer hunting." (I don't think God meant *that*.)

What Peyton told No Hair until the wee hours of Friday morning took discriminating interpretation of Bible do's and don'ts to a whole new level. God said take care of the elderly. He didn't mean take them for everything they're worth, take them to the cleaners, or take them out.

LeeRoy Gerard Maffini, our own Matthew Thatcher, was raised by his grandmother in a modest two bedroom home on Butler Mill Road in Sprague, Alabama. After a four-year absence, LeeRoy hit the doorstep with his Kappa Sigma T-shirt collection, rolled-up Roll Tide banners, and fresh-off-the-press Bachelor of Science in Finance diploma—only to learn that it was no longer his doorstep.

Jewell Maffini told her grandson it was called a Reverse Home Mortgage with Consolidated Debt Management.

LeeRoy Maffini told his grandmother it was called You've Been Had, MeMaw.

Turned out that not having her LeeRoy home to cook and clean for left Jewell with too much time on her hands. She met up with a bank of Cleopatra slot machines at the nearby Fortune Casino. That filled her void, but emptied her piggy bank, and just when she thought she'd never get a Double Mummy Bonus Round to dig her out of the financial ditch she'd jumped into head first, she met a nice man from the So Help Me God Church playing the Cleopatra machine next to hers, and he pulled her out of the ditch.

What she needed was prayer. And supplication. He told her that by his knowledge, her chambers would be filled with all precious and pleasant riches, which sounded like a Double Mummy Bonus Round to Jewell. God would see her through this. It said so in First Maffini 2:16. God told her to sign right here. And here. And here.

Bless her heart.

LeeRoy hightailed it to Beehive to explain the Principles of Investment to Reverend Marion Beecher. He summarized his entire college career, everything from Securities Analysis to Monetary Theory, and he threw in big concepts like convertible arbitrage, esoteric fixed income-trading strategies, and where the hell were they supposed to live? In the end, he demanded Reverend Beecher give back his grandmother's money and property, and the reverend said he couldn't do that, but he could give LeeRoy and his grandmother jobs. Having never set foot in a church, having never once cracked the spine of God's Word, and not knowing a single stanza of *Blessed Be the Name*, LeeRoy landed a job as the new Minister to the Elderly. Straight commission. For every estate he brought to the church, LeeRoy received eight percent off the top, and quarterly dividends of prime-plus-two off the interest each of his accounts earned. Jewell's new job was to hang out in small Alabama casinos, butter up marks, then toss them to her preacher grandson.

LeeRoy was a born salesman. Jewell was having the time of her life. The good Reverend Beecher hit his knees every night, praying that his Golden Boy wouldn't grow weary of schmoozing little old ladies in dank, dark, smoky Alabama casinos. Over the next two years, the accounting staff, along with everything else at So Help Me God, grew. It took an additional eighty-seven auditing souls to help count the blessings.

God is good.

About then, twenty-two-year-old Peyton Beecher, who hadn't been seen or heard from in Beehive for three years, called home. She was in a pickle. She and seventeen of her biodiversified friends had trekked across several states by foot, doubling their number along the way, until they reached Williamson County, Texas, where they were intent on saving the Coffin Cave mold beetle. The beetle, a troglobite, was a cave-dweller, and one of the last two cave habitats on Earth that the obscure insect called home was on the chopping block, slated to be paved over to build a straighter path to the new Walmart Supercenter.

Within twenty-four hours of arriving, the thirty-four environmentalists were all behind bars charged with first-degree homicide (times six each), possession of drugs (times a hundred each), drug paraphernalia, drugs for resale, and drugs for recreational use. They hadn't found beetle one; instead, they'd stumbled on a body dump. They needed My Cousin Vinnie; they got Reverend Marion Beecher, who said he'd send a team of cracker-jack lawyers, foot the bill, and save the endangered hippies (but if he heard one more word about the damn bugs, the deal was off), if they would all agree to bathe before they got on his new Boeing 727 and if Peyton would agree to come home, settle down, and get married.

God joined LeeRoy and Peyton together, but a few years later the Almighty Dollar, or the Republicans, or the Choctaws, or the lobbyists, or the PACs, or the real-estate developers put them asunder. If the doors hadn't closed on the small Alabama casinos, LeeRoy would still be behind a pulpit instead of Matthew Thatcher behind a microphone. And the Maffini's would probably still be married and living in Beehive. And the Bellissimo wouldn't be feeding wealthy elderly people to the So Help Me God Pentecostal Church.

* * *

"We can't just march into the church and shut them down," Fantasy said.

"Right." If No Hair had any hair on his head, he'd be pulling it out. "They're tight. They've been at it awhile, and they're good at it. Not only that," he said, "they're bound to have a few higher-up friends." He was elbows to knees; we were in chairs across from him. "We will not get into these people's politics."

No one in their right mind would get into Alabama's politics.

We were in Richard Sanders' office waiting for our Friday Skype call. Hard to believe he'd only been gone a week; it felt like a year. It was five in the afternoon here, five in the morning in Maui. Or wherever Mr. Sanders was. The three of us had gotten a combined eight hours of sleep the night before—we felt it and we looked it—and had been hard at it all day with So Help Me God.

Not to mention I had a few pressing personal issues.

Peyton Beecher Maffini told No Hair what she knew and what we suspected. The church was a façade meant to divert attention away from the real business at hand, the cash-cow Senior Assisted Living Center.

"She says they put on a big show to get them in the door of the nursing home." No Hair's tie was a field of blooming daffodils. "When they find someone who fits the profile, they bring them in through the first-class front half of the operation," he said, "rope them in, get them to commit, and as soon as the ink dries on the dotted lines, Peyton says they disappear."

"To where?" I asked.

"The back half of the operation," No Hair said.

"What happens back there?" I asked.

"She doesn't know."

"They're not tucking them in then putting pillows over their heads."

"Don't assume anything, Davis." No Hair said. "We don't know what they're doing."

"They can't be killing them," I said. "Dead people estates can donate, but dead people can't maintain residence and generate income."

"Says who?" Fantasy asked.

"The IRS," I said. "Tax code. They'd be caught in a week."

"Peyton doesn't know exactly how they do it," No Hair said, "and at this point she doesn't care to know. That girl knows two things: Whatever it is her father's doing needs to stop, and she'll help us in return for immunity for Matthew Thatcher."

"You didn't promise her anything, did you?"

"Davis." No Hair's eyes were so bloodshot they were making mine hurt. "I promised that girl the moon."

"Tell me you didn't promise her she could stay with me indefinitely."

"She's going to be at your place until we figure out how to shut down this end of it," he said. "That church is going to stop recruiting their old people here."

"So she's staying with me how long?"

"I don't know, Davis."

"Here's the big question," Fantasy said. "Are we going to tell Mr. Sanders about this?"

"I want to hold off on that," No Hair said. "We need hard evidence before we accuse Matthew Thatcher of anything, and that's something Peyton isn't going to give us."

"If she didn't believe he had a hand in it," Fantasy said, "she wouldn't be asking for immunity for him."

"What's her deal?" I asked.

"She loves the guy," No Hair answered, "and she's not going to give him up. We're going to have to figure that one out on our own."

"Mr. Sanders won't be home for another two weeks, right?" I had an idea. "Let's set Matthew Thatcher up. Let's put a mark in his face and see if the mark winds up behind the church." I was on a roll. This is why they pay me the big bucks. "The quickest way to figure out just what they're doing is to get in there. And to get in there, we're going to need some bait."

Fantasy and No Hair reacted with the enthusiasm of two stone-agers watching their redheaded cave friend light the first fire.

"Perfect!" Fantasy said.

"Good one, Davis." No Hair's bald head bobbed.

"We need a little old lady with a big fat portfolio," Fantasy said.

"There are plenty of little old ladies," I pointed out, "but where are we going to find one rolling in dough?" What were these two so excited about?

"You could roll her in dough, Davis," Fantasy said. "It wouldn't take you ten minutes at the computer to take an old lady, any old lady," she shrugged, "and make her an oil baroness."

"The widow of a banking tycoon." No Hair was grinning along.

He refreshed the screen on the laptop we were seated around, which had started blowing screen-saver bubbles. "Where are we going to find an old lady who'll go along with it? Someone we can trust with this information?"

"Hmmm." Fantasy tapped her lips with two fingers. "Where, indeed?"

They stared at me.

"What?"

They kept staring at me.

"No way," I said. "No way in hell. My parents would *never* agree to my grandmother getting into the middle of this. And if I tried to sneak it by them, they'd kill me dead."

They looked at me as if I'd suddenly refused to share my toys.

"You're both forgetting something." I shot up from the chair and began pacing. "I love my grandmother. *I* don't want her anywhere near this mess. I don't see either of you offering up your grandmothers to go sacrifice themselves to that crazy church!"

"My grandmother's the wrong color," Fantasy said.

"Both of my grandmothers passed away twenty years ago," No Hair said, "and for that matter, my mother passed away six years ago last March."

That shut things down. I walked to the wall of window behind Mr. Sanders' desk and lightly banged my head against the glass. No. No. No.

"Besides," Fantasy said gently. "We weren't thinking about sending in your granny, Davis."

I spun.

"We were thinking your ex mother-in-law," No Hair said. "Eddie's mother."

"She's perfect, Davis," Fantasy said. "She'll lap it up."

That she would. But if she agreed to be our shill and throw herself at the foot of the So Help Me God cross, at some point, I might have to be in the same room with her. Before I could convince myself it was a good idea or convince Fantasy and No Hair it wasn't, another voice boomed into the room.

The computer screen came to life and Richard Sanders filled it. "What is this about Matthew Thatcher's Porsche? What happened to that man's car?" Mr. Sanders was mad, mad, mad, and then some. Either the volume was set on XXL, or he was shouting at us. "I have exactly two minutes, and you three had better start talking."

We didn't say a word.

He kept going, barely stopping for air, for the next five minutes.

Thatch exited the building last night, saw his car (at least I put it back where it was supposed to be), had a gigantic fit, chased and batted at the twelve-year old valet with a long black umbrella (that boy hasn't been seen or heard from since), then used the same umbrella to pummel a Bellissimo limo that found itself in the wrong place at the wrong time, fired everyone out there including bellmen, doormen, and cab drivers who didn't even work for the Bellissimo, destroyed half of the outdoor lighting, threw a hundred sets of keys from the valet stand into the fifty-foot-high fountain, the night, and Beach Boulevard traffic, and in the process, ran off dozens of gamblers with his spittle and rage that the newspaper (Page Six) reported went on for half an hour.

There was a short pause when Mr. Sanders asked us to speculate as to how much volume we thought Thatch the Great generated for the Bellissimo's bottom line. We were still too stunned to speak, so he answered for us.

"Millions! A million in retail *alone*!"

He finished up with, "I think the three of you should work valet for a few weeks, and let's see if you can't learn to treat people's property with a little more respect."

When it was over and the echoes finally faded, Fantasy and No Hair turned on me.

"Let's look on the bright side," I said. "He doesn't know about Bianca shooting herself in the foot."

FOURTEEN

"I'll wait."

"It's going to be hours." Mary Ha Ha looked at her watch. "Several."

Fine by me. It was Friday night, and I didn't intend to go home to my wild woman houseguest until Bradley Cole understood that regardless of what else either of us had going on, there was nothing going on between me and Eddie the rotten, rotten, rotten snake. When I left the Bellissimo, I drove straight to the Grand Palace to tell him that, but I ran into a wall. A wall named Mary Harper Hathaway.

I stood at Wall's desk and got my first good look at her. Note to self: Don't base relationship insecurities on fifteen-year-old sorority photos. Time had not been this woman's friend. She didn't even look like the same person I'd done a thick exposé on.

"Why don't I have him call you when he's free?" (Patronizing.)

"I'll wait."

"He's already late for a meeting upstairs," she said. "You'll be waiting all night." (Parent-to-teenager.)

Which I was perfectly willing to do. I picked a spot on a sofa comfy enough for an all-nighter, where I could keep an eye on her and Bradley's door. I settled in.

Bradley's casino had four attorneys on staff, and they worked behind four different doors off a central reception area full of books, office furniture, and empty coffee cups. Mary Ha Ha, being a fifth wheel, had no door to work behind, so she worked from behind a desk in the big room. Maybe a desk, I couldn't really tell it was piled so high. One lit match in the middle, and the Grand Casino would go up in flames. I could see the top of a computer monitor, USB cords cascading down one side, and there must have been a landline telephone in there somewhere, because I could hear a muffled ring. One corner held a book the size of a Smart car: GOGO'S ENCYCLOPEDIA OF EVERYDAY LAW. It seemed odd to me that she would be referring to EVERYDAY LAW written by someone named GOGO for a case that was getting national attention.

"Is anyone following her?" I asked.

Mary Ha Ha peered between the mountains of folders. "Excuse me?"

"Do you have anyone following Bonita Jakes?"

"Who is Bonita Jakes?"

"The no-smoking woman suing the Grand? The pre-cancerous dealer?"

"No," Mary Ha Ha laughed out the word. "We're not following the plaintiffs." (Silly you.) "We're a little busy."

"She's Plaintiff Patient Zero, though, right?" I asked. "Hers is a stand-alone case coming up next week, and then the big tort one? Right?"

Her eyes narrowed to slits.

"So if you win the first one," I speculated, "won't you have a better chance of winning the big one?"

Her nostrils flared.

"What does her husband do?" I asked.

Mary Ha Ha took two deep breaths. She pressed her lips together into a thin line. "I wouldn't know what her husband does. If anything." (Kindergarten teacher.) "Or if she even has a husband."

"Where do they live?" I kept going.

Mary Ha Ha slammed a desk drawer. "Davis, right?" She stood. "It's Davis?"

I smiled (sweetly), nodded.

"I'm really, really busy." She gestured wide to display the chaos on her desk. "We're all busy, including Brad."

Brad?

"What about Jerry Springer?"

She walked around to the front of her desk, perched, crossed her arms and ankles, then stared at me. "Jerry Springer." (Deadpan.)

"The attorney. Jerry Somebody."

"McAllen."

"Right."

"No, we're not following him either, Davis. This is a class-action suit, not a television crime drama." (Condescending.)

Brad's door flew open. He took in the scene. "Davis." I could tell he was stunned to see me right there, right then, but Bradley Cole is a rock. Very professional. Very handsome. Very the man of my dreams. "Come on in. Have a seat."

Like I was his 6:30.

Of course, I totally lost it.

He jumped between me and Mary Ha Ha, probably so she wouldn't see me falling to pieces, and ushered me in, his hand burning through the small of my back.

Behind the closed door, I started blubbering. "Bradley!" I sucked in a huge gulp of air so that I might throw myself at his feet in one breathless ramble, and he stopped me with both palms.

"Davis, I can't talk right now, I have to get upstairs." He tipped my chin up, looked straight through to my heart for Eddie the Dog Crawford, didn't find him (because he'd *never* been there), then pulled me into a half-second hug before he let go. "I might make it back down here before tomorrow morning, and I might not. You can wait if you like." And then he was gone, but I could still smell him—sandalwood soap, the starch on his shirt, Christmas, a new pack of Crayons, puppies, home.

I sat in his chair, still warm, indulging in a few seconds of hysterical relief that clearly, enough time had passed that Bradley was willing to at least hear my side of the story and work this out, but that led to twice as much anxiety about what my side of the story was, and what it might take to work this out. To keep myself from taking the stairs two at a time and bursting into his meeting to profess my eternal love, I thought it better to take advantage of my surroundings. Since he'd invited me to wait. I began nosing around for clues, omens, signs, or anything edible. There wasn't a crumb of anything on his desktop, so I tiptoed to the door and quietly clicked it locked. I might as well look a little harder while I waited, and I didn't want Mary Ha Ha to catch me.

The Grand's Human Resource database said Bonita Jakes was indeed married, to a man named Earl Hump. Bonita and Earl Hump. No wonder she didn't use his surname. Her employment agreement was standard casino stuff: I won't steal, I'll tell you if I see someone stealing, and the moonlighting clause; I won't have another source of income. I hacked three local banks (not easy to do, thank you), before I found a joint account—a very nice one, a super-nice one, a little more than $600,000 sitting in it—listed under two names: B. S. Jakes and E. Z. Hump. (Here's hoping neither of them have monogrammed stationery.) The deposits were all blind, just transactions which traced to another account from yet another (hacked) bank.

Bingo.

The money was pouring in from Earl's Diesel Delivery, your one-stop-shop for barge delivery of diesel fuel to yachts and ships, serving Mobile, Biloxi, Gulfport, and New Orleans. He was a licensed USCG Captain, and his partner Bonita J. Shoof Hump, past secretary of the Mississippi Biodiesel Board, delivered truck-only fuel—tanker direct pricing—in the Gulfport area only, and only by appointment. They lived together in a mobile home in Gulfport, hardly distinguishable on Google Earth, because of the fence surrounding it. The fence was constructed of nine heel-to-toe diesel storage tanks.

Let me make four important points.

One: At the time she filed the suit, Bonita Jakes was in violation of her employment agreement with the Grand by having a second job, not to mention she was part owner of said second job.

Two: Computer hacking isn't for the faint of heart, and you

can't march into court with anything obtained illegally, which, technically, hacking is. (Illegal.) I have an undergraduate degree in Computer Information Science, although I didn't learn all this in Hacking 101. I learned it after it happened to me once (someone cleaned out my checking account buying Europasses and one of everything at a Hello Kitty store in Prague), out of boredom when I was a police officer in a city of four hundred (for the most part) law-abiding citizens, and going through the mother of all divorces. Now if you'd like to learn how, and you have some free time, or you're going through a nasty divorce, here's what you do: First of all, you have to have good Internet Protocol (IP) scanner software on your computer, which Bradley doesn't, because he's honest, and all other things good. Think of IP scanner software like an electronic 411 operator. ("Information for what city and state, please?" Then the operator gives you the number.) IP scanner software will do the same for a computer. ("Name of company, principals, locations, and any other keywords, please?" Then the software gives you a string of specific electronic address to choose from.) My favorite scanner software is Mad IP, because it's fast. You download it from the Internet onto your own computer (well, in this instance, Bradley's computer), then start stabbing in the dark. Once you locate the address, you temporarily replace your own computer's address with the new one (just a whole bunch of numbers and symbols, but you have to know where to find them in their system and where to put them in yours/Bradley's), then ask your computer to find an empty port on a computer, any terminal, at the new place, because you'd like to network your computer. There's always an empty one somewhere, usually an unused printer port. When you locate it, hook up, and just like that, you're in. You may as well have your own cubicle. While you're there, go into payroll and give yourself a raise. (Kidding.) (You don't really work there.) Nose around, gather the information you need, take screen shots of the really important stuff, don't change a keystroke, then—most importantly—walk out backwards, step-by-step, the opposite of how you came in. Undo everything you just did, or you (in this case, Bradley Cole) will get into trouble. Some people take wandering around their databases very seriously. Among them, the federal government. They call it high treason.

Pffffft.

Third very important point: Mary Ha Ha might be steering the Grand in the wrong direction. Their focus was on the tort case, because it was so big. At last count, one hundred twelve pre-cancerous souls. At her expert insistence, they were taking the offense. Trying to curtail the bloodshed. "Okay. We've been bad. We're installing a smoke-sucking system that will literally pull the hair out of your head. And we're going to pass out cash, cars, and Caribbean cruises to each and every one of you. Form a single line please." It looked to me like they should shut it down at the gate, with the single case coming up, and from a different approach—defense. Because last I heard (fourth and most important point), diesel exhaust and diesel fumes were way up on the list of carcinogens. Prolonged exposure might cause one to be pre-cancerous.

There'd be no way to pick between breathing second-hand smoke all day or inhaling diesel fumes all night as the source for Bonita Jakes' condition. I doubt a doctor could definitively determine it, and a jury wouldn't even try.

It had been almost two hours. I wrote Bradley a note, taped it to the frozen home page of Earl's Diesel Delivery on his computer monitor, put his door in the locked position before I pulled it closed.

Mary Ha Ha was still at her disheveled desk. She smiled at me. (Cat-to-mouse.)

* * *

The day was gone, replaced by a moonless night featuring thick, low clouds over the Gulf. The past year had taught me many things, including low clouds at night over the Gulf meant grab your Burberry rain boots tomorrow morning. Gulf rain was determined, purposeful, blowing in horizontally from the southeast, and, several times a year, running people out of their sea-level homes. A large slice of the Biloxi population pie gambled around the weather: If the forecast called for anything more than an inch, they checked in to the casinos to ride it out. If the rain had a tropical-storm chaser somewhere out there in the Atlantic, they packed heavily. The locals loved their rain, because the locals loved their casinos.

Beach Boulevard was packed with Friday night casino-hopping gamblers when I pulled my Bug into traffic. What I wouldn't give—my RED Valentino Paillettes tote, my mother's secret lemon pound cake recipe—to go home and sleep for twenty straight hours, but my new condo was minus Bradley Cole to warm the bed, and plus Peyton Beecher Maffini. She would be my houseguest for the foreseeable future, because without her insider knowledge, the So Help Me God monster might eat us alive, or worse, take six months to resolve. In addition to Peyton, I had a Bellissimo watchdog in residence, too, and he'd better get ready to sleep in a chair, because he wasn't sleeping on my new white sofa.

Fobbing myself into the parking garage at the Regent, it occurred to me that with Thatch the Great in residence too, I'd better remember to duck my head going in and out, so he wouldn't pull a "Don't you know me from somewhere?" Our parking spaces were miles apart, and instead of driving straight to mine, I idled around the parking-level corner and took a look at his.

Occupied. Thatch's parking place was packed out with a canary yellow Porsche 911 Carrera. I could smell his new car from inside my old one. He should write me a thank-you note. And put it in a muffin basket.

The guest-room door was closed. "What's she been up to?" I asked the Bellissimo bulldog, a guy named Baylor—mid-twenties, built like a bulldozer, dark hair, dark eyes, baby face—who No Hair had pulled off vault-guard duty for condo-guard duty. I'm not sure if Baylor was his first, middle, last, or all of his names.

"As far as I can tell," Baylor said, "she's watched about eight seasons of *Entourage* and eaten popcorn and ice cream all day."

I'm hanging out with her tomorrow.

"Other than that, nothing." He rocked his substantial weight from foot-to-foot.

"Nothing?" I asked. "She didn't ask for a phone? Didn't try to sneak out?"

He shook his head.

"Did the doctor come by?"

"Twice," he said. "Gave her thumbs up both times."

I staggered down the hall, waving goodnight to him, locked myself in my bedroom, kicked off my shoes, then pulled open all six French doors to let the ocean in. Next, I dug through my purse and located Laura Kasden's burner phone, something I'd been meaning to do all day. I powered it up to see that it had just enough juice left to listen to the three messages.

Message one, from the only person who had the number—*Laura, I'm going to be a little late for dinner, but one thing you need to know about me is I'm worth the wait.*

Message two—*I'm going to be tied up just a few more minutes, gorgeous. You wouldn't believe what jackasses these gamblers can be.*

Message three, obviously a butt dial from the Bellissimo entrance—*What the--?*—and then the longest streak of cursing and threats I've ever heard in my life. If I repeated it, I'd have to wash my mouth out with soap for a month. Not only that, I knew he'd gone home to find his prisoner had escaped, and he couldn't have reacted to that with anything less than hellfire and brimstone.

Matthew Thatcher had himself a bad, bad night.

Time for my next chore. I turned, walked to the bathroom, opened the linen closet, grabbed the ticking bomb in a First Response Gold Digital Pregnancy Test box that was screaming at me from atop a stack of hand towels, walked back to the French doors, and sent it sailing into the first sheets of rain.

The burner phone surrendered with one last beep, then went black. I dropped it into my purse. A clap of thunder cracked over the ocean. I reached back into my purse, retrieved the phone, then threw it out after the box.

* * *

Love is blind? Peyton Beecher Maffini's love was delusional.

The next morning, in various stages of sleepwear, we staked out opposite ends of the sofa during a Gulf soaker in full swing. I was tempted to wade out and snorkel around for the burner phone I'd tossed into the night so she could hear the messages Matthew Thatcher had left for Laura Kasden. This girl needed a big dose of reality to go along with the doses of whatever Jakeaway was giving her to keep her from scratching everyone's eyeballs out. After thirty minutes and several chocolate-frosted donuts each, I realized she believed she was still married to LeeRoy. She believed they were working together to bring down So Help Me God Pentecostal, and she didn't understand why we'd interfered.

(She'd be dead had we not interfered.)

"But Peyton," I said, "if that's true, then why were you tethered to the bed? Why was he keeping you prisoner?"

"We had a disagreement."

That was some disagreement. "About?"

In the World According to Peyton, when LeeRoy Maffini had taken the microphone job at the Bellissimo and changed his identity to Matthew Thatcher, their legal union had been one of the casualties, but he'd promised her it would be short term. He'd be right back to get her. Except he never went right back and got her.

With too much time on her hands, Peyton realized something was very wrong with the So Help Me God operation. She broke the news to LeeRoy in Biloxi, and he, too, was appalled. (He was most likely appalled that she knew.) He snuck her out of Beehive, hid her in a ratty apartment in Pass Christian, thirty miles from his active libido in Biloxi, and kept her busy and under his thumb by tossing her from one menial Bellissimo job to the next. All in the name of their mutual goal to expose the church operation and run away together. (He had no intention of doing either.) Deep in the dumpster shaft, Peyton decided she was tired of waiting. She was tired of hiding. She was tired of her father getting away with whatever he was doing. She vowed to do something about it if she ever escaped the garbage chute.

He disagreed on every point. Thus the disagreement.

"Peyton." I pulled a green throw pillow into my lap in case I needed it for cover. "I think you're wrong. I think LeeRoy's been stringing you along the entire time and has no intention of exposing your father's church. He's still very involved in the church operations."

"No," she said, "*you're* wrong. LeeRoy severed all ties with my father years ago."

"Who took you from the hospital, Peyton?"

The question surprised her. "He did."

"He, who?"

"LeeRoy."

I reached for my laptop and moused around until I found the photograph of her being wheeled out by an older man dressed in hospital garb. "Who is this?"

The color drained from her face.

I thought so.

We listened to the rain until she was ready. "I have a question for you," she said.

"Ask away."

"Do you live in this big place alone?"

I dropped what would have been my fifth chocolate-frosted donut. "I don't know, Peyton."

"Yeah," she said. "Men suck."

My head fell back against the cushion.

"One more question," she said. "Do you look just like Bianca Sanders on *purpose*? Or by accident?"

"Accident." The sun broke through the storm and spread across my ceiling. "Bad accident."

FIFTEEN

"One condition."

"What is it, Eddie?"

My ex-ex-husband and I were in the Coffee Shop on the corner of Main and Banana in Pine Apple. Word had gotten out that we were together again (woo!), and every living, breathing soul in town developed an urgent desire for a cup of the lukewarm, lethal, black sludge from the Coffee Shop's two-burner drip coffeemaker that had never, once, I'd-bet-my-life-on-it, been cleaned. The coffee tasted like rust and had a blue glow. The line at the counter for the nasty stuff had been steady and chatty since I'd arrived. "Hey there, Davis!" "Do you hear that? I hear wedding bells!" "Davis, does your daddy know you're here?" "Well, Davis Way and Eddie Crawford! As I live and breathe!"

Francine Simmerton, Coffee Shop proprietor who came with the coffee maker back in the '70s, had been the latest of our negotiation interruptions.

"Listen, Eddie, Davis." She laid her neatly folded apron beside the cash register. "I'm going to have to run to the Pig and get more Maxwell House. Just give people decaf till I get back, and don't steal my tips, Eddie." Francine was probably going to the Piggly Wiggly, Pine Apple's only grocery store, to get on Pine Apple's only loudspeaker. Just in case someone hadn't heard that Eddie and I were together again at her place.

"It might be more than one condition." Eddie the Ass was laid out on his side of the booth like it was a bathtub. "First of all, she gets to keep the clothes."

"No one will want clothes your mother has worn, Eddie."

His face froze in concentration while he tried to decide if he'd won that one or not.

"And second of all, you've got to pay whoever has to take over her job at the diner while she's gone," he said. "That cash register doesn't run itself, you know, and I've got too much going on to fill in for her."

"Minimum wage," I said. "And for one forty-hour week. That's it."

"Make the check out to me."

"No."

"Then pay me cash."

"No."

"Are you mad at me about the other day?"

I didn't bother.

Eddie picked up the paper-napkin dispenser, turned it sideways, and made sure his hair was messy enough. He peered over it. "I want you to hook me up with Bianca."

"That's never going to happen. I couldn't if I wanted to."

"Yes, you could."

"Forget her, Eddie," I said. "First of all, you'll be arrested if you get within ten miles of her, and second of all, she'd never agree to it. She's moved on, Eddie, and you need to move on. Third of all," I took a deep breath, "I would lose my job."

"You could get another one."

Again, I didn't bother.

He kept his hands going the entire time, playing with toothpicks, Louisiana Hot Sauce, and stir sticks. It occurred to me that Eddie Crawford might have ADHD, to go with his long list of documented flaws, including chronic lethargy, substance abuse, gambling addiction, and rattlesnake DNA.

I glanced at my watch. I'd hit the road thirty minutes after Peyton Beecher swallowed her morning Happy Pill, drove the two hundred miles to Pine Apple well above the posted speed limit, then visited with my parents for ten minutes.

"Davis, you look positively green." (My mother.) "You need better makeup."

Now I'd been going over the details of the Bea Crawford Beehive Sting with her rotten, rotten son for an hour, with all of Pine Apple popping in and out.

I was only negotiating with him because if there was one person on Earth whose company I'd rather not be in more than his, it was his mother's. I was so ready to hit the road again. I will always love Pine Apple, but two hours was about all I could take. Two minutes was all I could take of Eddie.

"Okay." Eddie lovingly massaged his jaw. "When I bring Ma down there for this slot tournament thing," he said, "you have to go to dinner with me in that new restaurant Bianca likes."

"To what end?" I asked.

"What end? It's in the middle of downstairs!" He looked at me like I was daft. "You're the one who works there, Davis."

He was talking about Violettes. But Violettes had opened after Eddie'd been asked to leave the Bellissimo and never ever come back. He shouldn't even know about it, much less that Bianca guzzled her martinis there. I made a mental note to run facial recognition on him to see if he'd been sneaking in. Then I mentally scribbled through it. I didn't care.

"No."

"Look it." Eddie pushed his sugar-packet building blocks aside and leaned in. "Bianca and me are," he focused on something just above my head, "soul mates. And we have unfinished business."

"Unfinished business is the only kind of business you know, Eddie, and how is going to dinner with me going to finish your business with her?"

"Maybe we'll accidentally run into her." He winked. "And wear your dark hair." He winked again.

I knew Eddie's language, so I started speaking it quickly, lest I kill him at the Coffee Shop and be stuck in Pine Apple for days. "This isn't about Bianca or dinner, Eddie. This is about money. If I'm right, your mother will win the slot tournament and she'll get to keep all that money. Think of yourself as her agent," I said. "She'll give you a cut."

"How much?"

"How much of a cut will she give you?" I asked. "That's between you and her."

"No," he said. "How much will she win in the slot tournament?"

"A thousand."

"Dollars?"

"Yes, Eddie. Dollars."

"Because she can't cut me in on a trip to Mexico. She doesn't want to go to Mexico anyway."

I watched Eddie's gears turn as he contemplated the upside of Bea winning a trip to Mexico. An all-expense-paid vacation for him.

"She's not going to Mexico, Eddie. Just Biloxi for a few days, then Beehive for a few days."

"And you'll be with her the whole time?"

"Not the whole time." Thank goodness. "But most of the time."

"How are you going to get the old-folks home to take her? She's only fifty," Eddie said. "Or sixty." This was when Eddie Crawford began counting on his fingers.

"Let me handle that." I knew exactly how old Bea Crawford was, because she and my mother were the same age. Fifty-seven. Bea, however, was at least a hundred pounds overweight, so she waddled like an eighty-year-old duck. And she was the only woman left in America who still gave herself a home permanent wave every six weeks, leaving her with seven or eight haphazardly placed piggy-tail curl clumps on her huge head, easily adding two decades to her look. Possibly the worst in the aging department—while Bea Crawford might use the words "skin" and "care" regularly, she'd never once used them together. Bea had the skin tone, texture, and complexion of a watermelon slushy. She had no lips. My challenge was for Bea to pass the filthy-rich test. We were covered on the old-woman front.

"When is this slot thing?" Eddie asked.

"Thursday."

His head jerked. "We already missed it."

"It's every Thursday, Eddie."

His head bobbed with a basic understanding of the Gregorian calendar.

"Isn't today Thursday?"

Strike what I just said.

"Today is Monday, Eddie. Bring your mother on Wednesday so I can take her shopping." The words tasted like ground sloth soup. "And don't plan on staying unless you have the money for a hotel room."

"She's staying with you at your place, right?"

"Correct." Incorrect. She was staying at my place, but there wasn't a chance in hell I'd be there with her. Bea Crawford was going to get a crash course in So Help Me God Pentecostal Churchery from my other house guest, recently enlightened and currently cooperating Peyton Beecher, and I had no intention of attending. I had the resources to get myself a hotel room, and I fully intended to.

Eddie puffed his chest out, stretched his neck, and growled. Clearly, he'd reached his physical and mental limits for the day. I dug for my keys. "Got it, Eddie? Do you know what to do and when to do it?"

"Let's get something straight, Davis." His finger was in my face. I slapped it away. "You don't tell me what to do anymore. We're not married, you know."

"Yes, Eddie. I know." I stood. "Have her there on Wednesday morning."

I headed for the door.

"Don't forget about our dinner."

I kept going.

"Make it Friday."

He said that to my back too.

"Say, Davis?"

My hand was on the door.

"Did you get things worked out with your sissy lawyer boyfriend?"

* * *

I drove straight to the courthouse and snuck into Judge Grafton Clemmer's courtroom. In session, standing room only. Bradley Cole, in the blue pinstripe I'd sent to the dry cleaners just two weeks ago, was seated at the defendant's table, whispering to his co-counsel, Kirk Olsen. I could see he'd had his hair cut sometime over the weekend. (Bradley Cole. I don't keep up with Kirk's hair.)

Mary Ha Ha was nowhere in sight.

To the right of the witness box, which was full of precancerous Bonita Jakes, who was studying the floor, stood a projector screen. It was projecting an aerial view of Bonita's home, diesel tanks around it like circled wagons.

* * *

"Have you been crying?" Fantasy swiveled around in her chair.

"Minimize that screen," I fell into my chair, "or I'll start crying."

"Gladly." The offensive computer display featuring my ex-ex-mother-in-law slid into swarming fireflies.

Monday was coming to a welcome close and Fantasy had been trapped in the office for most of it turning water into wine. Or Bea Crawford into Leona Powell. Same thing.

"Are we about set?"

Fantasy laced her fingers, flipped them, pushed her arms out, and stretched like a cat. "What the hell is a GOBAHIP?"

I held up a finger. "Go Bama," I racked my brain and found the rest, "Health Insurance Program."

After a long minute, Fantasy asked, "What is *wrong* with Alabama?"

I shrugged.

"The state-funded health insurance program is called Go Bama?"

"Go figure."

"Well, Leona Powell's a card-carrying member now," Fantasy said. "I've got her all set up. Driver's license, Social Security card, Medicare, Roll Tide Healthcare," she said. "You name it, Leona's on the roster. Now all you have to do is roll her in dough."

"It's going to take a lot of dough to cover Bea."

"Agreed," Fantasy said. "And she needs several medical conditions, too."

"Embarrassing medical conditions," I added. "I'll embarrass the crap out of her first thing in the morning."

"Yeah. Let's call it a day." She pushed back from the desk. "I have got to get home and spend some time with the boys."

"Anything going on?"

"Other than we haven't had a minute off in a month?" she asked. "No."

But her face said yes.

"You could use the night off too, girl."

"I wish," I said. "I've got to make a Bianca appearance," I took a peek at the clock, plenty of time to get blonde, "and I plan on making it a quick one. But then I have to go home to Peyton Beecher and a security thug."

"Well, I have to go home to a bitchy husband and three hungry kids who barely remember me and probably haven't brushed their teeth in a week," Fantasy said. "Trade."

"Done."

"Hey," Fantasy began putting computers to sleep so that she might go home to the unhappy, unfed, and unbrushed, "I've taken ten calls for you on the office phone."

I perked all the way up. "Really?"

"Eight from No Hair chewing me out because you didn't have your cell phone," she said, "and one from Bianca about the thing tonight."

Hopes dashed.

"Bianca sent the outfit she wants you to wear," Fantasy said, "and you're not going to like it."

I waved that off. I sat across from my ex-ex-husband for an hour this morning. Bianca could have me wearing a feed sack and I wouldn't care.

"I do have my cell phone," but even as I said it, it occurred to me that today was the first day since ninth grade it hadn't rung itself stupid. Uh-oh. I reached for my bag and started the dig. I hit pay dirt with the burn phone, which was supposed to have drowned in the rain.

Fantasy caught my eye, then tossed me a brand-spankin' new phone. "I got a homeless guy three times before I shut it down." She stood, took two steps in my direction, then leaned down to whisper. "He called."

"Why would a homeless guy call me?" I whispered back.

Fantasy stood and tapped a foot.

I grabbed both of her wrists and shook her all over. "What'd he say? What'd he say?"

"I didn't talk to him, Davis. This is between you and Bradley. *You* need to talk to him." She patted me about the head. "See you in the morning."

"*Davis,*" then there was a pause, "*I don't know what to think about us and at the same time I don't know how to thank you for what you've done for the Grand.*" Another long pause. "*I'm willing to hear your side of the story and I can tell you mine right now. Eddie needs to go. Away from us.*" Pause. "*I don't want you anywhere near him, and I don't want to be anywhere near him.*" Pause. "*I want to see you, Davis, I miss you.*" Pause. "*I'll be in court all week, so it'll have to be Friday night. I'll meet you at Violettes at eight, and we'll go from there. Can you make it?*"

Can I make it? I'd go through hell, tarantulas, or appendicitis to make it.

When I'd gathered my wits enough to stand, I made my way on wobbly, grateful, hopeful legs to the closet, with a whopping fifteen minutes to get changed and go blonde. The Bellissimo-sponsored fashion show to benefit puppies, or wild boars, or guinea pigs, that Bianca had signed herself (me) up to chair needed to be planned by committee over cocktails. The committee had been appointed in descending order of the area's largest snobs starting with the Mayor's wife, number-one snob, the President of the Junior League, number one-and-a-half snob, and the Lieutenant Governor's wife, who was actually kind of nice after a few drinks. I saw my outfit and wondered how in the world I was going to plan anything wearing the nightmare in front of me. There was more hanger than there was dress. It was made up entirely of electric blue silk crepe ruffles. It was as thin as air. It plunged and twisted and wrapped, and when I touched it, it fell to the floor in a puddle.

* * *

With each passing day, I felt sorrier and sorrier for the oil guy who'd lost the condo we—*we*!—now call home. Other than the parade of uninvited guests and the fact that the man who owned it with me was noticeably absent, I fell more in love with my new living space every time I found a new nicety. I couldn't wait to show Bradley Cole what all I'd stumbled on.

Dark and early on Tuesday morning, I stumbled into the shower. I loved the shower anyway because it was so large, you could park a motorcycle in it. (But I wouldn't. I wouldn't ride a motorcycle through the rest of the condo to get it to the shower.) What I discovered was if you bolted straight up at three in the morning feeling absolutely whack, you could race in there dragging a pillow and blanket and stretch out on the cold tile mumbling, "mind over matter mind over matter mind over matter" to yourself.

Which I did.

I woke up hours later, feeling like I'd slept on ice cold tile. (I had.) I threw the pillow and blanket out, turned the water on, which is when I found the blue button on the control panel. Ice

Shower. Pressing the small blue recessed circle instantly turned the shower water from 105°F to 70°F.

Which I did. Several times.

"Buck up, girl." I could see my teeth chattering in the mirror.

When I could brave the world outside the bathroom, I saw I'd missed eight calls, six with accompanying messages. The calls had come in on top of each other for eleven minutes beginning at seven-ten. No Hair and Fantasy hadn't left messages. Bianca left five I deleted without listening to. Bradley Cole left one. I pushed the button.

"Davis." I heard him inhale sharply. *"You're on Page Six again."*

I pushed a third button, this one bringing my laptop to life, then went straight to *The Sun Herald.*

I'd worn the blue dress backwards. The X was supposed to be in the front, to cover the girls, and the horizontal ruffles were intended to be in the back, to cover one's ass. The caption read, "We can't wait to see *this* fashion show!"

It took me a minute to brave the world past the bedroom door, and when I did, my first instinct was to get back in the bedroom, stack the furniture against the door, and never come out again.

Baylor the Security guy was duct taped to a ladder-back kitchen chair. My spent taser gun was on the floor several feet away. Peyton had chewed through her leash. It was eight o'clock in the morning.

SIXTEEN

"Look it, Bea." I blew across the top of my six-dollar caramel macchiato. "You don't need to know any details."

We were at Regis Beauty Salon in the Edgewater Mall at noon on Wednesday, where three stylists, plus the salon manager, were giving Bea their all. They'd turned off the Walk Ins Welcome sign, because they had plenty on their hands. The one trying to saw through my ex-ex-mother-in-law's inch-thick toenails was sweating. Bea, also sweating and wearing a plastic tarp and a mint julep pore-minimizing mask, was being nosy. One of her specialties.

"You look it, Davis. If I'm going to walk around with gray hair," Bea licked at the mint julep in the corners of her mouth, "I believe you can at least tell my why."

"It's not gray," the salon manager said. "It's called Pure Diamond, and the color will come out silver." She cautiously prodded Bea's head with a small wooden stick. "Very classy. You'll love it."

"It itches." Bea made a move toward her chemically-soaked scalp and about ten hands came out of nowhere to slap hers down.

"It's the straightener and the stripper that itches," the manager said. "Your hair is the color of Cheetos, ma'am; we have to get that off first. And I'm trying my best to unfurl it."

After that, it was an Edward Scissorhands Revival. Seven wispy inches of hair hit the floor. Pure Diamond was slapped on with paint brushes, seared in, then shampooed down the drain. Hair dryers blew, the mask came off, and the wax went on. In the end, Bea liked herself without a moustache—she couldn't stop tapping her fingertips across her smooth upper lip—and by all accounts, it was a marked improvement. But when that first strip of wax came off, Bea let out a war cry, then drop-kicked the poor girl trying to hack through the callouses on her heels. That chick flew across the room. It took two and a half hours, four hundred dollars (big tips), and a squadron of professionals to run Bea Crawford through the clean-up shop.

Next, it was the Lancôme counter at Dillard's. I slipped the girl a fifty. "We need spackling compound for the skin, grout-type stuff," I whispered, "and she has to leave here knowing how to use it." No way was I helping Bea put her face on. "Idiot proof," I said. "And give her paint-by-number instructions."

"I prefer cake mascara." Bea spilled all over, under, and out of the director's chair.

The terrified girl cut her eyes at me. "What happened to her eyebrows?"

"It was a fryer mishap." Bea fluffed her silver hair.

Thirty minutes and another two hundred dollars later, I swear, Bea Crawford looked half human. From the neck rolls up, anyway. She was still wearing a sweatshirt featuring a glittery cat over salmon-pink stretch pants with lavender Crocs on her feet. But we were making progress.

We found one clothing store that could accommodate all of my ex-ex-mother-in-law. One of the Chico's salesgirls asked me what I wanted to do with the clothes Bea wore in, and I told her to burn them. We left there with a new twelve-hundred-dollar wardrobe that fit, camouflaged, and for the most part, consisted of endangered-animal prints.

You can't win 'em all.

Last stop, the Naturalizer shoe store. I didn't even know they made women's shoes in double-digit sizes.

Leona Powell, I must say, looked like an over-the-hill well-to-do plus-sized model. I, on the other hand, looked like a pack mule trailing behind her with the day's loot. To look at Bea—posture, grin, twinkle—was to see how good she felt about herself, maybe for the first time in her life. I couldn't help but snap a picture in front of the mall fountain, and Bea was more than happy to pose. I zipped it to my sister, and texted, "*Guess who this is?*" under the photo.

"*This is a miracle,*" Meredith texted back.

* * *

"You have to come let me in."

"Davis," Fantasy said. "Where's your card key? First your gun, now your card key."

Fantasy and I used the only entrance in 3.2 million square feet that didn't have a camera watching. Of course, a swipe card was involved, issued by Mr. Richard Sanders and Mr. Richard Sanders only, and of course I occasionally misplaced mine.

On the way to our office, Fantasy opened her mouth to lecture me, and I said, "Please, don't. I've been with Bea for hours."

"You've been with *Leona*," she corrected me. "Where is Leona? You didn't kill her, did you?"

"She's at the dentist getting five decades of plaque jackhammered off her teeth," I said. "Her sorry-dog son will be taking her to my place after, so she can sleep it off. And there's plenty of room now that Peyton's jumped ship."

"That Peyton is nuts," Fantasy said.

"Amen."

"Not that Bea and Eddie aren't," she added.

"Amen again."

Bea and Eddie would be at my place without supervision, and it wasn't sitting too well with me, but nothing was sitting too well with me these days. At the moment, food-court lunch from the mall. Baylor was still in sick bay recovering from the ass kicking he'd received from my last house guest, and I set about drumming up a big thug substitute to keep an eye on my current house guests until Baylor was back on his feet. The worst of it, Baylor told us, was the duct tape. (No Hair: "Why do you have so much duct tape, Davis?" I didn't know I had any. At all. Of course, I didn't know I had a tea kettle or a potato smasher, either.) No Hair found the Happy Pills Peyton had stopped taking between the keys of the antique typewriter in the guest room. He'd made the executive decision that we would not attempt to chase Peyton down a second time—our plates were full—but he did put extra security on my neighbor, Matthew Thatcher.

Peyton. Pfffft.

* * *

Instant Wealth 101.

First, change the date on your computer. (Bottom right, right click.) Back it up a few decades. Begin concocting data, financial and personal. Fast-forward date, enter more data. Google, then Photoshop a few life events: graduation, engagement, bank error in your favor. Hack, then plant life events in newspapers archives. Zip date up. More financial information. Society page, only daughter marries Kooter Kasden. Change son-in-law's name to Philippe. (Why be married to a guy named Kooter?) When subject's at the gates of the big five-oh, begin sprinkling in pesky medical stuff—flu every other year, a three-day hospital stay for bronchitis, broken wrist, hemorrhoid surgery. (Ha ha.) Keep up with the medical stuff, increasingly dire, toss the word "obesity" around. Work your way to the mother lode—the inheritance.

Leon Larose, former Studebaker dealership mogul, dies peacefully in his sleep.

Leaves it all to his favorite granddaughter, Leona.

She's sixty-six years old, and she's worth a mint.

* * *

Finally, he answered.

"Bradley." It came out on a whoosh of air.

"Let me put you on hold a minute, Davis."

He put me on hold for nine minutes.

"Sorry."

"Me, too," I said. "I'm so sorry."

"I meant I was sorry I left you on hold so long."

"I'm sorry for *everything*, Bradley."

It was Wednesday evening, and I was Laura Kasden (Philippe's former wife) again. I had checked myself into a Bellissimo double-suite: two luxury guest rooms connected by a giant living room. Ocean view. Two full baths and a powder room. Wet bar. Laura's mother, Leona Powell, was supposed to be behind door number two, but she was at my condo, and she'd better not be snooping around. I left her with a big security guard whose name I didn't catch. I looked up, way up, at him.

"I'm just going to call you Baylor if that's okay with you."

He shrugged.

"Her son?" I pointed to Extreme Makeover on my sofa. "Is not allowed through that door." I pointed at the door.

Baylor II nodded.

Extreme Makeover piped up, "You can call me the Silver-Haired Fox, young man."

He shrugged again.

She patted my marshmallow sofa. "Come on over here, boy, take a load off."

I got out of there as fast as I could, locked myself up in my Bellissimo suite, showered, wrapped myself in a Bellissimo robe and my red hair in a Bellissimo towel, dialed Bradley, and now I'd been staring into the starry Gulf night for nine minutes while he had me on hold.

"I don't think I overreacted, Davis," Bradley said. "The man was standing in front of you naked."

"You moved out."

"No, I didn't. I put some space between us. I didn't move out."

"I'm there, and you're not there, Bradley. It feels a lot like you don't live there."

"Why are you saying 'there'? Are you not 'there'?"

I sighed. "I'm at the Bellissimo tonight. Long work story."

"I have a long work story of my own," he said.

"We need to talk, Bradley. I need to talk to you."

"Is it about Eddie?"

"No. No, Bradley. It's about us."

"Eddie *is* us, Davis. There are three of us."

"Exactly what I need to talk to you about."

"I don't understand."

"Because," I said, "three of us." A soft bell chimed. "I need to talk about three of us." I made my way across the room to the door.

"Davis, have you slept with Eddie?"

I threw open the door and shouted, "NO!" at the same time.

Matthew Thatcher google-eyed me wearing a bathrobe, yanked the long-stemmed rose he'd been biting from between his teeth, then asked, "Are you naked?"

"*What*?" Bradley yelled.

Oh, dear Lord.

"Is that *Eddie*? Are you kidding me, Davis? You have Eddie in your hotel room?"

"NO!"

"Are you not happy to see me?" Matthew Thatcher's heart was breaking. "You *invited* me!"

I invited you to *call* me, stupid. Not show up.

"Davis," Bradley said in my ear. "Maybe we should talk later when you're not entertaining."

* * *

"Let me get dressed. Then we'll meet somewhere." I had a death grip on the phone that no longer connected me to Bradley Cole. "My mother's asleep." I gave a nod to door number two, that thank goodness, wasn't full of my sleeping mother. Or Eddie Crawford's. Or Kooter Kasden's. Or anyone else's.

"Oh?" He craned and peered. "I saw you had someone with you."

Someone needed to block this guy from access to guest information.

"This is just a guess, Laura, but are you upset about something?"

I was shaking from head to toe, fighting the fit I was this close to. Bradley Cole and I couldn't get it together to save our lives, and I needed a moment alone to suck it up.

"It's my mother." I clapped my hand over my mouth, and let out the sob I'd been holding.

"Oh, you poor thing!" He was on his way into my hotel room, arms wide open. I knocked him back into the hall.

"I don't want to wake her up!"

"The piano bar downstairs." He pointed gun fingers at me and winked. "I love jazz. And if you're nice, I'll take you for a ride in my new car. That will make you feel better."

I closed the door, fell against it, then slid down to the carpet.

* * *

The piano bar, Ivories, was packed, dark, smoky, loud, and gave Matthew Thatcher maximum exposure. Every three seconds someone new stopped by to goo at him, and while he schmoozed, I tossed more of my drink, literally, on the floor. I doused the carpet with a whole glass of wine. Matthew Thatcher noticed I was empty, waved, snapped, and pointed for another.

"So what's the problem?" His eyes were all over the room. I don't think he'd looked at me once. I probably could have worn the bathrobe and skipped the two hundred dollars of medium-spice brown.

"Have you ever known a lottery winner?" I raised my voice to clear the amplified saxophone, and with that, he was all mine—heart, body, and soul.

"Did your mother win the lottery?"

"She might as well have." I looked away. Sighed, Scarlett-style.

"Tell." He turned his back to his adoring fans. "Tell me all about it."

He was a dog on a bone.

"We had no idea my great-grandfather had that kind of money."

He lapped up every word.

"And my mother's gone crazy with it."

His tail was wagging.

I put my wine glass to my lips, tipped, then lowered it. "She bought too much house, for one thing," I said. "She has a twelve-bedroom pillared mansion in the middle of corn field. She probably couldn't give it away," I said, "much less sell it."

He placed a comforting paw on my thigh. There, there.

"And she stays confused."

"How do you mean?" he asked.

"Her health is failing."

"Ooooh," he howled.

"She's at a different doctor's office three or four times a week."

He was slobbering.

"And half the time, she shows up at the wrong doctor's office."

He kept inching in. I feared for my leg. He looked like he wanted to wrap himself around it.

"I don't want to move back home," I said. "When I left Alabama, I said no more," I sliced through the air with both hands, "and I meant it."

He mouthed the word *Alabama*. "Is she on GOBAHIP?" He wiped his brow and snapped his fingers in the air for another drink.

I nodded.

"Does she have any other close family?"

"Distant," I scrambled. "Estranged."

"I can't wait to meet her, Laura. She's going to love the slot tournament."

She did.

She won.

Silver-haired Leona Powell, jangling a ton of gaudy costume

jewelry in a zebra-print jacket over black palazzo pants, left the old folk's slot tournament the next day with a thousand dollars in cash and a new best friend, a very large-eared man named McKinley, who'd introduced himself the second we cleared the door, practically sat in Bea's lap the whole time she banged away on the slot machine, and who would be picking us up at ten the next morning to give us a guided tour through old folk's paradise, the So Help Me God Senior Living Center, where he lived.

"I've never been to Beehive!"

I'd never seen Bea giddy, and I never wanted to see it again.

"You're going to love Beehive, Leona. It's this side of heaven!" McKinley Weeks and Matthew Thatcher showed no signs of knowing each other. "We have the best burger in the south. Have you ever heard of Our Daily Burger? It was in Southern Living. Do you like cheeseburgers?"

"I like everything!"

(Obviously.)

"And Leona, when you get back Friday night," Mr. Microphone said, "I'm going to take you girls to dinner at Violettes to celebrate."

Rut Ro.

* * *

"I swear, Davis." Bea had her cash spread out on the backseat leather of a Bellissimo limo as I accompanied her back to the condo after she had her photo taken with a big check and two of everything at the big buffet. It was bad enough she was staying at my place another night, no way was I going to stuff her into my car to get her there. "I never thought these words could come out of my mouth," she said, "but if you keep this up, one day I might forgive you for all you did to my son."

SEVENTEEN

"I HAVE A REPUTATION TO UPHOLD!"

Dr. Malibu Ken nodded along with the tirade. He agreed on every point.

"EVERYONE LOOKS UP TO ME!"

Not everyone.

"THIS IS A TRAVESTY! A TRAVESTY!"

The dogs were barking their little heads off, angry with me, too.

"This" was the Page Six photo album—four mortifying shots—of me, cut through the middle by blurred ovals framed in electric-blue ruffles.

"I can't *wait* to tell Richard what you've done!" She hissed the words and threw the newspaper. The dogs ran for cover.

"Now, Mrs. Sanders." No Hair didn't want Bianca to kill me, so he accompanied me to the Elvis floor. "Let's not get ahead of ourselves." No Hair's tie had penguins dressed up as hockey players on it. "It was an honest mistake on David's part."

"Whose side are you on?" I asked No Hair. "It's Davis."

"You shut up," Bianca said.

Dr. Doolittle rolled his eyes, tisk, tisk, tisked, and openly coveted No Hair's huge frame. "Do you take anabolics?"

We all turned on him. He tapped his loose lips.

"You're going to make this up to me, David."

"It's Davis."

"I want you dressed to kill kissing smelly babies and smellier homeless people. I want you in the restaurants, the bars, all over the casino and everywhere else spreading my goodwill and charm until you make this right." Her hands and good foot were flying in all the directions she wanted me in. "You turn this media nightmare around this minute." She huffed, reached for her cigarettes and martini, then shooed us away. No Hair led me by the elbow. We almost made it out. "And you're getting *fat*, David. Lose five pounds before the weekend. I don't care how you do it." We each had a foot out the door. "And find me a damned assistant!"

* * *

We were watching for Bianca's former damned assistant at all choke points, running facial-recognition round the clock, plus screening all vendor traffic and employment applications. We didn't have time to chase her down, but we did want to know if she dropped in on us. History repeats itself, so it was safe to assume that Peyton hadn't left my place for a change of scenery. She'd left with a task at hand.

Who was her task?

The smart money would be on Matthew Thatcher/ Mr. Microphone/LeeRoy Maffini; she had to be all kinds of new pissed at him. But she could have just as easily given up that quest and set new sights on Bianca, or one of us. For all we knew, she may have redirected her anger at its origins—her parents.

The only thing we knew for certain was that Peyton was resourceful, resilient, and deceptive. And while the underlying objective behind her vendettas might have merit—saving moldy beetles wasn't an unworthy cause—she went about righting wrongs in an increasingly destructive manner. She was a ticking time bomb.

"Let's say she's back in Beehive," No Hair suggested. Fantasy and I were on the new gold sofa and he was giving our old gold sofa a run for its money on Friday morning, just after Breakfast at Bianca's. "She's going to see you coming for a mile, Davis."

Yep.

"It's a tour through an old folk's home, right?" Fantasy asked.

"How much time are we talking about?"

"Leave here in an hour." I looked at my watch. "Thirty minute flight, two-hour tour, and thirty minutes back. Four hours max?"

"I could go as Bea's assistant," Fantasy offered.

No Hair looked lukewarm on the idea. He turned to me. "You think Samuel would be up for it?"

Just the thought of my father put my world back into perspective.

"He knows Bea well enough to be an interested brother-in-law, or cousin," No Hair said, "and he'd be as good as any of us at peeking behind the curtains."

"I'll call him," I said.

* * *

Text number one: *I need to cancel dinner.* Response (one second later): *No.*

Text number two: *Are we still on for dinner?* Response (an hour later): *Yes.*

* * *

Tilda Reyes Bunker was barren. To pass the time, since there were no wee ones, she quilted. Tilda and her husband Cyril lived in Oak Hill, Alabama, population thirty-seven, seven miles east of Pine Apple proper. Cyril bred and trained beagles for rabbit hunting, so the Bunkers didn't have a blade of grass in their acre of yard. They had dog pens, dog runs, dog houses, dog feeders, hundreds of scattered, limp, rabbit retriever dummies, but no grass. Month after month passed, and still no babies, and no grass, so month after month, Tilda made quilts. When the quilts piled up and threatened to overrun the house, Cyril began building quilt racks, then he built a covered front porch that had almost as much square footage as the house and moved the quilts out there. Every morning, he dragged them out. Every evening, he dragged them back in. In between dragging them in and out, passersby pulled into their dirt drive and purchased the quilts. The Bunkers filled the cookie jar with quilt money, until they had to buy another cookie jar. And then another, and then more.

Every once in a while, it looked like it had snowed at the Bunkers and only at the Bunkers, because one of the beagles would sneak up to the porch, steal a quilt, then invite his beagle friends to help him rip it to shreds. Batting everywhere.

To offset the dogs, Tilda quilted cats. Cats sleeping, cats playing, cats chasing mice, cats eating cheese. When all of Wilcox County had all the cats on their beds and across their sofa backs they could possibly want, Tilda branched out. Northern Star, Double Wedding Ring, Pink Lemonade, Oak Leaf, Grape Basket, and Dutch Doll. But she snuck a small cat in there somewhere on every quilt; it was her trademark.

The toaster had to be put away to make more room for cookie jars. Then the bright yellow Tupperware Servalier canisters. Cyril put his foot down when Tilda unplugged his coffee percolator to make room for another cookie jar, which is when the Bunkers opened a checking account at Pine Apple Savings & Loan. The cookie jars, one by one, were relocated to the dog shed, where the dogs, one by one, broke them, until there were no more cookie jars. But there was a ton of money in the bank.

Cyril had the dog business down pat, or he got tired of cleaning dog pens, or tired of having no grass. Whichever, he became more invested in the quilting. He tinkered with her machines, kept her scissors sharp, fetched fabric, and learned to cut on the bias, thread a machine, and sew a straight seam, because Tilda was really making a name for herself and bringing in more money with the quilts than he ever brought in with the dogs. He cut back to one stud and two brood bitches, and took to the dining room to sew with his wife.

It was from the dining room window, on a sunny November morning, that Cyril watched Tilda, age fifty-one, drop the Christmas Cactus quilt she was hanging over a rack on the porch, then race across the two lanes of Pine Apple Highway chasing after a litter of nine that had dug out and made a run for it. She was hit by a Little Debbie truck barreling around the curve. None of the pups were hurt.

Cyril had no kids, no siblings, and both his and Tilda's parents had passed on one after another, every two years for the past eight years, until they were all four buried behind Friendship Baptist Church in Pine Apple. And now Tilda. At the time of the parents' deaths, the Bunkers inherited land: forty-two acres from Tilda's side and a connecting sixteen from his. When he buried Tilda, he got a dining room full of sewing machines and quilting frames, a living room full of fabric, thread, and batting, and three bedrooms of floor-to-ceiling finished quilts. By then, there were so few pups that there would surely be grass in the spring. And Tilda not there to enjoy it.

It was time for Cyril to do some housecleaning, and he started with the pups. The ones that escaped and caused Tilda's untimely demise would be his last litter. It was January 1980, and one of the coldest on record. So on the morning he was supposed to deliver the last two pups to Bo Cordell, a rabbit-hunter in Furman, Alabama, ten miles on the other side of Pine Apple, he wrapped the pups up in a Texas Star quilt before he left the house, so they wouldn't freeze in his Dodge Ram truck, because the heater hadn't worked in the truck since Tilda had passed and he just didn't have the energy to fix it. He didn't go anywhere anyway, and surely one day it would warm up.

The pups protested being held captive in the quilt, and Cyril wasn't anxious to get out in the cold just yet either, so he made another cup of coffee and let the pups run around the house. He grabbed a pair of scissors. He cut four thirteen-by-nineteen squares into a Patchwork quilt, then sewed five-eighth-inch seams on three sides, to make two deep quilt pockets. One for each pup. Not wanting them running around loose in the truck cab, Cyril whipped out the zipper foot and sewed in twelve-inch nylon zippers along the tops. Thinking there had to be a better way to haul them out to the truck than holding them under his arms like potato sacks, he seamed the borders of the cut-up quilt to fashion, then attach, shoulder straps.

And that was the day Tilda Reyes quilted cotton luggage was born.

Five years later, Tilda Reyes was a household name, with 1,200 distributors nationwide. Cyril's business was Pine Apple's largest employer and he was Wilcox County's Most Eligible Bachelor. Five years after that, with no warning whatsoever, he sold out—lock, stock, and barrel—slinking out of town in the middle of the night, never to be seen or heard from again.

Until fifteen years later, when Pine Apple Police Chief Samuel Way found Cyril Bunker in a topiary garden, at two o'clock on a Friday afternoon, at the So Help Me God Senior Residence Center in Beehive, Alabama.

* * *

I looked at my watch. It was five o'clock on the same Friday afternoon. Fantasy was on the phone.

"What? Is he a prisoner?"

I couldn't hear the other side of the conversation.

"I'll be there in two hours to get him, and I'm bringing my lawyer." She hung up and turned to me. "Those people don't believe I'm Cyril's long-lost niece."

"Wait till they see you."

"Can you throw me some paperwork together?" she asked. "A photo of me on his knee?"

I turned Fantasy into Betty Bunker, with a driver's license, Social Security card, Sam's Club card, and a notarized letter of Power of Attorney. I back-dated, then spit out a last will and testament. I folded the thick document into thirds and rolled it under the wheels of my chair a few times. I passed it all to Fantasy.

"Change my name, Davis."

It was the first time I'd laughed all day.

We'd been at the computers non-stop since the call came in from my father. I could have stretched out on the floor and slept, but instead, I pushed back from the desk and said, "Showtime."

Fantasy said, "Go get 'em, tiger."

I came out of the Closet fifteen minutes later Bianca blonde, in a Peter Pilotto halter dress, the Hope Diamond around my neck, and four-inch Tibi shoes that had translucent heels. I was a small fortune.

"Betty. Does this make me look fat?"

Fantasy didn't turn around to look. "Yes."

I picked up Baylor on the mezzanine level.

"How are you feeling?"

"I've been through worse," he said. "What is it I'm supposed to do tonight?"

"Look official." He looked like an official linebacker. "You're my escort." Everything he had on was black except for a starched white shirt. "This will be easy," I said. "Fantasy's making you go to Beehive, Alabama, and be a lawyer after this."

I marched into Violettes and got that done first. "I need three private dining rooms tonight."

All the sparkling silver everyone had been placing froze mid-air. One of the wait people actually dove under a table. I guess I did have some Bianca Image work to do.

"Mrs. Sanders," the Maître D' rushed forward. "We're—" he was going to say booked, but I guess he thought better of it "—delighted." And then there was a little bow. I spun on my translucent heels and Baylor huffed out with me.

"Where to?" He pulled at his shirt cuffs.

"Casino."

"How do I act like a lawyer?" he asked.

I was winking, waving, and blowing kisses to the world at large. "On this job, Baylor, you just wing it."

"This is so much more fun than guarding the vault," he said, "except for the duct tape."

It took thirty minutes to work my way to the really, really rich people gambling room, because I stopped every two feet. Chatted it up with a bridal party, tried on the bride's party veil to the delight of the crowd, posed for twenty pictures (one of which, surely, would make it to Page Six), put the lucky mojo on a $10 Triple Gold slot machine for a man who was, seriously, drooling, and even nosed in on a packed crap table and finished a guy's roll. I heard him begging for the dice I'd touched as I pranced away, Baylor on my translucent heels. In the Ridiculously High Stakes private gaming room behind a huge waterfall, I schmoozed a little more, ordered a dirty martini with a sidecar, and fake-smoked one of Bianca's skinny cigarettes. "Oh, Mr. Hasigawa!" He smelled like a garlic factory. "You are too much!" Then to Baylor through clenched teeth, "Get me out of here." It was time to get ready for my three dinner dates.

* * *

The Eddie dinner was at seven, Bradley Cole (OMG) at eight, and Matthew Thatcher later. I'm sure he'd let me know.

The challenges were numerous. Eating three meals is a challenge in and of itself. My hair color was a challenge, too. The restaurant was expecting Bianca, which Eddie Crawford, that ass, ass, ass, would love, love, love, and Bradley Cole wouldn't mind, I hope, hope, hope, but Mr. Microphone might look past his own nose job and notice a different hair color. My plan was to carry a large enough bag to fit a can of medium-spice brown in it and give my hair a good squirt before the Last Supper.

Eddie would be a piece of cake. The trick would be to liquor him up, then give him the slip. As soon as he sniffed around and didn't turn up his lost love Bianca, he'd hit the road. If I had any trouble with him, I'd call Security. He wasn't supposed to be there anyway.

The thing to do with Bradley Cole was propose.

Then for my last dinner act, I'll slap cuffs on Matthew Thatcher. "You're going to jail, you jerk, for using the Bellissimo to recruit the elderly for a crooked church, then robbing them blind and locking them up. And for treating that nutjob Peyton the way you have."

Piece o' cake.

I had the underground office to myself, because Fantasy and Baylor, Esq. were on their way to the airport to meet the plane that would touch down, spill out Bea Crawford, then head right back to Beehive to break out Cyril Bunker.

The way to go, when one outfit has to get you through multiple events, is black. I fingered through the racks in the Closet and went Armani. I squeezed myself into a shiny black off-the-shoulder silk drape dress and six-inch silver heels. (Louboutin.) During this process, I rehearsed parts of my pitch to Bradley Cole. I grabbed a purse, a black Valentino patent leather bow bag, then stuffed it with my Smith & Wesson 380 Bodyguard (in case I needed to shoot Eddie Crawford), a can of medium-spice brown, and a Chanel lipstick. I slapped on makeup, went simple with the jewelry (under twenty carats), and grabbed a pair of Fendi sunglasses that covered the top half of my head.

I had ten minutes to spare. I spent five of them on the phone with my father, and I spent eight at the computer, scanning the newswires for a ruling in Bradley's pre-cancerous case so I could congratulate him on his amazing lawyerly skills, then I watched a two-minute press conference on the courthouse steps held by the mass-tort attorney, Jerry McAllen, who promised that, in spite of Bonita Jakes' setback, he would seek and find justice for the almost two hundred poor souls he represented. At least half of the poor souls were crowded around him, nodding along, damn straight. Something familiar in the back of the crowd was making a beeline across the screen, trying to push and shove her way out of the camera's lens. I zoomed in, froze on her, and sent her to another computer screen. It was Mary Ha Ha!

Why was the lead attorney for the defendants hanging out with the plaintiffs?

I google-imaged Mary Harper Hathaway, just like I'd done two months ago, and just like two months ago, most of the results were more than a decade old. I zoomed in on an image of her at a sorority luncheon, copied it, and sent it flying to the other screen. I picked points, then ran facial recogware on the side-by-side photographs.

Mary Harper Hathaway and Mary Ha Ha were two different women.

EIGHTEEN

The general theme of the Bellissimo Resort and Casino is French Riviera, so a fancy French restaurant was a perfect fit.

A weekly cooking show, broadcast by WLOXTV 13, featuring Violettes' head chef, Alphonse-Henri Beaumont (who was really Bubba Newman, from Lafayette, Louisiana. I did his background check), was local must-see-TV, and the restaurant had been featured in *Southern Living, Gulf Coast Style*, and *Bon Appétit*. Violettes had its own Cessna Citation Mustang, dedicated to flying in first-class delicacies from points beyond the five-star kitchen. The restaurant was almost invitation only, as opposed to reservations only. The price tag on dinner for two was in the thousand-dollar range.

I stepped through the carved wooden doors, opened by guys wearing white gloves (and black clothes), into the bar. The dining room—as far as I'd ever been— is behind the bar. Bordering the dining room, behind a curved wall, are the private rooms, seven or eight of them, three with my (Bianca's) name on them tonight.

The bar itself was an ornate mahogany number that stretched the length of the room, with open arched doorways on either side. The only direct lighting in the room came from above the bar, where a massive backlit stained-glass mural of nothing in particular hung from brass chains.

It was an abstract of butter yellow, soft pink, and pale-green wispy shapes, and it was probably a collaboration between an artist and a shrink, designed to be artsy, and, at the same time, make people gamble more: the yellow and pink were muted Bellissimo colors, (remember where you are), and green is, of course, the color of money.

A piano sits in the middle of the room, a piano rumored to have cost more than a million dollars. Also mahogany, more than 100,000 hand-cut polished diamonds formed a grandly illuminating thin line of sparkles all the way around. It was further accessorized by a nearly naked woman who played go-to-sleep music. When she fell asleep on the diamonds, she was relieved by a Calvin Klein boxer-brief model, and he played go-to-sleep music until she woke up. The side walls of the bar were floor-to-ceiling wine racks. Three, four thousand bottles of wine.

The bar was where Bianca liked to hang out when she didn't have a roughed-up foot.

The dining room had weathered-white walls, and everything else was one shade darker, but still white. It was dramatic, formal, full of pricey art and ornately carved mirrors, and all the tables and chairs were Queen Anne. The lighting was a huge brass chandelier in the middle, and baby brass chandeliers above individual tables. All very Parisian.

"Your first guests have already arrived," a tuxedo man said, then presented the door to a room named Champs-Elysées.

Guests? Plural?

"Serve us quickly," I whispered. "I don't care if you have to bring other people's food."

"Of course." He bowed.

Bea did a double take when she saw me, and I did a double take when I saw her.

"Fancy," she stared at my shoes.

"What are you doing here, Bea?" I asked.

"I want to eat at the bar, Davis," said Eddie. "I didn't come here to be locked up with you two in here."

Here's exterior wall was a solid sheet of glass that looked out on the sparkly Gulf. The sun was sinking, the moon rising, and the shrimp boats were returning. It was breathtaking. *Here* had piped-in piano lullabies, beautiful toile linens, silver, crystal, paper-white china, soft lighting from brass sconces on the wall, and two faceless waiters. The food, however, was another story.

"Don't ask what's in it, Ma. Just eat it." He stuck a fork in it.

"Don't double dip in my dinner, Eddie." Bea poked her fork in his arm.

I looked at my Cartier watch. The big hand was on the second diamond. I had fifty minutes left with these two. "Okay, Bea." I sipped sparkling French water from a crystal flute. "Spill."

"Well, you know," she talked with her mouth full of chunky veal-foie gras pâté garnished with a white truffle chutney (it looked like Hamburger Helper to me), "all this time we've thought Cyril was living on a cruise ship in Hawaii." She pronounced Hawaii with at least two Rs in there, then she turned to Eddie. "See if you can get me some saltines to go with this. And a Pepsi." Back to me. "Cyril just dropped off the map." She dabbed at the corners of her mouth using the cuff of her leopard-print jacket for a napkin. "And if he hadn't," she said, "he'd've been burned at the stake."

Probably. Cyril Bunker had been Public Enemy Number One in Wilcox County all my life. Legend has it one day he was there, the next he was gone. He didn't say bye, he didn't tell anyone he was selling his land to miners, he practically gave the bag business to China, who stopped hiding a cat in the design. He was an Alabama Turncoat.

"Stripped off that land, you know?" Bea talked with her mouth full. "Biggest eyesore ever? Sold off that bag business? Took his money and hit the road without so much as a howdy-do or a kiss my ass." The waiter whisked Bea's liver away and replaced it with a plate of unmentionables. "Hey!" she stopped him. "I'm gonna need that fork! Give it back!" He didn't blink. He returned her *salade* fork.

(How do I know the name of that fork? Four semesters of French.)

"Pissed off everyone in three counties." Bea waved her *salade* fork at me. "Turns out," she said, "he's been in Beehive this whole time." Eddie Crawford was plowing through the carafe of table wine like it was sweet tea and he'd just mowed the north forty.

The big hand was creeping toward the fourth diamond. I could *feel* Bradley Cole making his way to me.

"Did you talk to him, Bea?" I asked.

"Nope." She turned to her son. "Get me a French cookbook for Christmas." She turned back to me. "Your daddy said two words to him, then the nurse boy who was rolling Cyril's wheelchair got that thing in gear and shot off like a rocket," she used her fork to demonstrate, "and we didn't see Cyril again." She pointed the fork at my ex-ex-husband. "Sit up straight, Eddie. Were you raised in a barn?"

"Do they have toothpicks here?" Eddie asked.

Bea got a mouthful of something she didn't like, prompting her to find her dinner napkin.

The big hand was almost on the sixth diamond.

"What's your overall impression of the place, Bea?"

She turned to me. "I love it. They have a beauty parlor. I'm going to keep this color." She patted her silver-fox locks. "I signed the paperwork," she said. "I'm moving in."

"Where's the paperwork?"

"Eddie." Bea used her *salade* fork as a pointer. "Reach into my pocketbook and get those papers for Davis."

There were two documents: a deed transfer, and a comprehensive health care power of attorney. Leona had signed both.

Seventh diamond.

The waiters seemed to pass through the walls. I never heard them enter or exit. Dishes appeared, then disappeared. Eddie Crawford asked every one why there weren't baskets of butter rolls like at Olive Garden.

"Listen," Bea addressed the head waiter, "I've got to save myself for another dinner later. I don't want that whatever." Bea waved away a tour of cheeses and wines. "I'll just take a bite of dessert."

"Madam, this is dessert."

"Are you kidding me?" Bea pulled back. "I want some real dessert."

"We also have a banana crème brûlée with meringues, and an apple-almond tart tonight."

"*What*?"

"Apple pie or banana pudding, Ma," Eddie said. "Bring her one of each. I'll eat what she doesn't. And buddy," the waiter waited, "I gotta go drain the dragon."

"Excuse me, sir?"

"Make a wee?" Eddie laughed at the waiter's stupidity.

The water boy spoke up. Or maybe it was the water girl. The person assisting the waiter spoke up. "The men's lounge is in the bar."

"Perfect." Eddie pushed back from the table, then remembered his manners. "Excuse me, ladies." He stood. "And I don't mean *you*."

I reached for my gun. This was as good a time as any to rid the world of Eddie Crawford.

Bea wrapped her pudgy fingers around the waiter's arm. "Bring two of the banana puddings."

The big hand was on the tenth diamond. The waiter bent to my ear. "Your eight o'clock is here, Mrs. Sanders."

* * *

Not only did I not know how to tell Bradley Cole, I had no idea how he'd react.

Four private doors and around a curved wall down, I stepped into a perfect replica of the room I'd just (thank goodness) left, this one named Trocadéro, but with two dramatic differences: a more easterly and pending-twilight view, and Bradley Cole. I stood there, shaking all over, until he looked up from the call he was on and met my eyes.

And just like that, we were good.

I lobbed myself into the seat beside him, using the walls, the waiter, and the table to get there. I needed oxygen. Bradley pointed to my blonde hair and winked. He mouthed, "*Bianca*", then reached for my hand. He switched phone ears, put an arm around me, and pulled me to him.

I fell in, and wanted to die there.

He kissed the top of my head. He spun his phone upside down, still listening, and whispered, "I ordered us coffee and dessert." He barely, barely kissed me. "I have to leave for Vegas in an hour."

Oh, no.

"Other voices need to be heard, Kirk."

Kirk started a speech. Bradley Cole laid the phone on the table and kissed me. For real.

Next up? Classic, epic, total destruction of the best reunion ever in the history of relationships: No Hair's big fat bald head came in the door. Just his head. "Davis? Can I speak to you for a minute?"

I shook my head against Bradley's chest.

No Hair stared at me.

"Right," Bradley said to his phone. "I don't disagree."

It took everything I had to follow No Hair out. I turned to steal a glance at Bradley. He looked up and gave me the okay—he'd be here when I got back. I grabbed the doorframe to keep from falling in the floor.

No Hair cleared his big throat.

I followed him to the door of an empty private dining room named Mont St-Michel. "This had better be good."

"It is," he said, "or I wouldn't interrupt." He told me security had notified him Eddie Crawford was on property (get him off), and so were Fantasy's three boys (help).

"Why?" I whispered.

"Because her husband had to be in New Orleans," he whispered back. "He's," No Hair's huge head rocked left-to-right, "upset."

"What do you want me to do about it? Leave dinner to take care of Fantasy's kids?"

"No," he said. "Fantasy can take care of her own kids when she gets here, but that means she'll be handing off Cyril Bunker to you."

"Where are they now?"

"They're fifteen minutes out."

"Of?"

"Landing."

"I thought you said they were here."

"They're on an *airplane*, Davis."

"What are Fantasy's kids doing on an *airplane*?"

No Hair threw both arms in the air and shook them. "Fantasy and Cyril Bunker are on an airplane, Davis, headed here. Fantasy's *kids* are in the arcade."

"Who's watching them?"

"No one!" No Hair said. "Because I'm here playing Password with you!"

"You're babysitting?" I hid my smile.

"You think this is funny?"

I shook my head. Not funny.

"We haven't even gotten to the funny part yet."

Bianca Sanders had spilled her guts to her husband about the Page Six porn shots of me, then about her little gun accident, and No Hair told me to get to the office right now for the Skype call coming in from Mr. Sanders.

"He doesn't want to talk to me. He wants to talk to *you*." No Hair grabbed my wrist and looked at the diamonds. "You have seven minutes. Get going."

"What about Bradley?"

"I can't worry about your romance right now."

"Then worry about this," I said. "I'll be late for the dinner with Mr. Microphone if I go all the way to the office and get on a Skype call."

"Davis." No Hair whispered through clenched teeth. "Work it out."

I worked my way back to Trocadéro, for two more minutes of working it out with Bradley Cole, only to find someone in my chair.

"There you are," that ass, ass, snake, rotten bastard ex-ex-husband of mine said. "You forgot these." He waved Leona Powell's church paperwork. "I took my mother to your place. She's sick." He shook the ice in his glass. "*Sick* sick," he said. "Disgusting."

My eyes found Bradley's.

And just like that, we weren't good anymore.

Bradley stood, dropped his napkin on the table, and made for the door. He stopped a foot from me, then turned. "Eddie."

"Dude." Eddie banged his chest with his fist, then shot two fingers in the air.

Bradley turned to me. "Davis."

"Bradley, no." I whispered the plea. "Don't do this."

"I can't fight this, Davis." His hand passed between me and rotten, rotten, Eddie. "I don't think you can either."

"I can explain." I kept my voice low, because this was none of Eddie the Sloth's business. "He's sniffing around for Bianca, Bradley. That's all. And work. He's hanging around hoping to run into her, and he's here because of a case we're working on."

"And I guess his mother's at our place because of a case you're working on?"

I opened my mouth, but he stopped me. "Don't, Davis." He looked at everything but me. "Just don't."

Bradley Cole walked away.

Eddie Crawford was in the middle of an apple-almond tart. The other dessert dish had been licked clean. "He's mad at you."

I shot him between the eyes.

(No. I didn't.)

* * *

I tried to beat up the elevator. I couldn't catch my breath.

"Suck it up, Davis," I said. "Suck it up." Ten minutes on Skype saving my job, then thirty minutes of dinner with Mr. Microphone saving the world, then I'd be free to devote the rest of my life to saving my relationship with Bradley Cole.

I couldn't see the rest of my life without him.

Richard Sanders' angry face filled the computer screen. "Start talking, Davis."

I started talking, I kept talking, I talked a little more, and as the big hand crept toward the second diamond on my watch, I'd worked my speech from Bianca to Beehive.

"This is Alabama's problem, Davis. Not ours."

"It is our problem, Mr. Sanders."

"Then connect these dots for me, Davis, I don't understand what this has to do with *us*."

"The church gets their old people here, Mr. Sanders. At the Bellissimo. We're their recruitment center."

"What? How?"

How? Mr. Microphone. But I couldn't very well go there right now, seeing as how Mr. Sanders (a) adored him, (b) was on the other side of the world, and (c) I was almost thirty minutes late to meet How for dinner. "It would be best if I explain how when you return."

Richard Sanders looked mighty skeptical. "Is there something you're not telling me, Davis?"

Well, Bradley Cole just walked out on me for the second time in two weeks, but I doubted he wanted to hear about it. "That's it for now, Mr. Sanders."

"I'll see you next Friday, Davis."

"Yes, sir."

"Work things out with Bianca before I get home."

Right. Anything else?

I had something else. I dialed Bradley's number and wasn't surprised when he didn't take my call, but he had to know, so I left a message at the beep. "Bradley. Listen to me. She's not Mary Harper Hathaway. I don't know who she is, but I know she's not Mary Harper Hathaway. Please be careful." One last deep breath. "I love you, Bradley, and I'm—" his voicemail cut me off.

Sorry. I was going to say I'm sorry.

* * *

The third private dining room, this one named Eiffel Tower, was a French buffet. No visible tablecloth. There had to be two thousand dollars of French food in front of Matthew Thatcher. He was wearing a wireless earbud. And a suit. “Hey, you!” He swallowed. “I was beginning to think you’d stood me up.” His fork hovered over several French casseroles. “Where’s your mother?” He stabbed at something small, slick, and shiny in an oval dish.

“She’s not feeling well,” I said. “She won’t be joining us.”

“Sorry to hear that.” He didn’t sound sorry.

The waiter scooted the chair beneath me and poured me a glass of sparkling water.

“Are you hungry?” Matthew Thatcher asked.

“Starving to death.” I grabbed a *salade* fork and dug in.

“Delicious, right?” he asked. “I eat here at least two or three times a week. Try the saumon fumé.” He pointed with his knife. “Try everything.”

I tried everything that wasn’t brown or pink.

“When did you go blonde?” he asked. “Do you know who you look like?”

I forgot about my hair! I fell face first into a plate full of French food.

NINETEEN

"Welcome back."

Fantasy was sitting in a hospital chair.

I was lying in a hospital bed.

"What happened?" I bolted upright. "Why are we here?" I inventoried my limbs. I patted about my head. "Did Bianca make me come here?" I pulled the blue gown away from my chest, stuck my head in, and thank goodness, didn't find DDD boobs.

Fantasy stood, then closed the space between us. "Honey," she took my hand in hers, "you've been sick."

"I don't feel sick."

"You've been very sick."

"If I'm that sick, where are my parents? Where's Bradley?"

"Davis." Fantasy peeled our hands apart. "You were poisoned."

"*What*?" I didn't feel poisoned; I felt confused. And thirsty. "*Poisoned*? Antifreeze? Snake venom? Cyanide?"

"Banana pudding."

Poisoned banana pudding? I pushed her out of my way and tried to climb out of the bed, but the room started spinning, so I rocked back. Flashes of dinner—white linens, forks, red wine—were coming back to me. "I'm not the only one who had the banana pudding! Are we all in the hospital?" I tried to remember who all I'd seen the oval dish of golden meringue peaks in front of. I was having trouble remembering who all I'd had dinner with. "Where's Bradley?"

She passed me two things: the results of my blood work and the front page of *The Biloxi Sun Herald*. The headline read: "Bellissimo's Violettes to Reopen After Fatality."

She helped me up, she dressed me, she drove me home.

"Davis. Say something." We were at a red light. I could see the Regent a block away. "You're scaring me."

"What day is it?"

"It's Tuesday, honey."

"So I've been in the hospital since Friday night?"

She nodded, then took a left. I dug through the Patient Property bag for my parking-garage fob. I'm not sure how we got from the garage to the condo, but No Hair was waiting inside. I wondered how and why so many people had access to the condo. I watched the look that passed between them. Hers was *handle with care*; his was *gotcha.*

I took a hot shower, pulled my wet hair back, dressed in my favorite sweats, and joined them. Fantasy poured me a cup of hot coffee.

"What happened?" I asked No Hair.

"Have you ever heard of cassava?"

"No."

"It's a South American root imported for desserts, mostly tapioca. The banana pudding you were served was made with cassava, which won't hurt you if it's cooked properly. It's toxic when it's not."

Boy, I'll say.

"Do you remember any of this?" No Hair asked.

"It's coming back to me in bits and pieces." And bananas. "Was it an accident," I asked, "or intentional?"

"That," No Hair said, "is what we don't know. And if it was intentional, who was the target?"

I honestly didn't know. "Have funeral arrangements been made?"

"The funeral is on Thursday, Davis. We're doing everything we can to get to the bottom of this," No Hair said, "but for now, you need to lay low. Rest up."

"You've been through a major trauma, Davis." Fantasy patted

me: head, shoulders, knees and toes. Pat, pat, pat.

I looked from one to the other. These two never handled me with kid gloves. Neither held back. Today they looked like if they exhaled too hard, I'd crumble. If they moved to fast, I'd crack in two. "Did I almost die?"

"No, Davis." No Hair's tie was stark white with a small eyeball in the middle, against a stark white shirt. "You didn't almost die."

"Four days of my life are gone, No Hair. What's your definition of almost dying?"

"You were in a medically-induced coma, Davis, which they say *saved* your life."

I did feel rested.

"You slept through the bad stuff, honey." Pat, pat, pat.

No Hair rose to leave. "I'm going to run--"

I waited.

"Maybe," he suggested, "you should talk to someone, Davis. You know, a shrink-type someone."

"I don't want to talk to anyone."

"Sorry about all this, Davis."

Fantasy walked No Hair to the elevator. Where they whispered.

* * *

She steered me to the marshmallow sofa and tucked me under a blanket. My discharge paperwork and blood work results from Biloxi Memorial were on the table in front of me.

Much later, she asked, "How do you feel?"

"Empty."

She pressed her lips together. Pat, pat, pat.

"Were you with me at the hospital?

"Only the first few hours," she said. "Then they locked you up and wouldn't let anyone but family in, and that was every few hours for a few minutes at a time."

"Was my family there?"

"When I got there today, a nurse told me your mother had been there the whole time and didn't leave until this morning."

"She must have my mother mixed up with someone else's mother."

"No, Davis. She said your mother took it pretty hard."

It struck me as odd that I'd finally done something to drag a little compassion out of my mother.

"She told No Hair she would never make another banana pudding."

That sounded more like my mother. Blame the banana pudding. "So No Hair was there?"

"No, honey. I think he checked in on you."

I waited for Fantasy to tell me who else was there, who else took it pretty hard, who else checked in, but she didn't. Because, I suppose, no one else was there, no one else took it pretty hard, and no one else checked in.

Silent healing time passed. A lot of it.

She made me Frosted Cherry Pop Tarts. They tasted like Frosted Cherry Cardboard. A quick squall blew in from the Gulf and we watched it cross the sky.

Eventually, she began gathering her things. "I have some news. Good news, for a change."

"Let's hear it."

"No Hair hired Baylor for us."

"Really?" I asked. "Why?"

She shrugged. "He's cute."

"He is cute."

"Muscle, maybe?"

"We have plenty of muscles."

She agreed. "I guess No Hair hired him, Davis, because he needed help. You were—" she didn't say it, "—and I had to spend a little time at home," she said. "It was get my butt home, or get a divorce lawyer."

"I can't talk about Bradley right now."

"I didn't say anything about him, honey."

"You said 'lawyer'."

"Come here." I fell into her big hug and stayed there. When I woke up again, I was all tucked in on the sofa, the sky was dark, and Fantasy was gone.

* * *

The ABC, NBC, CBS, and FOX affiliates moved their reporters, microphones, and mobile satellites from the entrance of the Bellissimo, where they'd been camped out for days, to the entrance of the Grand Palace Casino. They joined CNN, CNBC, MSNBC, and E!, who were already there.

I watched with a bottle of wine, my first adult beverage in two months, so the images on the television were a little blurry, and I intended for them to get a lot blurrier.

"In a stunning turn of events," Lila Medina, WXXV Gulfport, wearing a hot hot pink tight tight sweater, reported, "a federal judge has dismissed without prejudice the class-action suit against the Grand Palace Casino for allegedly failing to protect its employees from secondhand smoke."

"What does that mean, exactly, Lila?" Sheldon Ortiz spoke from behind an anchor desk.

"Well, Sheldon," on-location Lila said, "it means that the almost two hundred plaintiffs in this case can bring the same charges against the Grand, but at a later date. The court's ruling means the rights of the plaintiffs aren't waived or terminated, rather, they're postponed. But for now, Sheldon, the show is over." Lila was panting.

"Does this have anything to do with the ruling against Bonita Jakes, whose complaint against the Grand was dismissed?" He struck a different, more ominous, pose. "Or is this about the blow the Grand's legal team has been dealt?"

"Grand Palace attorney Kirk Olsen spoke briefly at a press conference earlier today." The screen was split between Sheldon and Lila. "Here's what he had to say."

Kirk, who'd been sitting beside Bradley Cole in Grafton Clemmer's courtroom last week, was now in my living room. He looked like he hadn't slept in a week, and had four microphones in his face. Someone holding one of the microphones asked, "Is it true that your parent company in Las Vegas is going to offer a settlement to the victims?"

"They're not victims," Kirk snapped, "they're petitioners. And no comment."

A different microphone asked, "Do you think, Kirk, that the judge postponed this trial because your legal team has fallen apart?"

Kirk was offended. "Absolutely not."

Lila Medina didn't believe a word of it. Neither did Sheldon Ortiz. Neither did I.

TWENTY

On Wednesday, the day before the funeral, I woke early, packed an overnight bag, and drove home to Pine Apple. In an effort to start living my life in a completely different way, one that might yield different results, I drove straight to the home I'd grown up in, which is to say I went to see my mother first, instead of driving directly to the police station, my usual route, to see my father first.

"Child." Mother held the door open. She took my bag. She asked if I needed a sweater. She fixed me hot chocolate. Any minute, I looked for her to break out the Crayons and coloring books. When she finally stopped fussing over me, she sat beside me at the kitchen table that had seen a thousand bowls of tomato soup, two thousand grilled cheeses, and three thousand hours of homework. "Why didn't you tell us you were pregnant?"

"Mother." I slumped in the chair. "I didn't even tell myself."

"So your young man never knew?"

I ran my thumbnail down a long groove in the wooden table.

"Well, honey," my mother said. "These things happen for a reason." She went on to tell me God had plans, rainbows come after storms, lights are at the end of tunnels, and never run with scissors.

She asked me if I wanted to talk about my time in the hospital.

I did not.

I thanked her for being there.

I asked her if she'd told Daddy and Meredith.

Yes. She had.

Mother folded and refolded a kitchen towel. "I failed you girls by not talking to you more."

None of us would forget the day the seventh grade P.E. teacher explained womanhood to Meredith, convinced her she wasn't dying, then called Daddy to come get her because no one answered at home.

"This isn't your fault, Mother."

She matched the edges of the kitchen towel and folded it to postage-stamp size.

"Do you ever think of moving back to Pine Apple, Davis? Maybe Biloxi is just too big." Mother's hands looked so old. "You should talk to your father. He says he's ready to retire, and what he means is he's waiting on you." Mother's neck was...falling. "You and Meredith could have fun like you used to when you were girls."

"What?" Meredith banged through the kitchen door. "Are you two talking about me behind my back?" She hugged me from behind and kissed the top of my head. "Heard you rolled into town." She scraped up a chair. "How's tricks?"

I couldn't help it; the muscles in the bottom half of my face moved. My sister.

"So that Mr. Microphone guy is dead, huh?" Bells on every word.

My mother, in honor of her hero Ronald Reagan, kept a jar of jellybeans on the kitchen table between the napkin holder and the salt and pepper shakers. Meredith reached for it, then began digging out the red ones.

"Stop picking through the jellybeans, young lady."

She waved mother off. "Deader than a doornail?"

"He's all the way dead," I said. "He's a goner."

"Daddy says his last act on Earth was dinner with you."

Meredith collapsed on the table, playing dead. Jellybeans flew through the air, Mother let out a yelp, and I couldn't help it, I laughed. Which made Meredith laugh. It got so funny, even Mother was laughing. "You girls stop it!" She dabbed her eyes with a paper napkin. "Lightning will strike you!"

It was good to be home.

* * *

So Help Me God, I needed out of Pine Apple. Two hours, and I was about to lose my mind. There was no way in hell I was spending the night.

We were at Mel's Diner around a rectangular table that seated six: me, Daddy, Mother, Eddie the Dog, Mel (my ex-ex-father-in-law and proprietor of this health hazard of an establishment), and Wilcox County's Prodigal Son, Cyril Bunker, home at last. The man was three hundred years old. He might be, stretched out, four feet tall. He wore Mr. Magoo glasses, his clothes swallowed him, and white fluffy hair sprouted from all sorts of places about his head it shouldn't have.

"Oh, she'll love the place." Cyril spoke at the speed and volume of growing grass. "They put on the dog when you get there." His poor fingers were just mangled. He brought his coffee cup to his mouth in such a corkscrew way that my mother's hands kept shooting out to assist.

Bea Crawford, a.k.a. Leona Powell, checked into the So Help Me God Senior Living Orientation Center on Sunday morning while I snoozed away in Biloxi Memorial's Critical Care Unit, and no one had heard a peep from her since. No Hair sent her in with a satellite cell-phone-in-a-picture-frame (very James Bond) and instructions to check in at least twice a day, but she had yet to make contact. Bea's loved ones were slowly getting curious. Concerned would be way down the road.

"They roll out the red carpet for the first weeks." Cyril stretched every word to the breaking point. I noticed we were all dipping and swaying with each elongated syllable, freezing in anticipation between words, and wondering if we ought to check him for a pulse when he finally finished a sentence. "In a few days," ("*ddddaaaaaayyyyyyssssss*") "she'll get transferred to the therapy building," he said, "then she'll be ringing that picture off the wall wanting someone to break her out." ("*Oooooooooouuuuuuuuttttttt.*") It took Cyril a full twelve minutes to impart the thought.

"Tell us the whole story, Cyril," my father prompted.

"Oh, hell." Eddie Crawford lit a Marlboro. "Ma will be dead before he finishes the story."

"Shut up, Eddie." (Me.)

"Hey!" He stabbed the air with his lit cigarette. My mother squealed. "Don't blame me because you got dumped."

Just then, the door burst open and the long, distorted shadow of my Granny Dee fell across the length of the table. My sister scooted past her and found a barstool. "Geesh, Louise," Meredith said. "She made me bring her."

Granny Dee shuffled to the table. "Cyril Bunker, you handsome devil. Welcome home."

He looked at Granny through his Coke-bottle glasses. A wide grin spread across his face, then the whole row of his top teeth fell into his lap.

* * *

We moved the party to the police station, and we didn't invite Meredith, Eddie, Mel, Mother, or Granny Dee. Meredith was happy to be released, Eddie crawled back under his rock, Mel dove into a vat of Bombay gin, Mother said she'd bring us lunch, and Granny Dee insisted on coming with us. "I'm not letting him out of my sight," she whispered to me. Everyone in the room heard it except for Cyril Bunker.

My desk, the desk I walked away from more than two years ago when my father fired me, had not been touched. I stood beside it, knowing that if I pulled out the chair and sat down, I might never get up. I'd grown up in this room. My father, who was studying the floor as I studied my life, was growing old in this room.

"I love you, Daddy."

Daddy's eyes were shiny.

"Is this where you prepare prisoner meals, Samuel?" Granny Dee was helping Cyril walk, which was hilarious, because Daddy needed to be helping her walk, and I needed to be helping Daddy walk.

Oh, the circle of life.

We were squeezed into the kitchenette, because that's where the electronics were.

"Good grief." The dusty computer's software hadn't been updated in forever and I had to turn the keyboard upside down to bang out the cracker crumbs and a rubber band. "Don't you even play solitaire, Daddy?"

"Candy Crush!" My grandmother shouted.

Eventually, I weaseled my way into the Bellissimo's system and began pulling up images and transferring to a power-point slide show. We had to move Cyril to an office chair, roll him over, pump him up in the air, and get his nose on the monitor before he could see anything. In the middle of all that, he asked my father how long it would take to get his driver's license renewed, because it's not like he had all the time left in the world.

"I'll look into it, Cyril."

"Now, Mr. Bunker." I sat beside him. "Have you ever seen this man?"

"No."

"You don't want to see him now, Cyril," my grandmother said. "He's laid out on a slab at the morgue."

"Granny!"

She shrugged.

"Are you sure, Mr. Bunker?" There were thousands of images of Matthew Thatcher in the Bellissimo system to choose from, and I gave Cyril more than a hundred chances to recognize him.

"Nope." "No." "Don't know him from Adam." "Still don't know him." "Sorry." "Is he a singer?" "Never seen him." "Now, him I know."

I woke up. "What?"

"Go back one."

I went back one. It was Matthew Thatcher back in his LeeRoy Maffini days. Without the nose job, with auburn hair.

"He's a preacher."

"He's a dead preacher," my grandmother said.

Mother spread out a bright yellow tablecloth that smelled like summer and insisted we all wash our hands. She put out a platter of chicken salad and pimento cheese sandwiches, a dish of miniature sweet pickles, and a plate of toffee cookies. She had vanilla Ensure for Granny Dee and Cyril, a thermos of coffee for Daddy, and a cold Dr. Pepper in a bottle for me, a drink I loved as a child, a drink she had to drive to Sissy's Shell Station on Turkey Holloman Road to buy, and a drink I hadn't touched since college.

My father said, "You'd better enjoy this while it lasts."

"I'm going to milk it for everything it's worth, Daddy."

"That's my girl."

Cyril Bunker ate slower than he talked. "It's these *teeth*," he said. "Like trying to eat with rocks in your mouth."

My grandmother suggested he lose them, because we were practically family. She wallowed all over the word *family*.

Between bites, Cyril managed to identify McKinley Weeks, the church emissary who'd attached himself to Bea at the old people's slot tournament last week ("Another preacher," Cyril said) and Jewell Maffini, who'd started all this mess, because she'd been my mark a lifetime ago (two and a half weeks ago) when No Hair made me go to the Mystery Shopper tournament instead of moving. If I'd never seen this woman's picture, maybe Bradley Cole and I would still be together.

"How do you know her, Cyril?"

"Well. I found a cookie jar. It was in the year of our Lord nineteen aught nine."

Oh, dear Lord.

"No," ("*nnnnnoooooooooooooo*") "it was nineteen and eighty-nine."

Dodged that eighty-year bullet.

My mother called about supper before the poor old guy finished.

Cyril, in his early sixties, on his way to his lawyer's office in Montgomery to sign the last of the paperwork selling the Tilda

Reyes quilted luggage line to a soft-goods manufacturer in LaGrange, Georgia, stumbled out to his old dog shed and into an overlooked cookie jar full of hundred dollar bills. Early for his meeting, the cash burning a hole in his pocket, he made a pit stop at Jupiter's Gold Casino, just outside of Montgomery, where he met Jewell Maffini. He never made it to the meeting with his lawyer. The next day, he came to know Jewell in a carnal way—my grandmother angrily scooted her chair away from him with that, but she must have forgiven him, or forgotten, because after she woke up from her catnap (head tipped back, mouth wide open, snoring), taken during the grisly drawn-out details of Cyril's carnal education of Jewell, Granny scooted back in—and it was on the afternoon following all the carnal business, at a Double Diamond Dare slot machine, when Jewell convinced Cyril it was wrong to sell the Tilda Reyes line to foreigners. Cyril didn't think Georgia was a foreign country, to which Jewell brought up all that is right and holy in Alabama. Football. Dogs versus Tide. He couldn't argue with *that*. Cyril made the mistake of telling her, football notwithstanding, that if he didn't sell the line, he couldn't keep his property up, the taxes alone were killing him—and here he launched into a forty-minute diatribe about Amy Carter, only child of Rosalyn and Jimmy Carter—and the next thing the poor old guy knew, he was locked up in Beehive, Alabama, in therapy from twelve to fourteen hours a day.

I really needed to know about the therapy, but I really wanted to get back to Biloxi, and Granny Dee and Cyril really, really needed their meds.

My father walked me to my car. He told me he believed, with everything he had, that one day soon, when the time was right, I'd bring him a baby to bounce on his knee and call him Papa.

TWENTY-ONE

Bright and early the next morning, I stomped to the foyer to shoot the elevator control pad because it wouldn't stop buzzing. I was wearing a T-shirt and yesterday's makeup. I thought I'd grabbed my robe, but I was trying to get my sleepy arms into the sleeves of a pillowcase.

"David." She hobbled right past me—jewel-encrusted platinum and polished-wood walking stick—and into the living room. She surveyed my beautiful home with indifference. "Where do you *sit* in here?

There were three hundred places to sit.

"Anywhere you'd like, Mrs. Sanders."

"I'd like coffee."

Baylor was standing in front of the closed elevator doors. "*Sorry*," he mouthed. Then he waggled his fingers around his head, indicating he'd tried to call.

"*What's going on?*" I asked.

"*She thinks I'm her new assistant.*" He made crazy circles.

"Are you speaking to me?" Bianca had settled herself in the middle of my marshmallow sofa. "Are you speaking *of* me?"

"No, Mrs. Sanders."

I stumbled to the kitchen and started a pot of coffee.

"Artesian water!" Bianca shouted.

"You bet!" I held the carafe under the tap until it was full.

The elevator dinged again. The doors parted and a wardrobe entered—a rolling rack stuffed with clothes and a cart on wheels stacked with shoe boxes on its heels. The elevator doors closed. I wondered what would come out of the elevator next. Giraffe? Marching band? Bradley Cole?

From the kitchen, I could see the back of her bottle-blonde head, her good foot, going ninety-miles an hour, and a plume of smoke curling into the air. I poured us both a cup of coffee, stumbled in, served her, then sat a comfortable distance away and waited.

"This casino event, David, the slots affair." She used my Vietri saucer for an ashtray. "Surely you don't imagine I'm going to let you humiliate me again."

"What slot affair, Mrs. Sanders?"

"The large tournament." She rolled her eyes at out-of-the-loop David. "They've asked me to help," she said, "and of course, I agreed to."

"What, exactly, Mrs. Sanders, have you agreed to?" What have you signed *me* up for, Bianca?

"David." She tapped ashes into my dishes. "My husband needs me and I will not let him down."

I held up a finger. "Excuse me." I took off down the hall. I couldn't poke my phone fast enough. I said, "Start talking," when he answered.

"Davis," No Hair said, "plain and simple. We need you if you're up for it."

"She wants me to be her at the slot tournament."

"I know." He sighed. "I know."

I spent the next two or three minutes behind the closed door of Bradley's closet, my face buried in his shirt sleeves. Her husband needed her and I could not let him down. If I wanted to keep my job. I didn't need to sit around here thinking anyway. I trudged back to Bianca.

"I do not have all day, David."

"It's Davis." My coffee had cooled.

"You could use some lessons in hostessing."

I'd left her alone for all of five minutes. I smiled. Sipped my tepid coffee. "It was nice of you to bring the clothes here, Mrs.

Sanders. I'm glad you felt like getting out."

Bianca took a deep and shaky drag off her second cigarette on my brand new white sofa in my brand new condo. "This coffee is dreadful."

"Would you like me to go get you coffee, Mrs. Sanders?" Baylor, guarding the clothes, asked.

"I'd like you to stand over there and pretend you're not here, young man." She snapped at The Help. "I'm here to talk to David." She turned back to me. "The ice cream dip event." She lowered her voice. "I want Richard to be very, very impressed. Do you hear me, David? I want you on top of your game." She stubbed out her latest cigarette. In my Vietri saucer. Again. "The tippy top. Do you understand?"

I understood. Bianca missed her husband. His three-week journey would be complete at the start of the tournament and she was hoping if I looked like a million bucks, he'd run to her. (Sick, really, if you think about it too long. Or at all.) I also understood that as her foot had healed, she'd come down with an increasingly dire case of cabin fever, which was why she was here. And lastly, sadly, I understood long ago that I was the closest thing to a girlfriend Bianca had.

"So this is where you live, David?" Bianca looked down her nose.

"It's Davis. And yes. I've only been here a few weeks. Would you like me to show you around?"

"No."

Work things out with Bianca before I get home.

She turned at the elevator and used her cane to point to a Louis Vuitton garment bag. "Your funeral attire." She dug into her Prada bag and extracted a folder. She placed it on the demilune table beside the elevator. "This is from Marketing."

Funeral?

* * *

I sat down at my computer. I had two cyber chores before I left for the funeral, neither of which I wanted to start, much less complete. I flipped a mental coin, and went with the creepiest one first. I knew how to dress up as Bianca and work a crowd. I'd learned how to walk, sit, drink, smoke, criticize, whine, converse, and flirt as Bianca. And then there was the other list: Don't hug, guffaw, or commit to anything. Don't sign autographs. (My handwriting was "heinous.") Don't *slouch* like a teenage boy. Don't eat hors d'oeuvres. Don't scratch, tug, or sneeze. Ever.

One thing I didn't know how to do as Bianca, or Davis, however, was emcee an event, and the Double Dip tournament was three full days of mistressing ceremonies. I zipped through an hour of Mr. Microphone-at-his-finest video. I jotted down some of his better lines and got a bead on the timing and attitude of it all. I rehearsed in my pink polka dot bathrobe with a round hairbrush.

Next, I went back in time to 1994, to the Chi Chapter of the Delta Delta Delta Sorority at the University of Mississippi at Oxford. There she was—cute, blonde, pearls—Mary Harper Hathaway. Something was off, way off, and I'd known it since the afternoon of Banana Pudding Day when, in preparation for my dinner with Bradley, I'd tried to catch up on his case, but what I caught was Mary Ha Ha hanging out with the plaintiffs and their lawyer, Jerry McAllen.

No way she should have been anywhere near them.

I smelled a rat. Then took a four-day nap.

The microscope accessory on my laptop was just the weapon I needed for rat hunting. I put it to good use examining the other pledged faces for any trace of the woman I knew as Mary Ha Ha, but nothing popped. It wouldn't be a stretch to think that the sneaky bitch who'd saddled up to Bradley Cole (and made my life a living hell) had visited a plastic surgeon or three through the years (Facelifts R Us), but still, I think I'd recognize her wide, flat forehead, her jagged hairline, her round face. Nothing. So, what sorority did the really smart girls pledge back then? Search engine (Google), search engine (Bing), search engine (Topsy), where I hit pay dirt. In the mid-nineties, brainiacs went Kappa Alpha Theta. And there she was. Kimberli Silvers.

Mary Harper Hathaway and Kimberli Silvers were both born in Jackson, Mississippi within months of each other: different sides of the tracks, different high schools, same college. They both received undergraduate degrees (BAs in History and International Relations, respectively) in 1998, they both moved to Boston, Massachusetts, where they graduated with law degrees from the Northeastern University School of Law three years later.

In the twenty-five years these young women walked the same paths, I couldn't find a hint of them crossing. I poked around in the *Boston Globe* digital annals long enough to find what appeared to be their only documented interaction, and it was a tragic one. Mr. and Mrs. Robert Hathaway, III, and their only child, Mary Harper, died in the fiery crash of a Cessna Caravan Turboprop, piloted by Mr. Hathaway, forty-seven, owner/operator, seven minutes after takeoff from the Plum Island Airport (2B2), four hours after Mary Harper received her law degree. An unidentified passenger, also aboard the failed flight to Jackson, Mississippi, was ejected from the plane before impact and found, still buckled in the seat, seventy yards away from the fuselage, then rushed to the trauma unit at St. Elizabeth's.

I'll be damned.

To: BCole@GrandPalaceBiloxi.com

From: davis@davisway.com

Attachments

Bradley. I put the condo on the market for $120,000.

I found the real Mary Harper Hathaway. The woman you are/were working with is named Kimberli Silvers. It's all attached.

I love you, Bradley,

D

He'd call. The condo appraised at one-point-two *million*, not one-point-two *dollars*.

I dragged the Louis Vuitton hanging bag down the hall, then lobbed it across the foot of the bed. I unzipped it, then zipped it right back. Eventually, I had to unzip it again. I sprayed my hair blonde, then stuffed it into a ridiculous hat.

* * *

The sun was waning on the cool cloudless day as the city of Biloxi bid farewell to Matthew Thatcher.

Beach Boulevard was closed for a quarter-mile on both sides of the Bellissimo; traffic was rerouted through the streets of downtown Biloxi. The city's Casino Hopper buses shuttled mourners. General public admission was granted to those wearing RIP Thatch T-shirts, a profile silhouette of him emblazoned on the back, available in seven colors at temporary kiosks set up on every street corner in zip code 39530. Two counterfeit T-shirt dealers had been ordered to cease and desist. Even in death, Mr. Microphone was bringing in Bellissimo bucks.

The quarter-mile, seven-lane, circular entrance was bumper-to-bumper Bellissimo limos on the inside lane, the entire fleet, drivers at parade rest beside their vehicles. A massive black hearse was parked under the porte-cochere, directly beneath the outdoor chandelier. Also massive. The only spots of color were the running-board lights of the limos, the braided red tassels on the porter's shoulders, and Matthew Thatcher's canary yellow Porsche 911 Carrera, on display in front of the fountain. The Porsche wore a fifteen-foot spray of red roses. The flowers dripped off the front end, arced over the car, then spilled to the ground off the back. Eight million exterior lights had been darkened for the occasion, the towering marquee's scrolling message board being the only exception which could be seen a mile out to sea. It flashed *Godspeed Matthew Thatcher*.

All eight entrance doors were held open for me by the red-tasseled porters. Baylor, head bent respectfully, was at my right elbow. Bianca had dressed me in head-to-toe Christmas red (Chanel), in a short, cap-sleeve dress with a slit all the way up one leg. It looked like it had been airbrushed on; I couldn't breathe. On my feet, five-inch red patent stilettoes, with a four-inch-thick ankle strap featuring—I swear to you—a clunky gold horse bit. On my head, a five-pound study in mesh and silk that cast a foot-wide cylindrical shadow on me, flopped over both my ears, and had a huge red tulle bow on top that was twice as large as my actual head. I wore Dior crystal-studded sunglasses and chocolate diamonds set in gold. The dark diamonds dripped off both arms, three fingers, from around my neck, and dangled from my earlobes to my ribcage.

I thought this was a humiliatingly loud and inappropriate (for the occasion) follow-up to last week's pornographic blue number I'd been photographed in. Bianca insisted it would wipe the offensive blue images from the public's mind, and I couldn't argue with that. This getup would wipe the public's mind clean altogether, then boggle it for years to come.

I stepped into the lobby, a 20,000 square-foot glass-domed conservatory, to see uniformed Bellissimo employees on the left and right, carving a pathway to the casino. I recognized every uniform—housekeeping, various restaurants, Security detail, casino cage—because I'd worn most of them at one time or another. There were at least a thousand Bellissimo employees holding up the lobby walls. Most were staring straight ahead, some shuffling restlessly, some whispering. (About my crazy red hat, no doubt.)

The casino took my breath away. I stepped in, tore off the sunglasses, and my other hand flew to my mouth with an "Oh!" Cameras clicked unmercifully. The only light in the casino was from the 3,800 slot machines. They'd each been set to their top-payout displays, triggering 3,800 blinking yellow jackpot lights. The effect was that of a meteor shower or the finale of a fireworks display. An 80,000 square-foot laser show. Behind red velvet ropes the T-shirted grievers stretched as far as I could see, a gold glow on their sad faces and T-shirts.

The only other light in the room was a single spotlight, aimed at an elevated stage in the middle of the casino floor, illuminating a microphone stand. At its base, a silver urn full of Matthew Thatcher. Two floor easels displaying economy-car-sized portraits of him held spots on stage right and stage left.

The funeral service, straight from Marketing, was a variety show featuring ten minutes each of Patti LaBelle, comedian Ron White, the Reverend Oswaldo Starkey, and Engelbert Humperdinck. None took the stage; they performed in front of it, either to the left or right, of the empty microphone stand. The Reverend's ten minutes were titled, "All Emcees Go to Heaven".

I spoke last.

The sound of my red-heeled footfall onto Matthew Thatcher's stage echoed off the darkened forty-foot ceiling. I stood in the spotlight. I reached for the microphone with heartache, just like Marketing told me (Bianca) to. I examined it wistfully, just like Marketing told me (Bianca) to. I licked it. (I did NOT!) I did, however, hold it at a forty-five-degree angle two inches from my mouth. (Just like marketing...) I waited until you could have heard a gnat whisper.

"Matthew. Thatcher. Loved. The. Bellissimo." I took a minute to get a hold of myself, just like marketing told me (Bianca) to. "The. Bellissimo. Loved. Him. Back."

Thunderous, deafening, prolonged applause.

On cue (from Marketing), I waved chocolate diamonds around to quiet things down.

"For the next fifteen minutes," I scanned the crowd to my right, "in honor of Matthew Thatcher," I scanned the crowd to my left, "all slot play is *free*!"

In perfect symphony, the house lights came up, Phil Collins' "You'll Be in My Heart" blasted from a thousand speakers, balloons and confetti dropped from the ceiling, and the slot machines reset in unison, creating an opus of bells and whistles.

Baylor rushed me out the back way and into a waiting dark blue van. In white block letters across the side of the van were the words LEE COUNTY CORONER. We still hadn't heard from Bea

Crawford, and the only thing we could come up with was to kill her, then haul her out on a gurney. (Kidding. They don't make Bea-sized gurneys.)

"Good God, Davis!" Fantasy was waiting in the van. "Who dressed you?"

"Take a wild guess."

She passed me my phone, a fistful of identification on a chain, and a dark blue coroner's jumpsuit. "Change clothes," she said. "You're hurting my eyes."

I checked my phone—no calls—and began slinging chocolate diamonds. "Anything show up on the feed?" I sent the hat flying to the back of the van.

"Nope," Fantasy said. "No Jewell Maffini, no Preacher Beecher, no Peyton Beecher."

I peeled off the red dress and began climbing into the morgue jumpsuit.

"How are you doing, Davis?"

I stopped mid-jumpsuit. "I'll be fine, Fantasy."

"You're going to need to deal with it at some point, you know."

"I will." I zipped. "Just not now."

We tore out of there, Baylor at the wheel, just in front of the hearse.

TWENTY-TWO

We found Baylor's special gift; he could flirt.

Our mortuary credentials got us past the front, middle, and rear checkpoints of So Help Me God's Senior Living Center—it didn't hurt that it was midnight-thirty; the guards barely looked up from their porn/pizza/paperbacks—but Hazardous Shipping and Receiving, the loading dock behind the Therapy Services building where the cadavers were picked up, had iron gates.

The guard—stick thin, goateed, with a nametag that read "Dannee"—practically climbed in the driver window to drawl, "Well, hey there, Cowboy," at Baylor. Who froze. Solid.

Fantasy leaned up and whispered in his ear. "You got this, Baylor."

Baylor saddled up and lassoed us right through those iron gates, and he will forever be known to us, from that moment on, as Cowboy. He was coming in handy in all sorts of ways. First of all, he was a good Bianca babysitter. Enough said. In addition, he looked like an action-hero movie star, and we liked having a driver. He was in his mid-twenties, so we felt comfortable bossing him around. ("I said no cheese, not extra cheese. Run back in there.")

Earlier, about mid-Alabama, he asked if he would get a gun. "No!" Fantasy and I said together. And not another peep out of him for twenty miles.

We made it through Therapy (straight up Stephen King material), and through residential (padlocks on the outside of every resident door), without much incident. In fact, Fantasy was the only incident during the first half of Break Bea Out. She was zipped in the body bag, riding on the gurney, and complained about the odor, lack of oxygen, and our gurney driving the whole time.

"Hush, Fantasy. You're supposed to be dead."

To which she replied, "This thing has no padding. My bones are bruising."

Finally, we reached the Orientation Suites (think Ritz), where we hoped to find Bea.

Hope was the wrong word, we *had* to find Bea.

There were at least a dozen closed doors. We were at one end of the hall between guest rooms *Andrew* and *Bartholomew*.

"Cowboy," I whispered, "we'll find Bea. You go run interference." He sallied off to the nurse's station.

We found her in *James the Lesser*, four doors down.

"You can't stay here, Bea."

"Why not?"

"Because you have a family," I said. "And a home. And you're not really Leona Powell. When they figure that out, you need to be long gone."

"They're so nice." She made no move to get out of the four-poster bed. "The food is so good." She hugged a pillow and pulled a comforter up to her chins. "This has been the best vacation of my whole *life*."

Fantasy was on guard at the window, peeking between the plantation shutters. "Vacation's over, Bea."

I was on guard at the door. I could see Cowboy at the nurse's station wooing a nurse. Seriously, he was about to get lucky with a ponytail girl wearing a stethoscope.

"Get up, Bea." I stuffed her things into her bag (Tilda Reyes, school-bus yellow and apple green paisley). "It was hell getting in here—"

"Hell for who?" Fantasy asked. "You?"

"—and it won't be easy to get out," I told Bea. "Come on."

One of those little designer pet pigs fell out of the bed and onto the floor. Then its twin sister. Upon closer inspection, those were Bea's feet.

"Fudge," she said.

We couldn't begin to get her in the body bag, so we unzipped it and tucked it over her, like a tarp, that mouth of hers going ninety-to-nothing the whole time. "Bea." I poked in the general vicinity of her larynx. "You're dead. Shut up and act like it." We banged into every wall. "Cowboy, give that girl her stethoscope back and let's get going."

He caught up with us and slapped a thick file folder on dead Bea.

"What's that?" I asked.

"*Somebody cut me a air hole!*" (Bea.) "*I'm gonna pass out!*"

"Suit yourself, Bea." (Me. Spoken through my teeth.) "But do it quietly."

"The Leona Powell paperwork." (Cowboy.) "Swiped it off that girl's desk."

See? Handy Cowboy.

We made it to the service elevator just as two nurses thumped around a linoleum corner. "Go, go, go!" We shoved Bea in the elevator and I poked the escape button several hundred times.

"Some days." Fantasy was pinned to the back wall of a service elevator by the gurney full of thrashing Bea. "I want to go back to prison."

"You were in prison?" Cowboy was impressed.

"*Davis is the one who was in prison*!" Thrash thrash. "*She's the jailbird.*" Thrash. "*And you'll be right back there when I die in this bag, Davis.*"

"Do we have a tranquilizer gun?" I asked.

* * *

My niece Riley was born on a noisy Tuesday, both she and her mother wailing their little lungs out, just in time to attend my swearing-in ceremony two weeks later on the afternoon of her baptism. It was an emotional day for my family, with both Meredith and me dedicating our lives to something other than our own happiness. I remember Meredith looking like someone had beaten the stew out of her, lots of barbecue, and feeling thrilled and terrified at the same time. I couldn't have known it then, but Bradley Cole was three states away taking the road less traveled too, as he took an oath to support, protect, and defend the Constitution.

Police officers and attorneys are a dime a dozen, but as it turned out, Bradley really meant what he'd sworn that day, as did I. Before we even met, our lives were ones of commitment, with a side of service to our fellow man. (And both marched our righteous ethical butts to casinos. Go figure.)

As a result, we went into our relationship eyes-wide-open about the fact that the other didn't punch a clock, get summers off, or leave it for Monday. We had careers that required us to run into the fire and stay until it was out. It was who we were and what we'd signed up for.

We'd shared one Christmas. We spent it in Biloxi, at home, just us. (My mother was so pissed.) In the middle of our Christmas Eve celebration that included our first tossing around of the L Word, clothing, and wrapping paper, his phone rang. It was only one of many times his work interrupted our lives, matched only by how often mine did the same. We parted with a kiss, a hug, and I promised I wouldn't peek at the big gift under the tree until he returned. Which was New Year's Eve.

On our six-month anniversary, we got up early and drove to New Orleans for the world's best gumbo roux, then spent the rest of the day in our kitchen over a simmering pot, laughing and crying (him over onions, me telling him the story of how my life had changed when I was sixteen), only for my phone to ring two minutes after we sat down to eat. He told me he loved me and to be careful as he wrapped my gumbo for later. I didn't make it home for three days. By then the gumbo was long gone and so was he, to Vegas, but the diamond and sapphire anniversary earrings (monsters!) were on the kitchen counter with a note: *Bradley loves Davis.*

We knew how hot the other's fire could get.

I knew what was keeping Bradley up at night. Was the Grand Palace negligent in regard to employee health and safety? If Bradley believed his employer was guilty, yet had to do his job to protect the huge corporation's assets anyway, he was ripped in two, and I knew it. So I'll give him that; he's in the fire. It's the man he is, and it's what he signed up for.

I was in the fire too. I'd get three, maybe four hours of sleep before I'd be Double Dipping it. We didn't have a clue who'd spiked the banana pudding, or why. Matthew Thatcher was dead. Peyton was out there somewhere. Then there was Alabama, the Heart of Dixie, my home, being taken for a ride, and the biggest inferno of them all, what I couldn't/wouldn't turn my back on, the elderly were being preyed upon. By a church. I had a job to do. It's who I am, and it's what I signed up for.

This was the first time Bradley Cole and I had been in the fire at the same time, and on the dark, cool drive from Beehive to Pine Apple—Fantasy and Bea fast asleep, Cowboy at the wheel staring into the night probably thinking about Stethoscope—I admitted to myself that we'd failed the test, and I contemplated, heart breaking, that we may go our separate ways from here. I don't love Bradley one spec less, but it became clear to me that we could only accommodate the other's obligations as long as they didn't get in the way of our own.

Two fires in one house at the same time may have burned it down.

I should have told him I was pregnant the morning I knew. Which was many, many, mornings ago.

Bradley should have had more faith in me than to believe I'd put what we have on the line for a man I never loved, and never would.

I don't think Bradley had any way of knowing I'd miscarried; I'd been locked up, family only. But he had to have at least suspected it might be me in the hospital. The news had Bianca hospitalized after a meal at Violettes. No way, no way in hell, he could have missed it, even from Vegas. But not acknowledging my email, when we both knew I couldn't sell the condo for peanuts without his signature, which he knew was Davis Code for Let's Work This Out, meant he didn't want to.

And with that, I'm not so sure I wanted to either.

* * *

No Hair's tie was a huge thumbs-up.

"Your tie is ridiculous, No Hair."

"How's that, Davis?"

"I like it," Cowboy said.

"I can't even see it." Fantasy yawned.

It was seven in the morning on Friday. We were in our underground offices, Fantasy, Cowboy, and I only four hours off the road and all in our pajamas, or maybe that was just me.

"Okay." No Hair was fresh as a daisy. I guess so. "Showtime. If anyone from the church is here to recruit new residents at the tournament, we have to catch them," he said. "In the act. Right here and right now. Keep your eyes and ears open. Watch everything and everyone. You two get going." He forked fingers at Fantasy and Cowboy. "Sweep the entire area for bugs or weapons. Go over the guest list for last-minute additions." Fantasy saluted, weakly. No Hair dropped down to one finger and aimed it at Cowboy. "You come back for Davis at nine." They hit the road. "You," he said to me, "sit down." He dropped his jacket across the sofa back and sat down opposite me. "How are you holding up?"

I picked at my pajama pants. "I'll make it."

"Have you heard from your fella?"

I shook my head.

No Hair rubbed his extra-large jaw. I could hear his whiskers. "Have you caught any news these past few days, Davis?"

"No." I studied the ceiling. Nine feet, maybe? "Why? Is he in it?"

No Hair shrugged. "The Grand Palace is all over the news," he said. "The smoking thing. Maybe look it up when you have a minute."

"He's putting out his fires, No Hair," I said, "and I'm putting out mine. I'm sure we'll talk at some point."

I showed No Hair the patient file on Leona Powell.

"How'd you get this?" No Hair asked.

"Cowboy swiped it."

No Hair switched to a defensive position and fired up the finger he loves to wag at me. "Don't start calling that boy a name, Davis," he said. Wag, wag, wag. "I don't know who you're talking about half the time and I get tired of trying to figure it out."

"Are we really taking him on full time?"

"Why?"

"Because he'll need his own sofa," I said. "I don't think we have enough room for another sofa."

No Hair blinked at me for several seconds. "Can we talk about sofas later?"

"You can't keep putting things off, No Hair."

He rubbed his big bald head, looked up at the nine-foot ceiling for help, sighed, shook his head, then reached for the Leona Powell file. Paper flew for a few minutes; he took financials and passed me medical.

Another cup of coffee later, No Hair said, "What we have here are the projected earnings on Leona Powell. They have her going in valued at six hundred and fifty thousand, they think she'll live another dozen years or so, and it looks like her long-term contribution to the *cause*," he used air quotes, "will be a million dollars directly, and they estimated her *healthcare*," air quotes again, "contribution to be half a million."

"That healthcare contribution," I said. "She's scheduled for cognitive, electroconvulsive, obesity, depression, animal, physical, occupational, and mental therapies." I looked up. "I've known Bea all my life, and there's no doubt she needs every bit of it. But what in the heck is animal therapy?"

"That's when they bring in Golden Retrievers for the patients to pet," No Hair said.

"And they invoice the state of Alabama for that."

"No." He passed me a Medicare worksheet. "They invoice the federal government for that."

I compared it to Leona's GOBAHIP worksheet. I stared at the patient number on both documents.

My brain began clicking. Click, click, click.

No Hair's phone rang. Ring, ring, ring.

Someone was coding themselves in the door. Door, door, door.

"Covey." Which is how No Hair answers the phone. Unless it's me. Then he answers, "WHAT?"

Cowboy dropped a folded page of newspaper on top of Leona's paperwork, then rode off into the sunset.

"Got it." No Hair hung up. "That was Richard," he said. "His flight has been delayed. He won't be in tonight. He's going to stop off in Vegas tomorrow, drop off the contracts, then be here Sunday. Go tell Bianca."

"Why can't he tell her?"

"I didn't ask," No Hair said.

"Why can't you tell her?"

"Because he said for you to tell her."

No Hair opened the newspaper and spread it out between us, probably to shut me up, which it did. Page Six was two half-page photographs, each with a small blurb of print. I was below the fold. Bianca wouldn't like that. It was me in the Christmas red big-hat getup as I stepped into the casino for Matthew Thatcher's funeral. My eyes were sparkling saucers, my chocolate-diamond on full display, the expression on my face one of amazed delight. On second thought, Bianca would be thrilled.

Worry not Highest of High rollers, as we welcome you to our fine city for the most exclusive of slot tournaments, the Bellissimo's Double Dip. This breath of fresh and sophisticated air, our own Bianca Sanders, will be behind the microphone for you hosting our biggest event of the season. If you're lucky, it will be your name on her lips as she announces the big winner.

The top half of Page Six, the lead photograph, was heart-wrenching, as if my heart wasn't wrenched enough.

Matthew Thatcher, known to all as Mr. Microphone, was laid to rest in the Urn Garden of the Biloxi City Cemetery on Thursday. Full story on page 2. Police were called in during the night, passersby fearing for the unknown mourner's safety. "We're checking to see if there's a law against sleeping on graves," Biloxi PD Officer Charles Price said. "Vagrancy, certainly, would apply, but to tell the truth, we all feel so sorry for her."

We found Peyton.

* * *

I had an hour alone in the office, two bottles of Miss Clairol Semi-Permanent Honey Blonde on my red hair, and a degree in computer science from UA Birmingham, which at this point, wasn't worth the paper it was printed on. To be a ninja geek, you had to get the degree, then run and jump into the trenches of research and development. I didn't, because I'd rather have a third eyeball. I may have had geek potential at one time, those tweenage years, but by eighth grade I was a solid 32C, and it was not to be. I didn't have the makings of an adult geek freak either, because I didn't like Ramen Noodles at all and I liked Red Bull even less. I'm a good hacker (pat, pat, pat myself on the back), but there again, anyone can learn to hack, just like anyone can learn to rebuild carburetors or make fondant icing.

So the times when I sat down at a computer and didn't get up until I found what I was looking for, I got a lot of credit I wasn't necessarily due. To me, it's no different than sitting down at the kitchen table with a 1,000-piece jigsaw puzzle, but when it's a cyber puzzle, you have a computer in front of you and the puzzle pieces are all over the house. Maybe a few in the basement. And the last piece might be taped under the mailbox across the street. It's a matter of knowing where to look, and to keep looking until something pops. If anything, past common sense, I had the patience and an eye for it. But patience and eyes aren't that rare, so I felt guilty when I turned up something and my father shook his head in amazement. ("Daddy, it's nothing. Really.") Or when No Hair was so stunned by my computer trickeries he got off my back for a few days. (His highest praise.)

Today's puzzle: Was someone in the Alabama government allowing the gross abuse in Beehive? (Yes.) Were they profiting directly? (Of course they were.) If this thing came back on me, would my family have to move to Oregon in the middle of the night? (Yes.) Can you get to Oregon from Alabama? (Doubtful.)

The Alabama Governor's Cabinet is made up of twenty-one members. It took me fifteen minutes to identify the one who was turning a blind eye to the Medicare and GOBAHIP fraud behind the So Help Me God Pentecostal Church in Beehive, and it took an additional two minutes to find her buddy, who was most likely sanctioning the home-equity scams.

I didn't uncover large wire transfers to secret accounts in the Caymans or proof of anyone allocating a million state dollars to build a hush-mansion for the mother of his secret love-child. I found, instead, take-out.

I needed to see the players together, so I asked myself, logging on, when was this group—every elected Alabama politician from Waterloo to Dauphin Island—in one place at one time? Governor's granddaughter's bat mitzvah? (Ha, ha.) Alabama-Auburn football game? (Yes, but I needed them isolated.) The signing of Alabama HB-56? *(¡Claro que sí!)*

The largest gathering of government officials in my home state since the last general election was a few Junes ago, when Alabama made national headlines by adopting the strictest immigration-crackdown laws on the books. We made Arizona look like they were leaving the lights on. Passing on the politics, I searched the photographs, looking for any anomaly—anything or anyone out of place on that summer day. No more than thirty clicks in, I found her. Dr. Brianna Barbosa, head of the Department of Revenue. I searched for separate images taken within five minutes, both ways, of the candid shot she'd been captured in on the steps of the Alabama State House on Union Street in Montgomery, and found her partner in a similar photograph taken in front of the Alabama Judicial Building on Dexter, four blocks away, Associate Justice Lee Garner, Alabama Supreme Court.

On that historic day, Dr. Brianna Barbosa and the Honorable Lee Garner were photographed in large groups of lawmakers, and both were holding take-out cups. From Our Daily Burger. In Beehive.

They wouldn't have driven a hundred miles for a burger. These two had business in Beehive.

* * *

"Crossword puzzles," my father said, "and magnet puzzles."

I had just enough time to check in with my father, who'd been debriefing Cyril Bunker between naps. (Cyril's naps. Although my father has been known to enjoy a good rainy Sunday afternoon nap, too.)

"What they're billing as cognitive therapy is nothing more than gathering the residents into a cafeteria-style room and passing out crossword puzzles."

"What?"

"Aromatherapy," Daddy continued, "which is one of their biofield therapies, is sitting in the same room with lit candles."

"I've never even heard of a biofield."

"It's a category of alternative healing therapies," my father said, "including music, same room, Frank Sinatra on the stereo, and magnet therapy, same room, magnet puzzles."

"How are magnets considered therapy?"

"I don't have a clue, but they categorize it as both biofield and cognitive therapies, and write it up and bill it as both."

"Doubling their revenue."

"Their revenues have got to be through the roof, honey. Cyril says they wake the residents from sound sleep to get them in the therapy room, and keep them in some manner of treatment until the day's done. If there's any grumbling or complaining," Daddy said, "they're moved to physical therapy. Very physical therapy."

"Is Cyril saying they're *abused* if they don't go along with the all-day crossword puzzles?"

"He described it more as a constant threat over the residents' heads. When the staff meets resistance, or insubordination, the patients find themselves in what sounds like very aggressive physical therapy until they agree to be compliant."

"That's abuse."

"Yes," my father admitted. "Yes it is."

"I feel sick."

"Get your ducks in a row, Davis, and turn this over to the feds."

"That's the plan."

"Watch your back."

"Always."

TWENTY-THREE

My Double Dip handler, a six-foot-tall marketing executive named Laney Harris, clearly wasn't a fan. Of Bianca's. I'd never even *seen* this girl.

She led me to my dressing house—no way this amount of space could be called a room—at a cool clip, and she walked fast, too. I plopped down across from her and tried to catch my breath, in a corner of the dressing house set aside for relaxation—refreshments, Barcaloungers, every flat surface hosting crystal ashtrays, a fresh pack of Bianca's ciggies, with gold lighters on the side.

"Have we met before, Laney?"

The woman's dark eyes narrowed to slits.

We'd met all right, and I (Bianca) had royally pissed her off.

"You might remember firing me?" She crossed her long legs the other way. "In front of a hundred people?"

(Didn't remember that.)

"Yet here you are!" I flashed my pearly whites.

"Your husband," she explained.

"He's a sweetheart." I glazed over with true love at the very thought of him.

(And the Oscar goes to Davis Way.)

Her jury was still way out.

"I've got to tell you, Laney," I leaned in, sincerely, "there are times when I go off my meds." Cowboy, a foot behind me, tried to cover laughing with coughing. "Today's not one of those days." I wagged a no-no-no finger. "I'm on every color pill they make. I apologize for my behavior that day, and I'd like us to start over." I stuck my hand out. "Bianca Sanders." She didn't move a muscle, and my hand was in the air. "How about a big fat bonus for having to put up with me for the next three days?" She looked at me suspiciously, and my hand was still out there. "Five thousand bucks."

Finally, the woman shook my hand. Fifteen minutes later, she cracked a smile. An hour later, we were BFFs.

Honestly, I take decent care of myself. I wear sunscreen. I throw out old lip gloss. I exfoliate. I drink tons of water, because it takes tons of water to make tons of coffee. Fifty people came after me like I'd never picked up a hairbrush in my life. I was cuffed and shackled to a salon chair, then ambushed by Bianca's New Orleans team from the Salon du Beau Monde on St. Joseph's. I was pummeled, marinated, and snipped on unmercifully. A girl trying her best to chop off my fingers asked, "Do you bury bones in the backyard?" The contractor for the remodeling job was the salon's owner, the man (?) named Seattle who did mine and Bianca's hair, and at his elbow, tsk, tsk, tsking with him, and not discreetly, was my assistant.

"I tell to her, and I tell to her." Seattle wore rings on every finger and bells on every toe.

"I feel ya, Seattle," said my assistant. "She doesn't listen to a word I say either."

My handler, Laney Harris, in a director's chair beside me, leaned in. "She really shouldn't speak of you that way, Mrs. Sanders."

"Please," I dabbed at my stinging eyes with a linen towel, "call me Bianca."

"What's her name?"

Her shot me a dirty look.

"Fantasia," I said. "And yes, she does have an attitude."

Attitude accidentally knocked into me, almost spilling me into Laney's lap. "Ooops." Fantasy said. "My bad, Bianca."

Laney scribbled.

I mouthed, *pink slip*, to Fantasia. (Fantasy!)

Laney stood. "Could we have the room please?"

Jackhammers, industrial sanders, and diesel-powered vise grips were all powered down, and the Pimp My Ride team happily took a cocktail break. Fantasy found a Barcalounger out of (within) ear shot, stretched out, then covered her head with a million-dollar dress from my wardrobe rack.

"She's fine," I stopped Laney, who was warming up to let Fantasy have it. "Let her stay."

Laney passed me a guest list. "Look over this," she said, "while I tell you a little about the tournament."

The glossy ten-page roster gave me fifty names, accompanying photos, Bellissimo player numbers, the amount of money they had dropped/picked up here in the past six months, and where they were from. I recognized half of the faces, but not names. Blinks-too-much was actually Francine Poston from Arkadelphia, Arkansas, and Jack T. Colton, from *Romancing the Stone*, was really Ernie Fish, from Marietta, Georgia. I'd have rather not known that.

"This event is the brainchild of the late Matthew Thatcher." Laney crossed herself, Catholic style. "And it's an absolute cash cow." She handed me a spreadsheet, dotted yellow in places. "The entry fees pay for the entire tournament."

$25,000 multiplied by fifty was a very long number typed out.

"Now, the production costs are high," she said, "but the three-day spike in casino revenue is ten times what the tournament costs." She leaned over and pointed out a highlight. "Profits go up twenty-seven percent, handily covering the expenses, which include custom software and graphics for the tournament slot machines, labor, transportation, hotel, and food costs."

My brain calculator was spitting out numbers all over the place.

"And just to cover all our bases," she said, "we charge a hundred spectators twenty-five-hundred dollars each to watch."

I had one of those pricey spectator invitations on my desk.

"We do that," Laney said, "as a means of enticing them to participate in the tournament next year. You know," her hands danced, "the hoopla and all. A catch-the-tournament-fever thing."

Clever, Mr. Microphone. I crossed myself, Catholic style.

"And the spectators go to the casino between tournament events and contribute to the bottom line, too." Laney pointed out another highlight. "Now," she said, "I'll let you in on the secret."

For the next fifteen minutes, I just listened.

The first year, the tournament only drew twenty players, probably because the entry fee had so many zeros. Matthew Thatcher (cross, cross, cross) had proposed they let *two* players win, talked Mr. Sanders into it, and it paid off, because participation for the next year, and every subsequent year, including this one, was cut off at fifty players. First-come, first-serve.

The inaugural-year theme was Planes, Trains, and Automobiles. The invitations were die-cut jumbo jets and the ballroom had been transformed into a ritzy airport terminal. The servers were decked out as almost-naked flight attendants, Matthew Thatcher (cross, cross, cross) the pilot. There was the guaranteed million-dollar tournament winner, the player among the twenty-five who racked up the most points, but during the last round of play a lady—not the million-dollar winner—lined up three cars on her slot machine. Surprise jackpot. She won a peacock blue Rolls Royce Phantom Bespoke. The crowd, the media, and especially the lady who won the car were thrilled. From then on, the tournament sold out before the formal invitations arrived in the mail.

The following year, the theme had been Pay the Rent. The ballroom was given a bank-lobby remodel; the servers sexy bank tellers, Matthew Thatcher a loan officer. One player won the million, and another player lined up three run-down tenement houses in his slot-machine window, winning a 2,200-square-foot penthouse apartment on the Upper East Side with a Central Park view.

The year after that, the theme was Silver Lining. The cocktail talent had to be flown in from Vegas last-minute, because while Southern girls didn't have a problem with the silver bikinis and five-inch heels, they fell all over themselves trying to hold up the forty-pound rhinestone and silver-feather headdresses. Matthew Thatcher wore a silver tux. A thirty-year-old woman won the million and her husband lined up three gold bars on his slot machine, winning ten pounds of 2 ounce 99.99% pure Engelhard gold bars.

The press dubbed them Mr. & Mrs. Lucky.

Last year the tournament theme was City Life, the slot machines housed in a custom-built open-air tour bus, the staff dressed as cab drivers in fedoras and high heels with not much in between, Matthew Thatcher a subway conductor, and the surprise win went to the man whose slot machine lined up three palm trees on little patches of dirt surrounded by water—a beachfront mansion on a private island in the Caribbean.

"Mrs. Sanders?" Laney waved a hand in front of my face. "Bianca?"

"Cool beans." I said it on a whoosh of air.

Laney nodded. "It's fun."

"Do I have to dress up as an ice-cream cone?" Bianca had already chosen every stitch of clothing I was to wear, all the way down to nude thongs and the stick-on fake bra things that felt like slabs of raw chicken. ("The only acceptable undergarments David, aside from the obvious fact that you need Spanx.") (She's the one who needed Spanx.)

"Well," Laney said, "we tossed that around, and given the amount of time we didn't have, we decided we'd like you to be your glamorous self." She tucked the stack of photographic tournament history back in her leather portfolio. "We just need you to be beautiful."

"What was Matthew Thatcher going to wear?" My guesses: a banana split, milkshake, or root beer float costume.

"We had him in a bright red tux," she said. "He was going to be a maraschino cherry."

I think I snorted.

"What's the big surprise win?"

Her eyebrows danced. "Come on." She actually held a hand out. "I'll show you."

I followed her around bends and curves to the stage entrance of the ballroom, at a much reduced pace than earlier. She paused at the door. "You know," she said, "if you don't mind me saying so, you've really changed." Her hand was on the doorknob. "Almost as if you're happy. About being here."

"It's the meds."

She opened the door and we stepped into Candyland.

The slot machines were powered down and wearing capes. Four security guards, in rainbow sherbet tuxedoes, were on point around them.

"May I?" The lime-green security guard nodded.

Laney pushed back the lemon-yellow drape from the first machine. The play area of the slot machine was full of ice cream: single scoops, double scoops, and triple scoops. I saw one, a double dip on a sugar cone, wearing a sparkly sprinkle diamond topping. It was diamonds. The surprise was diamonds. Someone would leave this tournament with a million dollars, and someone else would leave with a really nice rock.

The welcome reception, an hour later, was held in a room adjacent to the ballroom, decked out as an old-fashioned soda shop, the servers in short skirts, halter tops, and roller skates. The soda-shop drinks they were rolling around with were spiked, and they weren't serving burgers and fries. They were serving caviar on matsutake mushrooms.

I wore an Aidan Maddox silver beaded dress, strappy silver mirrored-leather Jimmy Choos, the chicken-cutlets bra, and a wireless microphone hidden in a small diamond brooch. Instead of a bodypack, the transmitter was a rhinestone ring I tapped off and on.

"Showtime," Fantasy had a hand on the door.

"Have fun, Bianca," my new BFF said.

I stepped in and within a minute, you could have heard a flea sneeze.

"Welcome to the Double Dip slot tournament." I raised a Waterford crystal flute full of Krug champagne and promised the excited attendees the time of their lives.

* * *

At eleven that night, down in the bunker, I was busy getting out of a Stella McCartney gold brocade dress and matching platform pumps (my dogs were *barking*), while everyone else was stretched out on the gold sofas.

"Cowboy," Fantasy said, "you haven't been here long enough for a sofa. Move."

"Well?" No Hair asked, when I fell into the seat Cowboy had warmed up for me wearing yoga pants, flip-flops, and a sweatshirt.

"I had a ball!" My words came out on a laugh. It *was* fun, and it was distracting. In the middle of the first round of tournament play, a mental picture of Bradley Cole popped into my brain, and I honestly felt a stab of guilt when I realized I'd been so caught up in the excitement I hadn't thought of him in hours. My ear-to-ear smile slid off as I picked up my heart, and Cowboy, who was proving himself to be good at having my back, had jumped, thinking something was wrong.

"You were great!" Fantasy said. "Bianca's stock rose through the roof, girl. She'll be lovin' all over you tomorrow."

I could use some all-over lovin'. Not necessarily from Bianca.

"Who authorized five-thousand bucks to the marketing girl?" No Hair tapped a gigantic foot.

My good-for-nothing coworkers pointed at me. No Hair's nostrils flared.

"So?" I changed the subject. "Did we catch anyone?"

"As of yet we don't have anyone in or near the tournament who has any obvious connection to Beehive," No Hair said, "including our own staff. But seven of the spectators didn't check in for the first round, so we'll take a hard look at them when they do. And these two players popped." He passed out eight-by-tens. "They're the most likely candidates for the church scam, so I've put round-the-clock surveillance on them. This first one, Florence Cole, age sixty-eight, is from Beaumont, Texas. She's a widow and lost her only son in the Gulf War seven years ago. Her closest relatives are a set of nieces in the Los Angeles area and she's from Cadillac money."

"She's a perfect Beehive target," Fantasy said.

"Yes, she is," No Hair agreed.

"What's Cadillac money?" Cowboy asked.

"Her family owned Cadillac dealerships in Texas." No Hair rubbed cash fingers in the air. "This is her first year in the tournament."

"Dragonfly." They all looked at me. "She had a dragonfly pinned on her shoulder at the tournament today. I thought it was a bug and tried to knock it off."

No Hair took a deep breath. "The other player who could have a big Beehive bullseye on his back is this guy," he said. "A man named Otis Cummings."

"Hush Puppies."

Fantasy asked if he had a dog on his shoulder.

I told her he was *wearing* Hush Puppies.

"What are hush puppies?" Cowboy asked.

"Shoes," No Hair and I said.

"He's sixty-six years old, from Augusta, Georgia, and his family was in the peppermint candy business," No Hair said. "Big bucks." He shifted his weight. The whole room slid starboard. "He wrote his three sons out of his will a decade ago."

"Peppermint money." Cowboy looked like he could taste it.

"Watch them both." No Hair shifted his weight again, and the room slid port. "Stay sharp. If anyone from Beehive is here to recruit these people, we're going to intervene."

Aye, aye, Captain.

The room settled, then grew still, too still, except for throat clearing (No Hair), yawning (Fantasia), and eyes darting (Cowboy).

"I'll do it." I said it on a long weary sigh.

"That would be best," No Hair said. "I know you're tired, Davis. We're all tired and we all have to be right back here bright and early tomorrow, but maybe it'll go quickly."

"That," I said, "or one of you will have to get out of bed and identify my body."

"I'm going with you," Cowboy said. "I'll identify your body." He jangled car keys. "Ready when you are."

It was a twelve-mile drive, but with Cowboy at the reins, we were there in a blink. We parked at a praying angel with a six-foot wing span.

"Stay back a little bit, Cowboy."

The flip-flops were a bad idea. My achy feet turned to ice as I made my way through the winding concrete paths. I knelt down beside her and put my hand in the middle of her back. "Peyton," I whispered. "Come on."

Her lips were blue, her eyes red, her skin almost translucent. She was slack and prone on the cold ground.

"Let me help you up," I whispered. "Come with me. Get some sleep," I said. "We'll get you something to eat, some clean clothes, a warm bed, then I'll bring you back in the morning."

Cowboy scooped her up like a rag doll.

* * *

One might think after my day, my week, my month, my *life*, I'd pass out before my head hit the pillow, but when I climbed into the empty bed, sleep wouldn't come at all. It might have been the dull buzz ringing in my ears because of the slot-machine din earlier, but that wasn't it. Tonight's insomnia was brought to me by the letter B, for Bradley, and by the letter P, for Paperwork, because something I'd seen earlier had been waiting patiently at my brain door all day.

I wasn't about to get out of bed, sneak past Peyton (in the guest room again) and Cowboy (sleeping on my marshmallow sofa again), then drive to work, but I did throw back the covers, pad across the room, and fire up my laptop.

I looked up Leona Powell's Bellissimo player number. 8709074.

What was Leona Powell's So Help Me God resident identification number? 008709074.

Hack, hack, hack into the church's Senior Residence Center.

I ran the resident identification numbers against the Bellissimo player list.

More than sixty percent of the So Help Me God residents had come straight from the Bellissimo.

And while I was at it...

How much did GOBAHIP shell out to So Help Me God last year?

Hack, hack, hack. Three-point-eight million.

How much did Medicare pay So Help You God during the same time period?

Firewall one, hacked. Firewall two, hacked. Firewall three, hacked.

Three-point-eight million.

They were billing Medicare and GOBAHIP simultaneously for the exact same therapy treatments.

So Help Me God was double dipping.

TWENTY-FOUR

Bianca Sanders was in a foul mood, which meant it was one of the seven days of the week. "Can't you be a little more reserved, David? Must you get in everyone's face and shriek, like a madwoman?"

I batted through the cigarette smoke. "Have you ever been to one of the tournaments, Mrs. Sanders? It's exciting. And the excitement is contagious."

"I would like to have a little dignity left when this event is over. And I'm telling you to use better judgment and conduct yourself with a little more *decorum.*" She tapped her cigarette ashes into a waste can full of paper. "Stop groping and fawning strangers, David."

"It's Davis."

She smoked.

"How's your foot, Mrs. Sanders?"

I only asked because I could see her warming up for round two. Obviously, her foot was better. For one, she'd traveled unassisted down thirty stories, the length of the mezzanine, behind Shakes, then two more floors down, where she scared us all to death by trying to beat the door down.

And she calls me a madwoman.

For two, she was wearing designer espadrilles in a very light creamy color no one but her would buy, because they'd get dirty the second they came out of the box, and I couldn't see a bulk of bandages under the fabric. She was working undercover today as a designer ghost, dressed head to toe in the same ivory color. She had on an eggshell trench coat, double-breasted, with wide floppy lapels, and pleated cuffs. (I want one. Pretty.) She had a wide silk scarf in a buttermilk color wrapped and tucked around her head, and milky-framed Cat Woman sunglasses. Until she yanked them off. "Don't change the subject, David."

She went on to instruct me to pack my bags for West Palm Beach, Florida. She'd booked us suites at the Willoughby. (Never heard of such.) We would leave by Bellissimo jet on Monday morning. Dr. Doogie Howser would be accompanying us.

"When will we be back?" I asked.

"After I've healed."

"From what?"

"I'm having my neck done."

(Snapped? She could have that done here.)

"The beach sounds lovely, Mrs. Sanders." It sounded harrowing. "Do you need me for security purposes?"

"No." She put her Cat Woman glasses back on, blew a plume of smoke big enough to set off alarms, and turned for the door. "I need your neck."

I grabbed it with both hands.

"Wear the lace peplum this morning," she said, "and for God's sake, don't make a spectacle of yourself."

I counted to ten. "The coast is clear!"

Cowboy popped up from behind a sofa and Fantasy came out of the closet. "What is her problem?" Cowboy asked.

"Doesn't matter," I said. "Let's finish these background checks."

"You have twenty minutes, Davis." Fantasy tapped her watch.

Nineteen minutes later, we had No Hair on speakerphone. I did the honors. "I've run today's new faces through the system and there are no Beehive connections."

"Okay." No Hair's booming voice made the phone shake. "We can't let our guard down, because whoever poisoned the pudding is still out there, but at this point it's safe to assume no one from Beehive is at the tournament. Matthew Thatcher was their in, and now he's out." (Cross, cross, cross.) "They haven't had time to regroup and we'll shut them down before they do."

Sirens blared from control central. "Hold on, No Hair." I ran in there. Every screen was flashing; we had a facial-recognition hit in the lobby.

"Who is that?" Cowboy was right behind me.

"That's Matthew Thatcher's grandmother." Fantasy was right behind Cowboy.

I ran back to the phone and took it off speaker mode. "No Hair," I said, "we spoke too soon. Jewell Maffini is in the lobby."

"I got her," No Hair said. "Have Baylor meet me."

Who?

On the way to the convention level to get gussied up for Double Dip Round Two, Fantasy chitchatted, which is how she starts when there's something she needs to get off her chest.

"What's up with Peyton?"

"That girl's a mess," I said. "Staring at the walls."

"Tell me there's security on her."

"Yes," I said. "No Hair has security outside my building, in the garage, and inside the door. They're on banana pudding patrol and suicide watch."

"Your poor condo."

"Tell me about it."

"She's wily," Fantasy said. "She could have easily pulled off the banana pudding business."

"And hit the wrong target," I said. "Which may be what her problem is."

"Or hit the right target," Fantasy said, "and regrets it."

"Could be."

"Man, it's getting cold out."

The elevator dinged and the doors opened to the convention level.

"What is it, Fantasy? Just say it."

She pounced. "You've given up on Bradley."

"No, I haven't."

"Yes, you have." She had a hand on the bouncing doors. "You're not being fair to him."

"*Fair*?" Fair? "He hasn't exactly been giving me the benefit of the doubt lately, Fantasy, which I don't think is particularly *fair*."

"You owe him the truth, Davis. You need to tell him."

She let the doors close and punched random numbers.

"You're avoiding him."

"I've been a little busy, thank you."

"No one's that busy."

The doors opened to a guest floor. Fantasy glared at three people who each had a leg mid-air. They decided to wait.

"Have you called him?"

I sniffed.

"Do you even know where he is?"

I shrugged. I think we were going down. "The last time we spoke he was headed to Vegas to hammer out a settlement deal, so I guess he's there." Now we were going up. "If that's changed I wouldn't know because he hasn't called."

"Why don't *you* call *him*, Davis?"

"Last time I checked, Fantasy, they still had phones in Las Vegas. He can call me if he wants to talk. And it's none of your business anyway."

Uh-oh. Mighta shoulda coulda worded that differently.

"What did you just say to me?"

And now we were in each other's faces. The doors opened *again*.

"GO AWAY!" We both screamed it. At No Hair.

"What the *hell*?"

No Hair and Cowboy had the dishrag that was Jewell Maffini between them. She looked to be in no better shape than Peyton. In fact, she looked worse.

"What is going on here, ladies?" No Hair's big head jerked back and forth between us.

"Nothing, No Hair." I smoothed my blonde hair. "We're fine."

He hairy-eyeballed Fantasy, then he hairy-eyeballed me. He

swept his arm out: After you, Mrs. Maffini. She stepped in hesitantly, found a corner as far away from Fantasy and me as she could, then squeezed herself into it.

"This is Jewell Maffini," No Hair said. "And she's here to talk."

"I'm sorry about your grandson," I said.

It started with a whisper, it worked its way to a wail. I mean it, the woman detonated.

Cowboy pushed C for Convention Level. "Never a dull moment."

* * *

For all the fun and frivolity on the outside of a slot machine—you can catch fish, choose your favorite Brady (Peter), or spin the wheel—they're all the same on the inside: motors, gears, graphics on spinning reels, computer chips, cash/voucher collectors, and wires, wires, wires.

The player puts money in. The machine eats the money. The player hits a button or pulls a lever, and a very long number randomly generated by a computer program tells the mechanical reels where to stop.

Most of the time, the reels stop on a combination that doesn't win—Sam the Butcher, Tiger, Carol Brady. But every once in a while, the reels stop on a winner—Marcia, Marcia, Marcia!

It's a cold, electrical, mechanical, computerized process on the inside, it's everything but on the outside. More and more, with video-display slot machines replacing traditional three-reel slot machines, they could, and did, put on a show.

The Double Dip slot machines put on a show like none I'd ever seen.

Tournament machines are different in a few distinct ways. One, they have a different computer chip; they're set to win and win and win. And win. Two, they're pre-loaded with credits, in this case a thousand credits per machine, each round. And three, they're on timers. After a pre-set amount of play time they come to a screeching halt. There is a fourth, and very remarkable feature of tournament slot machines—the tournament administrators know which machine will be the grand-prize winner beforehand.

The Double Dip tournament slot machines had made a huge splash during the first round of play on Friday night. When the third wheel fell into place, the screen suddenly burst alive, sending 3-D sprinkles everywhere. Chocolate sprinkles burst from scoops of strawberry ice cream, multi-colored sprinkles exploded from vanilla scoops, and shiny gold sprinkles appeared out of nowhere to top chocolate scoops. The sound effects that accompanied the sprinkles were incredible—cymbals, pinball trills, cannon booms, hand-bell arpeggios—and it happened every five seconds on fifty different machines.

I couldn't wait to see it all again and at the crack of noon Saturday, when I finally got it together enough to step through the curtain, the fifty players, their plus-ones, along with the hundred paid spectators and their plus-ones, broke into thunderous applause. They seemed very happy to see me and none of us could wait to see the slot machines in action again.

Three hundred bodies turned my way. I tapped the microphone ring on and hailed out to the crowd, arms open wide, "Who's ready for a Double Dip?" The crowd reacted as if I'd said, "A million dollars and a puppy for everyone!"

Two waitresses, dressed as cupcakes (teeny silver pleated skirts that looked like cupcake liners and six-inch strips of white organza for icing tops) each took one of my hands and led me down the stage steps, Miss America style, for my pre-tournament meet-and-greet. I worked the crowd as quickly as I could in an attempt to cover the room. I kissed cheeks, I squeezed hands, I hugged, I congratulated, I welcomed, and I took a sip of a lady's blueberry martini she promised me was delicious. (It was.) I showed the crowd my blue teeth, and they roared with laughter, then cupcake waitresses were sent scrambling. "I want blue teeth like Bianca!"

No Hair boomed into my earpiece. "Davis, don't eat or drink...hands you! Do you want to...in the hospital?" I pretended to fiddle with my Marco Bicego drop earrings, but I was really pressing my earpiece, because No Hair's big mouth was still going. "...watching by close-circuit, and threw...at the television. Tone it down unless...ripping your head off."

I squealed with delight as a player waved a phone in my face. "Mrs. Alexander! Is that your new grandbaby?" That baby looked like E.T.

Round Two upset the leader board. A woman from New Orleans gained a substantial point lead, having lined up triple scoops four times during the twenty-minute round—sprinkles bursting everywhere with spectacular fireworks sound effects—and second and third places were only a scoop apart. When the machines powered down, the contestants kept their seats as Armani-suited accountants from Deloitte recorded player scores. The accountants started at one end, I started at the other with a cordless mic.

"Good grief, Mr. Rosenberg! Give someone else a chance!"

He was dead last, but he enjoyed the attention so much, he forgot. I wished him luck for round three. Down the row.

"Elaine Vega! Stand up! Could we have a spotlight? What's this I heard about you?" I grabbed her hand and held it up high. "Everyone say hello to Mrs. Vega! Look at this ring! Elaine's a newlywed!" She turned fifty shades of red. "Elaine," I covered my mouth with my hand, "just between us girls—" (into a microphone for all to hear) "—this marriage business ain't all it's cracked up to be." The audience, who loved Bianca's husband, roared.

And on. Until the accountants finished and I'd let everyone know how much we appreciated their money. (Them being there! Them being there!) I made my way to the stage. Someone in the audience shouted, "We love you, Bianca!" I found him, made eye contact across the big room, and told him I loved him too. He beat on his chest with both fists. I announced current first, second, and third places with a drumroll soundtrack, and told them I couldn't wait to see them tonight.

The dizzy crowd exited the front and took a left for the banquet hall where they would have a fancy lunch, as a clean-up and overhaul crew entered through the back to repair and reset the room. Technicians came in from a side door and positioned themselves for the best possible views of the cupcake waitresses, who were clearing tables. Security entered through a different door to lock down the room while the techs switched computer chips in all fifty machines.

My marketing handler, Laney Harris, was waiting for me at the stage door after I said my goodbyes and good lucks to the tournament participants. "You're a rock star, Bianca." She handed me off to my assistant Fantasia, who looked like she'd seen a ghost.

I stopped dead in my Dolce & Gabbana tracks. Was it Bradley Cole?

Laney, no flies on her, said, "I'll leave you two alone." She shooed everyone out of the dressing house.

"Sit down, Davis," Fantasy said.

I collapsed into the salon chair.

"It's your grandmother."

I bent over double, like I'd been chopped in two.

"Not that, Davis! Not that!" She crouched to my level. "It's not that anything bad has happened." She tilted my face up. "Your family can't *find* her."

"Fantasy, you can't *hide* in Pine Apple!" I cried. "Something's happened to her!"

She passed me my phone. "Here," she said. "Get it together. Call home."

The door burst open, and Bianca came roaring in, dressed exactly like she had been this morning, except she'd been dipped in black paint. Black shoes, trench coat, sunglasses, and scarf.

I shot out of the salon chair. "No!" I yelled. "I'm not listening to it, Bianca. Get out!" I pointed for the door with a shaky hand.

She stood there statue still. She spun and left, Dr. Quinn Medicine Woman on her heels.

There goes my job.

* * *

It took a lot to rock my sister. When I got Meredith on the phone, though, she was a driveling puddle. "Oh, God, Davis! We can't find her anywhere!"

"Who else is missing, Meredith?"

"*What*? We're looking for Granny, Davis. We're not taking roll all over town."

"Where's Cyril Bunker?"

"How would I know where Cyril is? Again, Davis, we're looking for *Granny*."

"Go find Cyril. And let me talk to Daddy."

"Daddy's out looking," she wailed. "Call him on his cell."

Fantasy traded me a glass of water for my phone. She scrolled to my father's number, tapped, then handed it back.

"Daddy."

"Cyril's gone too," my father said, no preamble.

I was born on his page.

"Surely neither of them would try to drive, Daddy. They've got to be with someone. Who else is missing? Who's driving them?"

He must have had his window down, because I heard the crunch of gravel. Then I heard nothing until, "Eddie."

I made immediate plans to kill him. (Eddie.) Dead. Very, very dead.

"Eddie's Lincoln isn't in front of his trailer," Daddy said, "and it's only one o'clock."

Eddie Crawford, that total rat bastard, didn't roll out of bed until three, and everyone knew it.

"Where could they be? Have you checked Cyril's old property? Maybe they just took a ride."

"I tried that first," Daddy said.

"Have you tried Bates Turkey? Maybe they just went to Greenville for lunch."

"I called," Daddy said.

Oh, no. No, no, no.

"He's taken them to Andalusia, Daddy." I said it on a very long sigh. "They're at the Sweet Gum Bottom Wedding Chapel. It's where we eloped the second time." I almost choked on the words.

"Sweet Jesus." My father's foulest language.

He called me back five minutes later. That's where they were. My eighty-two-year-old grandmother and her eighty-eight-year-old beau were eloping. The officiate told Daddy that the bride and groom were napping on chapel pews, and he would conduct the ceremony as soon as they woke up. The man who drove them there had been drinking heavily and steadily, and the officiate was a little concerned.

"When you get there, shoot him, Daddy," I said. "Just get it over with."

I staggered to a Barcalounger and dropped into it. Fantasy perched on the arm of the Barcalounger across from me. The sudden silence was eerie. A twinkle sparked in Fantasy's eye and a smile crept across her face. I caught it.

"Ain't love grand?" she asked on a laugh.

We laughed until we decided it was time for blueberry martinis. "They're so good!" I told her. "They taste like pie in a glass."

"You'd better have two, Davis. You're going to have to get your butt to the Elvis floor and grovel."

Right. There was that.

TWENTY-FIVE

A criminal's number one fear is being caught. A criminal's number one relief is being caught.

Sometime during being cuffed, transported, and processed, they realize somewhere down the road there will be a decent night's sleep in it for them. Once they recognize they've turned the corner from hunted to trapped, the confessions begin spewing. As they confess, they name accomplices. They want you to know who made them do this—names, shoe sizes, all known baby-mamas—and where they, the *real* criminals, can be found. Many, by the time you get them in the box, can't wait to tell you all about it. They're tired of the burden, the guilt, and looking over their shoulder. The future suddenly looks brighter than the immediate past, as the future holds a like-minded community, three squares, and much-needed supervision.

None of this applies to drunks.

I've been in prison (a story for another day), and it wasn't that way for me, either, but there again, I'm not a criminal. Or a drunk.

Jewell Maffini had been carrying an extra-large load. She'd watched her grandson turn his back on all that she'd raised him to be, which was mild-mannered, unambitious, and careful. "Blend in, LeeRoy. It's safer." She'd watched him merrily walk away from his heritage—his Catholic faith, ginger-colored hair, and strong Maffini nose. What started out as a simple solution to their problems, and fun to boot, turned into something that took her grandson from her, and all she could do was stand by helplessly and watch as the

So Help Me God scams exploded, with her grandson, carrying a microphone torch, leading the way.

Jewell blamed herself. She felt certain that if not for her, her LeeRoy would be alive today. To make up for it, she'd do anything within her power to right the wrongs. Of which there were many.

No Hair let Jewell get settled in—cream and sugar? too hot in here?—and think about it, while he kept a closed-circuit eye on us, Double Dipping Round Two. He gave her just enough time to stew and when he stepped back into the room, Jewell began spilling her guts on video at about the same time Fantasy and I were enjoying our first blueberry martinis. Delicious blueberry martinis. Well-deserved blueberry martinis. Hard-earned blueberry martinis. You get my point.

At the same time, my family was scrambling to cover the fifty miles between Pine Apple and the Sweet Gum Bottom Wedding Chapel in Andalusia. I spoke to my father once and could hear the rest of my family in the background, after his patrol-car siren finally faded. "God, leave that off, Daddy. I'm getting a migraine." (Meredith.) "I'm a flower child!" (My niece Riley.) "Flower girl." (My mother.) "You don't want to be a flower child. It's flower *girl*."

No Hair asked Jewell if he thought our resident (literally, for me) flower child, Peyton Beecher Maffini, was capable of murder, and Jewell stated what we all believed, Peyton is capable of anything.

Fantasy and I locked the dressing house doors so no unwelcome visitors would barge in while we enjoyed our second, well-deserved, blueberry martinis. No Hair called as we contemplated a third round (hard-earned, blah, blah), and had me forward my So Help Me God zip files to him, which I did via laptop. "Good God, Davis." It took a while to download. "What is all this?"

"Ethidence."

"Are you drinking?"

The Office of the Inspector General for the Department of Health and Human Services, the FBI, and the Alabama Attorney General had been notified, and they were scrambling. In Montgomery, Alabama, the offices of Dr. Brianna Barbosa, head of the Department of Revenue, and Associate Justice Lee Garner of the Alabama Supreme Court, were being raided. Beehive, Alabama, was not going to know what hit it when one hundred fifty federal agents and two hundred healthcare workers swooped in, sometime in the next forty-eight hours. "We're almost ready," a federal agent said, then asked, "Who put this package together? We want to hire them." Which was good, considering I'd be unemployed the second the Double Dip tournament was over.

Documents were shuffled around in Las Vegas, Nevada, too, as Richard Sanders would soon arrive, then sign off on the Macau deal, and a text had come from my marketing handler, Laney Harris, to inform me Mr. Sanders would make it back to Biloxi in time to make an appearance at the Double Dip grand finale tonight, or at least for the awards ceremony afterward. GOOD NEWS. YOUR HUSBAND'S ON THE WAY! ;)

I wondered why *she* got my husband's schedule before I did.

Wait.

It would be nice to have Mr. Sanders back at the helm, but I hoped to be far, far away for the debriefing. If that chore somehow fell to me and Fantasy, he'd say, "Okay, ladies, let's hear it," and we would start babbling sweet nothings. "Garbage Cowboy. Bitch stole my gun. Banana Therapy. Don't smoke microphones."

We only made it halfway through our third lunch martini before we decided a nap was in order.

"Leth's see." Fantasy's arm zoomed in and out as she tried to focus on the big hand and the little hand. "We can sleep for oneth hour."

I was drunk.

* * *

The coffee woke me up. That, and Cowboy poking me. "Davis. Get up."

We'd slept for threeth hours.

"Bradley?" I sat straight up in my Barcalounger. "Bradley Cole?"

"Whaaaa?" Fantasy, hair out to there, shot straight up in hers.

"What time is it, Cowboy?" I stretched. "How'd you get in here?"

"I came through the ballroom," he said, "and it's three-thirty."

I resumed my previous position. "Plenty of time."

He picked up Fantasy's half-full martini glass and helped himself to a sip. Then he began spitting and spewing. "This is *horrible*. Have you two ever heard of this new thing they call *beer*?" He picked up a house phone. A minute later he said, "One of everything on the menu, heavy on the carbs, and send a bottle of aspirin."

He dropped a folded section of newspaper on me and with his foot, pushed my Barcalounger to a sitting position. He took two steps and did the same to Fantasy. There was groaning.

Page Six. *Bellissimo's Shiniest Star, Bianca Sanders.*

I flipped it around for Fantasy to see. "You look like a movie star, David."

"Bianca's decided to let you live," Cowboy said.

"Where's that aspirin?"

* * *

Coffee, showers, coffee, aspirin, jeans and T-shirts, coffee, and turkey clubs later, we assembled in Mr. Sanders' office.

"These are the personal effects from his desk, Mrs. Maffini." I put the box in front of her. We'd have to ship the photographs he had of himself to her on a flat-bed truck. The box was full of trinkets, a winter scarf, and a stapler.

Jewel Maffini was in her early seventies, but today she looked in her early hundreds. She wore a dark red cardigan over black knit pants, flat rubber-soled shoes, and her hair was a helmet of stiff, dyed, wheat-colored curls. She twisted the wool scarf into a ball and hugged it. "I'd like to see where he lived."

"That means seeing Peyton," I said.

"I'd like to see Peyton," she said. "I want to talk to Peyton."

Maybe the two halves would make a whole.

Maybe we could get them out of my place and into his.

Cowboy carried the box and the two of them left for the Regent.

"He's savvy enough to listen in. Right?" (Fantasy.)

"He's sharp," No Hair said, "but he can't hear through walls." He turned to me. "We hooked up your place with audio this morning."

The words sank in slowly. "I'm moving."

"Okay, ladies." No Hair's beady eyes narrowed to slits. "And I use that term loosely." He looked at the clock. "You have a couple of hours before you need to be downstairs for the tournament. I need to prepare for Richard's return and I'd like, very much, if you two would stay here, out of trouble, until it's time for you to get dressed." (Me. Fantasy was already dressed.)

We nodded.

"I mean it."

We nodded. Nod, nod, nod.

I knew what she was thinking. She knew I knew what she was thinking. We both knew that we knew what both of us were thinking.

"Okay," I said. "Come help me."

It was time to track down Bradley Cole. My heartbeat kicked up to the next gear. It might be past time to track down Bradley Cole. She was right. I should have done this days ago.

A big red light was blinking steadily in control central with a message on the landline phone. Only a handful of people even had the number and they only used it in extreme emergencies when all else failed, or when I accidentally misplaced my personal phone. And I had my phone in my hand.

The robot said, "You have three new messages."

* * *

Bea Crawford heard about my grandmother eloping in the checkout line at the Piggly Wiggly, Pine Apple's only grocery store. (She heard about it in the checkout line. Granny didn't elope in the checkout line.)

"Why didn't they tell anybody?" Bea asked Shirl, Pine Apple's gum-smacking cashier. "I've got a closet full of New York clothes and nowhere to wear them." She fluffed her silver-fox hair. "Call down there, Shirl." She claimed her grocery bag full of dinner—Cheese Wiz, Bam-Bam-Bama wieners, canned chili, day-old hot dog buns. "Tell them to hold up till we can get there."

Word got around, and a Pine Apple convoy threatened middle Alabama at an alarming speed, until they were all pulled over at mile marker 57 on I-65.

"Look it," Bea told the trooper. "We've got a town emergency and we're in a hurry to get to it."

"What town would that be?"

"Did your mother not teach you to say, 'Yes, ma'am and no, ma'am,' boy?

The trooper's fingers curled around the butt of his Sig 229. "No," he said. "She didn't." He was rethinking his decision to pull the line of beat-up cars over. "And I'd advise you to leave my mother out of this and answer the question."

Bea twisted in her seat. Her Ford Fiesta rocked. "We're from Pine Apple."

"Never heard of it."

She pulled off her Polaroids. "Where are you from, boy?"

"Cincinnati."

"What the hell are you doing in Alabama?" she demanded. "You're gonna get rode out on a rail if you go around telling people you're from up north."

"Cincinnati's not 'up north'."

"Don't you sass me, boy. Like hell it's not," she said. "We don't ask questions down here. We shoot Yankees on sight."

The trooper reached for the radio on his shoulder. "I'm going to need a wagon."

The first message left on the landline phone was from my ex-ex-mother-in-law, Bea Crawford. "Davis. We're in the lockup in Ascambia County. Need a little help."

"Did you give her this number?" Fantasy asked.

"Hell, no."

The second message was from No Hair's wife.

"Davis, Fantasy, this is Grace Covey? Jeremy's wife?"

Both our heads shot back and we looked at each other. Fantasy asked, "Who?"

I snapped my fingers. "No Hair's wife."

"Right."

"I'm having such a wonderful time with your darling boys, Fantasy."

Fantasy's hands hit the desk, fingers splayed and her mouth dropped open.

"The boys and I are watching a pirate movie," she said. "The costumes are spectacular." She took a breath. "We just watched a commercial I thought you all should know about."

Fantasy began tapping out a howler on her phone, thumbs flying.

"I can't get Jeremy on the phone," Mrs. No Hair said, "so I thought I'd leave a message for you girls. The television lawyer? The one who represents the people suing the Grand Palace? He's on television again." She paused. "It's pitiful, really," she said, "scared Kyle to death. The lawyer is in a hospital room with a young boy who is in *traction*, with a head apparatus that is truly frightful, because of injuries he suffered while riding a motorized scooter."

Fantasy and I looked at each other.

"The company is Scooteroo, located in Goodlette, Georgia."

I began logging on to all the computers.

"And one last thing," she said. "Fantasy, your boys are telling me they're allergic to both fruits *and* vegetables. Might they be pulling my leg?"

"I'm going pull somebody's legs," Fantasy said, "off." She read the return text from her husband aloud. "Fantasy. It's the Super Bowl before the Super Bowl. Saints and Broncos. Your boss said he'd take care of the boys until whatever you're doing is done. I'll be home late Sunday night."

The third message was from Kirk Olsen. Grand Palace attorney, Kirk Olsen.

"Davis," the machine said. "Kirk Olsen. Need you to call me as soon as you can." He rattled off a number, and Fantasy scribbled it down, because my head had hit the desk.

She dialed for me. She'd been dialing for me all day. He answered on the third ring.

"Kirk," I panted, "Davis Way."

"Davis. Good. Listen, I need to know if you've heard from Brad."

"I haven't," I said. "What's wrong?"

"I don't know that anything's wrong," he said. "Except he's been off the grid for," he paused, "today's the fourth day. I haven't been able to reach him."

"Isn't he at the settlement negotiations in Las Vegas?"

"He's supposed to be, but I can't get ahold of him."

"You can't get *ahold* of him?"

Fantasy grabbed me from behind. I didn't remember starting my run around the room. "Sit down, Davis." She shoved me into a chair.

I got ahold of myself. A little. "Tell me what's going on, Kirk." Fantasy placed a glass of water in front of me that I pushed away. The martinis, the coffee, Bradley Cole.

"Let's back up a week," Kirk said. "You put us on to Mary Harper, who is not Mary Harper at all."

"Right." Bradley got my message. "She's Kimberli Silvers."

"Correct. We didn't want to expose her until we could get a handle on her accomplice, Jerry McAllen. So Brad left with her for Las Vegas last Friday night, as planned."

Last Friday night. Banana pudding night.

"The plane only touched down, though," Kirk said, "before it turned around and came right back."

"They came back to Biloxi? Why?"

"They didn't come back. Brad came back."

"Why?"

"Why? Because you were in the hospital. He came back and stayed with you until you were out of the woods."

The world stopped spinning.

I pulled the phone away from my head and whispered to Fantasy. "Why would my family not tell me Bradley was there?"

After a beat, she asked, "Why *would* they tell you Bradley was there? Wouldn't it be a given he was with you? Would it even occur to them to point it out?"

"Did you know?"

She shook her head. I put the phone back to mine. My hands were shaking.

"Where is he supposed to be now, Kirk?"

"That's just it," he said. "He flew back to Vegas late Sunday afternoon to join the negotiations. That was the last time I spoke to him. He was in a limo on his way to dinner, but he never checked into his hotel room. The next morning, he didn't show, or the next, or the next," Kirk said. "For what it's worth," he said, "we can't find her either."

The world cracked.

"Who did he have dinner with?" I asked.

"Her."

The world blew up. Smithereens.

"He's in the hospital, Kirk."

"What?" (Kirk.)

"What?" (Fantasy.)

I went after the keyboard in front of me as if it could put the world back together. I could hear my own heart beating. My shaky fingers managed to pull up a list of Vegas hospitals. Patient search, patient search, patient search. Bradley, my Bradley Cole, was in the Desert Springs Hospital. Hack, hack, hack. Stable condition. Amanita Phalloides poisoning. Web search, web search, web search. Mushrooms. Bradley Cole didn't even *like* mushrooms. Neither did I. They're a fungus.

For this reason—mushrooms—and many other reasons, Bradley Cole and I belonged together.

"Davis?" The phone was on the desk. "Davis?"

"She's here, Kirk," Fantasy picked it up. "Give her a minute."

* * *

"I have to go to Vegas, No Hair."

He didn't react immediately.

"It's Bradley Cole."

He pushed away from Mr. Sanders' desk and walked around to me. He put his paws on my shoulders; I went from five-two to five feet. "Sit down, Davis. Tell me what's going on."

TWENTY-SIX

4:30: Kickoff Double Dip Final Round
Gift Baskets Delivered to Guest Rooms

Logistically, I couldn't get to Las Vegas.

We were holed up in Mr. Sanders' office.

Bradley Cole's phone would not ping a location, and I couldn't get any decent information out of Desert Springs Hospital to save my life. He was no longer a patient and that's all they'd say. No, they wouldn't fax his signature on the discharge papers so I could authenticate it. No, they didn't have time to watch their security feed and see who'd picked him up. No, they would not interview the staff who'd cared for him to ask if he'd mentioned my name.

Fantasy looked at commercial flights. Of course, there was nothing direct. If I left the Bellissimo now, I could catch a six-twenty out of Gulfport, and from there, my choices were either the Atlanta, Cincinnati, or Dallas airports to spend the night in, then catch a dark-thirty morning flight to Vegas.

No Hair pulled up the Bellissimo fleet schedule. Booked solid. Three of the four corporate jets were fueled up and flight plans had already been filed for post-Double Dip runs. After the tournament, the three planes were taking Bellissimo high rollers home to Raleigh, North Carolina, Charleston, South Carolina, and Frankfort, Kentucky. The flights were at or near capacity, especially the Frankfort flight, the only one not going in the opposite direction of Vegas.

"What's their big hurry?" Fantasy asked.

I pulled up the player names and their casino activity during the three-day tournament. Between the registered players on the planes, they'd dropped a combined quarter of a million dollars in the casino. None of them would be in the mood to be bumped.

"Just tell them engine trouble," Fantasy suggested, "or bad weather."

"No," No Hair said. "Let's look at that fourth jet."

"Mr. Sanders' plane," I said. "Halfway around the world." I surrendered with both hands. "How's that going to help?"

"No." No Hair tilted the computer screen so I could see a blue map of the greater United States with a little bitty plane over California. "He lands in Vegas in twelve minutes."

* * *

5:00: Player and Audience Cocktail Reception
Stella Lounge
Stack the Deck Jazz Band

"It never happened, Mrs. Sanders," I assured her. "I don't think they were ever in the same room at the same time."

Bianca was weepy, probably something Dr. Spock had given her, and she didn't take the news well that Mr. Sanders' return might be delayed again. However, she quickly changed the subject to her overall disappointment in how I'd "behaved" so far at the "casino whatever event," and she would *never* do another one of these, because she was exhausted from it.

(Really?)

She had a copy of Page Six with the headline "*Bellissimo's Shiniest Star, Bianca Sanders*" spread out on the table in front of her. I felt confident she would eventually get past how I'd "behaved." Not that I didn't fully intend to drop a line in the employee suggestion box as soon as I could get to it: Hire an emcee.

After that, she smoked and whined about not having an assistant. "The cowboy is tolerable," (puff, puff, puff) "but he runs off. As if he's being chased. He's here one minute," her lit cigarette arced through the air, "and the next, he's gone."

"How's your foot?"

She was wearing kitten heels, working her way back to her beloved stilettos.

"Scarred," she said, "for life." Which somehow reminded her of Peyton. "She was a good assistant," Bianca said, "other than she sulked, she shot me, and she was sleeping with Richard."

Which is when I assured her that Peyton was a one-man woman, and the man wasn't Mr. Sanders. The man wasn't even alive. (Cross, cross, cross.)

"I'm really ready for Richard to be home."

Bianca *never* said home. She said "Biloxi" or "this wretched place" or "the intolerable hell that is the South."

"I'll see you soon, Mrs. Sanders." I stood.

"Yes, David." She shooed me out. "Stop by the kitchen and have them bring me a fresh martini. This one has all but gelled during your rambling."

* * *

5:30: Casino Hosts, Stella Lounge
Bianca Sanders, Dressing Room

Fantasy and I ran past, behind, and under Shakes, then ran the length of the hall to our underground offices. I keyed the code wrong twice before she said, "Move."

I ran to the shower while she dialed for me, again, then talked for me, too.

"Laney, this is Fantasia. Bianca's assistant. She's running a little late. I don't think she's going to make it to dinner."

The zipper on my jeans was stuck.

"She says she's not hungry."

I did not say that.

"Look, lady. I'm just telling you what she told me."

In fact, I was starving.

"I'll get her there as quickly as I can."

5:45 Players to Magnolia Ballroom
6:00 Dinner Seating

I'd planned on a two-minute shower, but I stood under the hot water for at least ten minutes without moving a muscle, at which point Fantasy banged on the door. "Your dad's on the phone, Davis!" I grabbed a towel.

"We have newlyweds," he said.

"Please tell me they're not in a honeymoon suite somewhere, Daddy."

"They're in the back of my patrol car," Daddy said. "Snoring."

"Where's everyone else?"

"Meredith is driving Eddie's car, with your mother and Riley in tow."

I didn't ask, but he answered anyway.

"Eddie took a shine to the organist at the chapel and said he'd find his own way home."

"Poor organist," I said. "You do know half the town's locked up in Ascambia, right?"

"No, punkin'," he said. "They didn't hold them thirty minutes."

"I'm surprised they put up with them that long."

6:00 Carrot Ginger soup with Apple Pumpkin Seed Pesto

I had just applied Morocanoil Moisture Repair conditioner to my tortured hair.

"Hey," Fantasy said, "you're going to run out of hot water if you don't hurry."

I stuck my head out. "Is that what you came in here to tell me?"

"No. Kirk Olsen is texting you."

"What?"

"He says Kimberli Silvers and Jerry McAllen are actually married. And this is their third tag-team sting. He says their goal is his-and-hers settlements."

"Seriously?" I asked over the water. "Text him back," I said from under the conditioner. "Tell him we're trying to track down Bradley."

"He knows that, Davis. He says they got a warrant from Judge Clemmer to enter her corporate apartment and found transcripts of phone taps on both yours and Bradley's phones. And they found your Bellissimo passkey."

6:15 Endive and Pear Salad with Gorgonzola Cream Dressing

I don't know how long it had been, but I prayed.

"Davis? Are you ever coming out of that shower?"

"I might, I might not." I was waiting on the Morocanoil Moisture Repair conditioner to save my tortured hair and I was busy with a Higher Power trying to save Bradley Cole.

6:30 Roast Duckling with Poached Peaches
Pan Grilled Salmon with Sautéed Peas and Celery Root
Chateaubriand with Lobster Béarnaise Sauce

I made it to the salon chair in the dressing house, tongue hanging out.

Laney Harris wasn't happy, but she was savvy. She didn't fuss at me for being an hour late or ask why. She was dolled up for tonight's shindig in a hot-pink sleeveless dress with a chocolate-brown silk scarf draped about her neck, her dark bob swept up and slicked back, and chocolate-brown Tori Burch wedges.

"You look really nice, Laney."

"Why thank you, Mrs. Sanders." She winked.

Maybe she wasn't upset with me, but I didn't get off scot-free. Seattle had a fit about my extra moisturized hair. My slick blondy-blond Bianca hair, which there was a lot of anyway, was being heaped into a red-carpet updo, except it kept falling down. I felt certain they would pull it out before they got it up. Seattle threw his caulk gun on the floor and screamed at me in the mirror.

"I tell to you! Do not buy *les couleurs* and *les savon* at the market! Buy the *fruit* and *vegetable* at the market!"

Fantasia led him to a Barcolounger and tossed him a pack of Bianca's cigarettes. "She's shot people for way less than that, San Fran. You'd better button up."

Four girls—two with polish, two with leaf blowers—were attending to my toes, while another team of experts came at me with spatulas and paint brushes.

"Please," I said, "easy on the makeup. I hugged a woman this morning and she came away with four pounds of my makeup on her clothes." The guy with an airbrush machine strapped over his shoulder looked offended. "Simple makeup," I said. "Please."

"You're clogging her pores!" (Fantasia. Who was busy hooking Seattle up to a liquor drip.)

At six fifty-nine, a ninety-year-old woman presented me with several carats of pear-shaped diamond solitaire earrings on velvet and a tray of chicken-cutlet bras on a cutting board.

7:00 Ballroom Doors Open
Cocktails
Gulf Coast Symphony Orchestra
Final Round Double Dip

The dress left nothing, *nothing*, to the imagination. Nothing.

The designer was Herve Leger—whoever he is—and he called his creation Asymmetrical Sequined Bandage. No telling what his creation cost. It was asymmetrical, because it only had one shoulder, which meant the neckline was diagonal. (Dramatic.) Sequined, because, well, every bit of it was covered in sequins. (Shiny.) The bandage part, and I'm only guessing here, but think ace bandage. "Hold your arms up," then someone ballerina spins you until you're covered. That's not exactly how this dress worked, because it was not made of ace bandages, rather, creamy, stretchy silk, and it was in one piece, someone had already spun it. (Dizzy.) I would have named it Lopsided Twinkling Curve-Hugger. I doubt Mr. Leger would approve of my description, while I approved mightily of his dress, other than at the moment, it was hanging limp on a headless armless mannequin in the middle of the dressing house. (Creepy.)

The shoes were simple Chanel's, if you call two-thousand dollar five-inch-heeled shoes simple. They were winter-white leather, the exact color of the dress, with ankle straps and matching straps across my toes, which had just been painted OPI's "Teal We Meet Again" green. (The color of money.)

Whilst Fantasia and I had been knocking back blueberry martinis earlier in the day, a very talented decorating crew had been having their way with the ballroom. What had been "I Scream You Scream We All Scream for Ice Cream" was now "Nice Day for a White Wedding." Fairy lights and white organza everywhere. White linens, white china, and two-foot-tall white-rose topiary arrangements on the tables.

The white was set off by silver. Silver ware (silverware—one word), silver candelabras, and silver stanchions with connecting white velvet ropes cordoned off the slot machines. The waitresses were wearing white shiny ace bandages, too, but they'd split one shiny ace bandage between the fifty of them, where I had three bandages all to myself. At least two. Mine was a whole dress; theirs was a whole napkin. Their hair, too, was piled up like mine. Their toenails, peeking out from their Jimmy Choo strappys, were Teal We Meet Again green.

"Do you want to know?" Laney Harris walked me to the stage, passed me the jeweled microphone along with the tap-on, tap-off ring and went over what was left of the evening's itinerary with me one more time. "Matthew Thatcher always knew. He wanted to know."

The slot machines' reels had also been switched out during our Blueberry Martini Matinee. They'd gone from 31 Flavors to one—vanilla, and just one topping—diamonds. One of the machines had three special symbols, three little jewels that would line up for one lucky player. Laney Harris knew which one. (She knew which machine. She didn't know which player.)

"I really don't want to know, Laney," I said. "I'd rather be surprised."

"You're sure?" she asked. "You'll need to let the crowd know when it hits."

"Won't the person scream and holler?"

"You never know," she said. "The person might pass out."

"What happens if I drop it?"

"Drop what?"

"The diamond. At the awards."

Laney hesitated. "The winner doesn't get it tonight. It'll be delivered by armored courier tomorrow."

I was so disappointed. (I was so many things—scared for Bradley, anxious for this to be over, worried that I'd have to catch a plane wearing the twinkling bandage, exhausted, and a twinge of sorry that I'd missed my grandmother's wedding.)

"It's the insurance company's call," Laney said. "Not ours." She opened a leather portfolio, looked both ways, then let me peek. It was a beautiful sparkly solitaire.

"I'd like to have one of those."

"Wouldn't we all?" She tucked the portfolio under an arm, then pulled me to face her. She tucked a stray strand of moisturized hair back into the beehive on my head. "Good luck out there." She spun me toward the curtains. "Do Bianca proud!"

I froze and looked over my shoulder.

She winked, then pushed me through to the stage.

Cue the lights (house down, spot up), cue the orchestra (Elvis Costello's "She"), then deafening applause and a standing ovation.

I no longer remember how I got from a town of four hundred to *here*.

I did know the second this was over I would be with, or on my way to, Bradley Cole.

7:10 Welcome
Richard and Bianca Sanders

I floated. (Around the room.) Which was more like *ran* around the room.

"This old thang? I picked it up at a yard sale."

"I told him this morning, 'Richard,' I said, 'no goofing off. Get back here to see who wins this tournament.'"

"Say cheese!"

"Mrs. Conner, you look absolutely amazing. Monty Conner, you do not deserve her."

"All I know is someone's going to win a million dollars. I don't know a thing about anyone winning anything else."

"He's wonderful! Thank you! He's fourteen now, straight As, and plays lacrosse."

"I don't know what lacrosse is either."

7:25 Machine Assignments

The players drew. (Numbers. Out of a hat.) Which was not a hat at all; it was a silver bowl full of numbered, etched, crystal, goose eggs.

Each of the fifty tournament players came to the stage to be introduced and draw a number. They were lined up by current rank—lowest score first.

"You draw it, Mrs. Sanders." It was Emmett Reese (Furry Ears), from Baton Rouge, Louisiana.

"I can't do that, Emmett!"

The crowd weighed in. "Do it, Bianca!" "Draw the number for him, Bianca!"

A quick meeting among suits convened behind two solid white baby grand pianos in a corner. Accountants from Delloite, there to verify the wins, bent heads with Bellissimo legal eagles, there to protect the bottom line. They must have flipped a coin rather than discuss it, which would have led to conference rooms, thick documents, debates and mediation, because they gave me the go-ahead quickly.

"Oh, the pressure!" I dipped a hand into the goose eggs. I pulled one out. "Thirty-two, Emmett!" (Furry Ears!) "You'll play on lucky machine number thirty-two!"

7:45 Player Seating
Bianca Sanders makeup check

I ducked backstage for lip gloss.

Fantasy had an orange juice on crushed ice for me.

"STRAW! STRAW!" one of the powder and paint people yelled. "SOMEONE GET HER A STRAW!"

Fantasy leaned in. "The Georgia authorities have Mary Ha Ha and her husband."

"Any word on Bradley?" I slapped at anonymous hands that had moved in and were physically hoisting up my chicken cutlets.

Fantasy pressed her lips together in a smile and nodded. "It's all good."

I caved, she caught me, and someone yelled, "NO TOUCHING MRS. SANDERS! BACK OFF!"

"I'll show you some back off, lady." (Fantasia.)

I stumbled back to the ballroom.

8:00 Go Time!

The fifty players were seated. The audience, drinks in tow, were pressed against the white velvet ropes. I rang the opening bell and the machine display switched from the Double Dip Tournament graphics to play mode, and a spectator screamed it first.

"It's diamonds!" You'd thought someone had presented her with one. "It's diamonds! The surprise is diamonds!"

We counted down together and they were off. All fifty players beat the play buttons on their slot machines as if their very lives depended on it. I tugged the pearl-drop diamond at my ear and spoke to Fantasy, "Let's be players in this next year."

Sixteen minutes in, we were all about to drop. So far, Mrs. Dragonfly, who had a jeweled lizard crawling across her shoulder tonight, was the clear point leader for this round, because her slot machine almost couldn't spin anything but triple scoops, diamonds exploding everywhere, and much of the audience had migrated her way. Twenty minutes in, the screaming was unbearable. I stepped back to take it all in. I welcomed the focus on the tournament play, so I could be ignored for a minute. And breathe.

A chill of Bradley Cole anticipation ran through me when I realized the tournament was almost over.

"Are you hiding?" Someone shouted in my ear. It was Laney Harris. "Come with me."

She led me down the row. She pointed. "Watch."

Slot machine number sixteen was being played by the slightest little old man, Cornelius something, from Metairie, Louisiana. With two minutes of play left, he lined them up.

Diamond diamond diamond.

They were the size of baseballs on the screen, positively brilliant, and they sat there quietly on the three reels, as did Cornelius. He looked around to see if anyone else noticed, and found me.

"Congratulations!" I mouthed above the ridiculous din.

"Thank you!"

Someone else noticed the diamonds and the energy in the room, barely contained to begin with, doubled.

The slot machines, in unison, popped up the tournament graphics screens.

The Double Dip Tournament was finally over.

8:30 Dessert
Credit Meter Verification

It was hard to believe the players weren't passed out on the machines. I found it equally hard to believe I was still standing. The exhausted audience slowly peeled away from the white velvet ropes, found their seats, and fell into them. The shiny bandaged waitresses swarmed. Accountants and lawyers, machine by machine, verified the final round points. Champagne flowed freely. An army of white-gloved white-tuxed servers invaded the ballroom from all points carrying silver trays with silver domed lids.

Ben & Jerry, have a seat. In the back. Farther back.

It was ice cream, of that I was certain, and it was decadent—I had my own teeny silver spoon I carried around the ballroom double-dipping into every other dish—but past that, I'd never seen or tasted anything like it in my life.

Fantasy, in my ear, "Stop eating after people."

I picked up a few details between bites. Double scoops of Tahitian vanilla bean ice cream infused with Madagascar vanilla were in Waterford crystal goblets. The ice cream was sprinkled in 23K edible gold, then drizzled with Delafee chocolate from Switzerland. It was served with miniature chocolate-dipped petit fours (I ate twenty of those), passion fruit, and snifters of fifty-year old Hennessey cognac. I confess to having a few of those, too.

Fantasy, in my ear, "You're going to get fat."

The accountants finished recording scores, and scuttled off to tally. The players stumbled to their tables. My earpiece beeped again, and I asked, "What now?"

Fantasy, in my ear, "Look at the door."

My boss, Richard Sanders, wearing a black tuxedo, strolled in. It stunned us all so much, the only thing in the room you could hear was the ice cream melting.

He was alone.

He shook hands, slapped backs, found me, gave me a smile and a wink, then made his way to Cornelius Diamond Winner to congratulate him. Laney Harris passed him a cordless microphone.

My heart was pounding.

"Did I miss all the fun?" The crowd roared. "If you all will excuse me," he said, "I'd like to say hello to my wife."

He hustled me backstage.

9:00 Winners Announced

"Did you find him? They released him from the hospital. Where is he? Did you look for him?"

"Davis, slow down."

Davis fell down. A wooden box caught her.

Mr. Sanders looked around, found a straight chair, pulled it next to me, then sat down.

"I found him at the Grand Palace, Davis, and yes, he'd been released from the hospital."

"Surely, they didn't make him stay and work, after what he's been through."

"No," Mr. Sanders said. "He flew back with me."

But...where was he? My heart broke in two.

Someone yelled the time out—nine-oh-eight, the natives were getting restless—and Mr. Sanders waved them off.

"He said he'd catch up with you later."

My heart broke in four.

I wanted to ask Mr. Sanders if those were his exact words: catch up with me later. *Catch up* with me?

I'd dreamed it up. I made everything right with Bradley in my own little world. I had to hold the sides of the box to steady myself.

Someone yelled the time.

"Stay here, Davis," Mr. Sanders said. "I'll go announce the winners."

I nodded. I think I nodded.

It was dark and I was cold and I was alone, except for the orchestra's empty instrument cases. I scooted the shiny ace bandages back until I found a wall to hold me up.

What now? Where would I go from here?

Mr. Sanders' muffled voice snuck backstage. Muted applause broke out. Drum rolls and squeals from far, far away. I closed my eyes and rested the back of my head against the cold, cold wall.

My eyes popped open when I heard him say, "Scoot over."

My first frantic thought was there was nowhere to scoot to.

"Okay," he said. "Let's try this." Bradley Cole scooped me up, we sat on the crate together, and I finally found a good crying place. I'd been looking for one for so long.

"I brought you something."

The center stone was square. Baguettes bowed all around it. Tons of them. It was set in platinum, to which, I cried all the harder.

"Marry me, Davis."

Someone did leave the tournament with a great big rock.

Me!

Photo by Garrett Nudd

Gretchen Archer

Gretchen Archer is a Tennessee housewife who began writing when her daughters, seeking higher educations, ran off and left her. She lives on Lookout Mountain with her husband, son, and a Yorkie named Bently. *Double Dip* is the second Davis Way crime caper. You can visit her at www.gretchenarcher.com.

In Case You Missed the 1st Book in the Series

DOUBLE WHAMMY

Gretchen Archer

A Davis Way Crime Caper (#1)

Davis Way thinks she's hit the jackpot when she lands a job as the fifth wheel on an elite security team at the fabulous Bellissimo Resort and Casino in Biloxi, Mississippi. But once there, she runs straight into her ex-ex husband, a rigged slot machine, her evil twin, and a trail of dead bodies. Davis learns the truth and it does not set her free—in fact, it lands her in the pokey.

Buried under a mistaken identity, unable to seek help from her family, her hot streak runs cold until her landlord Bradley Cole steps in. Make that her landlord, lawyer, and love interest. With his help, Davis must win this high stakes game before her luck runs out.

Don't Miss the 3rd Book in the Series

DOUBLE STRIKE

Gretchen Archer

A Davis Way Crime Caper (#3)

Bellissimo Resort and Casino Super Spy Davis Way knows three things: Cooking isn't a prerequisite for a happy marriage, don't trust men who look like David Hasselhoff, and money doesn't grow on Christmas trees. None of which help when a storm hits the Gulf a week before the Bellissimo's Strike It Rich Sweepstakes. Securing the guests, staff, and property might take a stray bullet. Or two.

Bellissimo Resort and Casino Super Spy Davis Way has three problems: She's desperate to change her marital status, her new boss who speaks in hashtags, and Bianca Sanders has confiscated her clothes. All of which bring on a headache hot enough to spark a fire. Solving her problems means stealing a car. From a dingbat lawyer.

Bellissimo Resort and Casino Super Spy Davis Way has three goals: Keep the Sanders family out of prison, regain her footing in her relationship, and find the genius who wrote the software for futureGaming. One of which, the manhunt one, is iffy. Because when Alabama hides someone, they hide them good.

DOUBLE STRIKE. A VIP invitation to an extraordinary high-stakes gaming event, as thieves, feds, dance instructors, shady bankers, kidnappers, and gold waiters go all in. #Don'tMissIt.

Henery Press Mystery Books

And finally, before you go...
Here are a few other mysteries
you might enjoy:

BOARD STIFF

Kendel Lynn

An Elliott Lisbon Mystery (#1)

As director of the Ballantyne Foundation on Sea Pine Island, SC, Elliott Lisbon scratches her detective itch by performing discreet inquiries for Foundation donors. Usually nothing more serious than retrieving a pilfered Pomeranian. Until Jane Hatting, Ballantyne board chair, is accused of murder. The Ballantyne's reputation tanks, Jane's headed to a jail cell, and Elliott's sexy ex is the new lieutenant in town.

Armed with moxie and her Mini Coop, Elliott uncovers a trail of blackmail schemes, gambling debts, illicit affairs, and investment scams. But the deeper she digs to clear Jane's name, the guiltier Jane looks. The closer she gets to the truth, the more treacherous her investigation becomes. With victims piling up faster than shells at a clambake, Elliott realizes she's next on the killer's list.

FINDING SKY

Susan O'Brien

A Nicki Valentine Mystery

Suburban widow and P.I. in training Nicki Valentine can barely keep track of her two kids, never mind anyone else. But when her best friend's adoption plan is jeopardized by the young birth mother's disappearance, Nicki is persuaded to help. Nearly everyone else believes the teenager ran away, but Nicki trusts her BFF's judgment, and the feeling is mutual.

The case leads where few moms go (teen parties, gang shootings) and places they can't avoid (preschool parties, OB-GYNs' offices). Nicki has everything to lose and much to gain — including the attention of her unnervingly hot P.I. instructor. Thankfully, Nicki is armed with her pesky conscience, occasional babysitters, a fully stocked minivan, and nature's best defense system: women's intuition.

From the Henery Press Chick Lit Collection

BET YOUR BOTTOM DOLLAR

Karin Gillespie

The Bottom Dollar Series (#1)

Welcome to the Bottom Dollar Emporium in Cayboo Creek, South Carolina, where everything from coconut mallow cookies to Clabber Girl Baking Powder costs a dollar but the coffee and gossip are free. For the Bottom Dollar gals, work time is sisterhood time.

When news gets out that a corporate dollar store is coming to town, the women are thrown into a tizzy, hoping to save their beloved store as well their friendships. Meanwhile the manager is canoodling with the town's wealthiest bachelor and their romance unearths some startling family secrets.

The first in a series, *Bet Your Bottom Dollar* serves up a heaping portion of small town Southern life and introduces readers to a cast of eccentric characters. Pull up a wicker chair, set out a tall glass of Cheer Wine, and immerse yourself in the adventures of a group of women who the *Atlanta Journal Constitution* calls, "... the kind of steel magnolias who would make Scarlett O'Hara envious."

Available at booksellers nationwide and online

Visit www.henerypress.com for details

MACDEATH

Cindy Brown

An Ivy Meadows Mystery (#1)

Like every actor, Ivy Meadows knows that *Macbeth* is cursed. But she's finally scored her big break, cast as an acrobatic witch in a circus-themed production of *Macbeth* in Phoenix, Arizona. And though it may not be Broadway, nothing can dampen her enthusiasm—not her flying caldron, too-tight leotard, or carrot-wielding dictator of a director.

But when one of the cast dies on opening night, Ivy is sure the seeming accident is "murder most foul" and that she's the perfect person to solve the crime (after all, she does work part-time in her uncle's detective agency). Undeterred by a poisoned Big Gulp, the threat of being blackballed, and the suddenly too-real curse, Ivy pursues the truth at the risk of her hard-won career—and her life.

Available at booksellers nationwide and online

Visit www.henerypress.com for details

NUN TOO SOON

Alice Loweecey

A Giulia Driscoll Mystery (#1)

Giulia Falcone-Driscoll has just taken on her first impossible client: The Silk Tie Killer. He's hired Driscoll Investigations to prove his innocence and they have only thirteen days to accomplish it. Talk about being tried in the media. Everyone in town is sure Roger Fitch strangled his girlfriend with one of his silk neckties. And then there's the local TMZ wannabes—The Scoop—stalking Giulia and her client for sleazy sound bites.

On top of all that, her assistant's first baby is due any second, her scary smart admin still doesn't relate well to humans, and her police detective husband insists her client is guilty. About this marriage thing—it's unknown territory, but it sure beats ten years of living with 150 nuns.

Giulia's ownership of Driscoll Investigations hasn't changed her passion for justice from her convent years. But the more dirt she digs up, the more she's worried her efforts will help a murderer escape. As the client accuses DI of dragging its heels on purpose, Giulia thinks The Silk Tie Killer might be choosing one of his ties for her own neck.

CPSIA information can be obtained
at www.ICGtesting.com
Printed in the USA
LVOW04s1530190116
471354LV00018B/937/P